CANDACE CAMP

THE *Courtship* DANCE

HQN™

Recycling programs
for this product may
not exist in your area.

ISBN-13: 978-0-373-77564-4

THE COURTSHIP DANCE

www.HQNBooks.com

Printed in U.S.A.

CHAPTER ONE

No ONE WOULD have guessed from the way Lady Francesca Haughston moved through the Whittington ballroom that she was making the opening moves of her campaign. She strolled along in her usual manner, pausing to compliment a dress here or flirt with one of her many admirers there. She smiled and talked and plied her fan deftly, a vision in ice-blue silk, her blond hair falling in a cascade of curls from an upswept knot. But all the while, her dark blue eyes were looking for her prey.

It had been almost a month since she had vowed to herself to find a wife for the Duke of Rochford, and tonight she intended to set her plan in motion. She had made all her preparations. She had studied the young unmarried women of the *ton,* and through careful research and observation, she had managed to whittle the number down to just three whom she felt suitable for Sinclair.

All three of the young ladies would be here this evening, she was certain. The Whittington ball was one of the highlights of the Season, and, short of dire illness, any marriageable young lady would attend. Moreover, the odds were that the duke would be there, as well, which meant that Francesca could set her scheme in motion. It was time she began, she knew—past time. She had not really needed three weeks to sort out the possible brides for Rochford. There was only a rather small number of girls who could qualify to become his duchess.

But for some reason, ever since Callie's wedding, Francesca had been beset by ennui, curiously reluctant to pay calls or attend parties or the theater. Even her good friend Sir Lucien had commented on her sudden preference for staying at home. She was not sure of the reason for it; everything just suddenly seemed dull and scarcely worth the effort. She had felt, in fact, a trifle blue-deviled—a result, she had decided, of the fact that Callie, who had been living with Francesca while they sorted out a husband for her, was now married and gone. Without Callie's cheerful voice and fetching smile, Francesca's house was too empty.

Still, she reminded herself, she had vowed to make up for the wrong she had done to Callie's brother, Sinclair, fifteen long years ago. It was impossible to right matters, of course, but she could at least do the duke the favor of finding him a suitable bride. It was, after all, the thing at which she was most skilled. So she had come to this party tonight determined to begin the long dance of courtship on his behalf.

She strolled along the perimeter of the grand ballroom, a huge affair painted all in white and gold, floored with oak planks the color of honey, and lit by three glittering cascades of crystal chandeliers. Several gold stands of thick white beeswax candles provided more light, as did the gold-and-white sconces along the walls. All this brilliance was softened by the huge bouquets of crimson roses and peonies standing in vases against the walls, and twining in garlands up the banister of the magnificent staircase to the second floor. It was an elegant room, worthy of a palace, and it was rumored that only the formal ballroom made Lady Whittington willing to remain in this enormous and antiquated old mansion situated unfashionably outside Mayfair.

Francesca threaded through the crowd to the staircase, intending to use the vantage point of the second-floor railing to locate the young women she was seeking in the massive ballroom below. It was fitting, she thought, as she began to climb the curving stairs, that she should begin her campaign at the Whittingtons' ball. It had been here, after all, that she had ended things with the Duke of Rochford fifteen years ago. It had been here that her world had come crashing down.

The flowers had all been white that night, she remembered, masses of roses, peonies, camellias and sweet-scented gardenias, accented by glossy greenery trailing from the high vases. It had been a night of heady triumph for Francesca—she had made her debut only weeks before, and she was the undisputed Beauty of the Season. Men had flocked around her, flirting and begging for a dance, making extravagant declarations of love and paying flowery compliments. And all the while she had hugged her secret to herself, giddy with love and excitement—until the footman had slipped a note into her hand.

Now Francesca reached the second floor and took her place at the railing, where she could gaze down at the swirling dancers below. Things were much the same, she thought, as they had been that night so long ago. The dresses had been different, of course, the colors of the walls and the decorations changed. But the glamour, the excitement, the hopes and intrigues, had not altered. Francesca gazed out at the crowd without really seeing them, remembering instead the past.

"Is the party so grim?" a light, familiar voice said at her side.

Francesca turned and smiled at the blond woman. "Irene. How good to see you."

Lady Irene Radbourne was a striking woman with thick, curling blond hair and unusual golden eyes. At twenty-seven years old, she had been a spinster—and determined to remain one—until last autumn, when Francesca, searching for a suitable spouse for the Earl of Radbourne, had realized that Irene was the perfect match for him. The two women had spent their lives in much the same circle, so she had known the blunt, opinionated Lady Irene for years, but the two of them had not been friends until they had spent two weeks together at the Radbourne estate as Francesca sought to match the rough Lord Gideon to a well-bred wife. Now Francesca counted Irene as one of her closest friends.

Irene looked out over the multicolored crowd of dancers. "Is the new crop of marriageable young ladies so dismal?"

Francesca shrugged. Though she and Irene had maintained a genteel silence regarding the matter, Francesca suspected Irene had guessed that her matchmaking efforts were more a question of survival than amusement.

"Indeed, I have not really given them much attention. I have been quite lazy since Callie's wedding, I fear."

Irene regarded her shrewdly. "You *are* distressed, are you not? Is there aught that I can do?"

Francesca shook her head. "'Tis nothing, really. I am just remembering…a time long past. Another party here." She forced a smile, the charming dimple in her cheek appearing. "Where is Lord Gideon?"

In the six months the couple had been married, it was rare to see Irene without Gideon by her side. The pair had suited each other even better than Francesca had guessed; it seemed as if their love grew with each passing day.

Irene let out a little giggle. "He was waylaid by his great-aunt as we came in."

"Lady Odelia?" Francesca asked, appalled. "Good Gad, is she here?" She glanced around apprehensively.

"We are safe here," Irene assured her. "I do not think

she will climb the stairs. That is why I fled to the balcony as soon as I stepped out of the cloakroom and saw that she had cornered Gideon."

"And left him there?" Francesca asked, chuckling. "For shame, Lady Radbourne. What about your vows?"

"My wedding vows made no mention of Great-Aunt Odelia, I assure you," Irene retorted, grinning. "I did feel a twinge of guilt, but I reminded myself that Gideon is a strong man, feared by many."

"Even the bravest quail before Lady Odelia, however. I remember once when Rochford himself sneaked out the back door and went 'round to the stables when he saw her carriage out front, leaving my mother and me with his grandmother to face her."

Irene let out a burst of laughter. "I should like to have seen that. I shall have to tease him about that the next time we meet."

"How is the duke?" Francesca asked casually, not looking at Irene. "Have you seen him lately?"

Irene glanced at her. "A week or so ago. We went to the theater together. He and Gideon are now friends, as well as cousins. But surely you have seen Rochford, as well."

Francesca shrugged. "Only rarely since Callie's wedding. It was his sister who was my friend, really, not Rochford."

The truth was that Francesca had been avoiding the duke since his sister's wedding. The guilty knowledge of how she had wronged him had weighed on her, and every time she had run into him, she had been pierced with guilt anew. She knew that she should tell him what she had found out, that she should apologize for her actions. It was craven of her not to.

Yet she could not do it; her insides chilled whenever she thought of confessing and begging his pardon. They had at least achieved a kind of peace with each other after all these years. Not friendship, exactly, but something close to it. What if she told him and it brought back his anger? She deserved that anger, she supposed, but her stomach twisted at the idea. So she had taken to avoiding Rochford whenever possible, staying away from a party if she thought he would attend it, and when she did see him, taking care not to go near him. If they came face-to-face, as had happened once or twice, she had been stiff and awkward, escaping as soon as possible.

Of course, that must end if she was to have any success finding a wife for the man. She could scarcely bring him together with one of his prospective brides if she continued to avoid him.

"Callie told me that Rochford had been unfair to you," Irene began carefully.

"Unfair?" Francesca glanced at her, startled. "No. How was he unfair?"

"I know not," Irene admitted. "Something to do with Lord Bromwell courting Callie, I gathered."

"Oh, that." Francesca dismissed the idea with a flick

of her hand. "The duke had reason to be concerned. Brom's sister had certainly poisoned him against Rochford, but..." She shrugged expressively. "There was little I could do once they fell in love, in any case, and Rochford realized it afterwards. I am not so tender a female as to wither under a rebuke."

Francesca glanced out again over the crowd, and Irene followed her gaze.

"Who do you seek?" Irene asked after a moment.

"What? Oh. No one."

Irene's eyebrows lifted. "You are most diligent in looking for no one."

Francesca had difficulty dissembling with Irene. Something about Irene's forthright manner seemed to call forth an equal candor in *her*. She hesitated now, then admitted, "I was hoping to see Lady Althea Robart."

"Althea?" Irene repeated in surprise. "Whatever for?"

Francesca could not help but chuckle. "You dislike the woman?"

Irene shrugged. "*Dislike* is too strong a word. She simply is not company I would choose to keep. Too high in the instep for me."

Francesca nodded. The lady did seem a bit stiff. But she was not sure that pride would necessarily be a detriment to a future duchess. "I do not know her well."

"Nor I," Irene agreed.

"What about Damaris Burke?"

"The daughter of Lord Burke?" Irene asked. "The diplomat?"

Francesca nodded. "Exactly."

Irene thought for a moment, then shrugged. "I cannot say, really. I have never moved in government circles."

"She seems quite pleasant."

"Smooth," Irene agreed. "What one would expect, I suppose, from a woman who holds diplomatic parties." She glanced at her friend curiously. "Why are you asking? Do not tell me they have asked your help in seeking a husband."

"No," Francesca told her quickly. "They have not. I was just…considering them."

"Ah, then it is a gentleman who has sought your help?" Irene guessed.

"Not really. I have been thinking. On my own, as it were."

"Now you have completely aroused my curiosity. You are matchmaking for someone who has not even asked you? Is this another wager with the duke?"

Francesca blushed. "Oh. No, nothing like that. I had thought—well, there was someone I wronged once, and I had been looking to make it up to him."

"By finding him a wife?" Irene asked. "There are a number of men who would not thank you for that favor. Who is the man?"

Francesca studied the woman next to her. Of all her friends, Irene knew the most about her. Though Francesca had never confided in her about her own past, Irene's father had been a friend of Francesca's late husband, so no doubt Irene suspected how little happiness Francesca had found in her marriage, and Francesca had never felt it necessary to maintain a pretense to Irene that she had missed Andrew in the five years since his death. She had never told anyone about what had happened between her and Rochford so long ago, but she suddenly found herself wanting to confide in Irene.

"Is he the reason for your melancholy?" Irene persisted.

"I think that is caused by the rapid approach of my birthday," Francesca replied lightly, but then she sighed and said, "And a little by having hurt him when he did not deserve it. I am very sorry for what I did."

Irene frowned. "I cannot imagine that you could have done anything so terrible."

"I think he might differ with you," Francesca responded. She looked into her friend's eyes, warm with sympathy. "No one must know this—not even Lord Gideon, for he knows the man."

Irene's brows went up, and Francesca saw understanding dawn in the other woman's clear golden eyes. "The duke? You are talking about Rochford?"

Francesca sighed. "I should have known that you would guess. Yes, it is Rochford, but you must promise me that you will not tell anyone."

"Of course. I promise. Not even Gideon. But, Francesca, I don't understand. Rochford is your friend. What great wrong could you have done him?"

Francesca hesitated. Her heart felt like lead within her chest, the long-dead sorrow hanging there still. "I broke off our engagement."

Irene stared. "I *knew* there was something between you!" she exclaimed softly. "I just was not sure exactly what it had been. But I have never heard of this. I don't understand. It must have been a huge scandal."

"No." Francesca shook her head. "There was no scandal. Our engagement was secret."

"Secret? That scarcely sounds like the duke."

"Oh, there was nothing havey-cavey about it," Francesca assured her. "Rochford was always quite proper. He—he told me that he did not want me to be locked into an engagement during my first Season. It was the summer I made my come-out, you see. He said that I might change my mind once I had had a Season. I knew that I would not, but…well, you know the duke. He always allows for every contingency. And he thought me flighty, no doubt."

"You were young," Irene said.

Francesca shrugged. "Yes. But more than that—I have never been, will never be, a *weighty* sort." She flashed a smile at her companion. "A 'butterfly' is the way he described me."

"So you did not suit, then?"

"No, it was not that. Rochford was content enough, I think. He expressed no displeasure, at least. And I—"

She paused, her eyes seeing a different time, a faint smile hovering on her lips. "I was desperately in love with him—as only an eighteen-year-old girl can be."

Irene wrinkled her brow. "Then what happened?"

"Daphne happened," Francesca replied grimly.

"Daphne! Lady Swithington?" Irene stared at her. "Lord Bromwell's sister?"

Francesca nodded. "Yes. She was the source of the trouble between Rochford and Brom, the reason Rochford was so set against him becoming Callie's husband. I was not the only one fooled by Daphne's lies. Her brother believed, as well, that Rochford and Daphne were having an affair."

"Oh, no! Francesca…" Irene laid her hand on her friend's arm, sympathy warm on her face. "You thought she was his mistress?"

"Not at first. She told me straight out that she was, but I refused to believe her. I knew Rochford. Or I thought I knew him. I was aware that he did not love me as I loved him, but I believed he was too honorable a man to marry one woman and keep another as a mistress. But then, one evening—in this very house, in fact—I discovered that I was wrong. A footman brought me a note as I finished a dance. It said that if I went to the conservatory, I would find something interesting."

"Oh, dear."

"Yes. Oh, dear. I thought the duke had sent me the note. I imagined that he had some sort of surprise for me, something romantic, perhaps. He had given me a pair of sapphire earrings the week before, saying that they were the best he could find, though they could not match the brilliance of my eyes." She let out a sound, half laugh, half sigh. "Goodness, how long ago that seems."

"Do you have the earrings still?" Irene asked.

"Of course. They were beautiful. I did not wear them, but I could not get rid of them. I offered them back to him afterwards, of course, but he refused, with the blackest look."

"I presume you found him and Lady Daphne *in flagrante?*" Irene went on.

Francesca nodded. She remembered how she had felt, so brimming with love and eagerness, as she had hurried through the wide halls toward the conservatory. She had hoped that Rochford had found a way to steal some time alone with her. It had been even more difficult here in the city than it had been at home, surrounded as they were not only by chaperones, but all the *ton*, as well. Such a secluded tryst was not like him, of course; he was always supremely careful of her honor, unwilling to engage in any behavior that might damage her reputation. But perhaps, she had thought, tonight passion had carried him away, and the idea had sent a delicious shiver through her.

Francesca had not been able to quite imagine what it would be like to see Sinclair burn with passion. The duke was such a cool and elegant sort, ever unflappable in the face of the most major crisis, and correct to a fault. But there had been a time or two when he had kissed her, when his lips had pressed harder into hers and his skin had flamed in such a way that her own nerves had begun to jangle inside her, and she had wondered if something hotter, harder, stronger, boiled inside him, as well. He had always pulled away quickly, of course, but Francesca had seen a flash of something in his eyes—something hot and almost frightening, but in a somehow delicious way.

"I went into the conservatory," Francesca recalled now. "I said his name. Sinclair was at the far end of the room, and there were some orange trees between us. He started toward me, and I saw that his ascot was in disarray, his hair mussed. I did not understand at first, but then I heard a noise, and I looked beyond him. Daphne had come out from behind the trees, as well. Her dress was unfastened down the front to the waist."

Unconsciously, Francesca's face hardened as she remembered the moment. Daphne's hair had been partially undone, straggling around her face in tangled curls. Her flimsy chemise had been unlaced, and her full white breasts had spilled flagrantly out, almost completely uncovered. She had smiled at Francesca like the cat that had just gotten into the cream. And Francesca had shattered inside.

"When I saw them, I realized what a fool I had been. I had not been so deluded that I believed that Rochford was madly in love with me. He had, after all, pointed out to me all the very practical reasons why he and I were a good match. He had not spouted declarations of love or written odes to my smile or any such foolishness. But I believed that he cared for me. I had been sure that he would never harm me or treat me with anything but respect. And I had known that I would be such a good wife to him, make him so happy, that someday he would come to love me as much as I loved him."

"Instead he had been bedding down with Lady Daphne while he was engaged to you."

"Yes. Well, no, not really. It was all a lie. But I did not know that at the time, and I could not bear what I believed to be true. No doubt there are other women who would have ignored it, reasoning that they would still be his duchess, even if another had his heart. But I could not. I broke it off with him."

"But in fact Daphne had arranged that little scene and sent you the note?"

"Yes. She told me at Callie's wedding that it had all been a lie. He had not slept with her, just as he swore to me then that he had not. I did not believe him when he tried to tell me that, of course. I refused to listen to him. And afterwards, when he called on me, I would not see him."

"And that is why you married Lord Haughston?" Irene asked shrewdly.

Francesca nodded. "He was everything that Rochford was not—full of romantic words and extravagant gestures. I was his stars, his moon, he told me." She gave a little grimace. "His words were like balm to my wounded heart. This, I told myself, was what love was really like. So I married him. Our honeymoon was not yet over before I realized what a mistake I had made."

"I'm so sorry." Irene slipped her hand into Francesca's and squeezed.

"Well, 'tis long past now," Francesca replied, and forced a little smile.

"I can scarcely believe that Lady Daphne admitted that she had lied to you."

"It was not done with any good will, I can assure you. I think she wanted me to realize what an idiot I had been. I am sure she hoped I would regret throwing away my chance to be a duchess."

"And, instead, of course, what you regretted was having misjudged Rochford. The hurt you did to him."

Francesca admitted, "His pride must have suffered greatly. He would have hated having his honor impugned, even though he knew he was not at fault."

"Oh, Francesca…what a terrible thing. Certainly he was not the only one hurt."

"No. But at least I was at fault. One could say I deserved what happened to me. I was the one who believed her lies. I was the one who would not listen to the truth when he told it to me. But Sinclair had done nothing wrong."

"And you think finding the duke a wife will set this right?" Irene asked.

Francesca recognized the skepticism in her friend's tone. "I know it cannot make up for what I did. But I fear that… What if it is because of me that Rochford has never married?" She colored a little. "I am not saying that I think his heart was forever broken. I do not rate myself so high as to think no other woman could take my place. But I fear that I led him to mistrust women so much that he has not wanted to marry. He was already used to being alone, I think, and it was easier, perhaps, for him to live that way. Sinclair came into his title at such an early age, and he had already learned that people courted his favor simply because of his title and wealth. I think that is one of the things he found appealing about marrying me—we had known each other since we were children, and I was not in awe of him. I knew him for himself, not for his title or anything else. But then, when I did not believe him, when I acted in a way that must have seemed a betrayal to him, I fear that he became even more distant and distrustful."

"That may be, but if he does not want to marry…"

"But he must. He knows that as well as I do. He is the Duke of Rochford. He must have an heir, someone to inherit the title and estate. Rochford is far too responsible not to realize that. I will simply be helping him to do what he knows must be done." She threw an impish grin at her companion. "And you, more than anyone else, cannot deny that I am adept at bringing to the altar even those who profess a determination not to wed."

Irene acknowledged her words with a wry smile. "I will admit that you are expert at joining even the wariest together. However, I cannot help but wonder how the duke will take to this plan."

"Oh, I do not intend for him to know about it," Francesca responded blithely. "That is why you must not tell even Gideon about this. I am sure that Rochford would consider it a great interference on my part and would order me to stop it, so I have no intention of giving him that opportunity."

Irene nodded, looking amused. "It should not be difficult to find women eager to wed the duke. He is the most eligible bachelor in the country."

"True. I am certain that any number would wish to become his wife, but not just anyone will do. I had to find the right woman for him, which has proven to be a more difficult task than I had expected. But, then, Rochford is deserving of only an extraordinary woman, so it is no wonder that there are not many of them about."

"Althea and Damaris are two of them, I gather. Who else have you picked out for him?"

"I have narrowed the field to three. Besides Damaris and Althea, there is only Lady Caroline Wyatt. I must talk to the three of them tonight and decide on how to throw each of them together with the duke."

"What if he doesn't like any of them?" Irene asked.

Francesca shrugged. "Then I shall have to find others. Someone is bound to suit him."

"Perhaps I am being obtuse," Irene began, "but it seems to me that the best candidate would be you."

"Me?" Francesca cast a startled glance at her.

"Yes, you. After all, you are the one woman whom we are certain Rochford would want to marry, given that he has already asked you once. If you were to tell him you had discovered the lie, that you were sorry for not believing him…"

"No. No," Francesca said, looking flustered. "That is impossible. I am almost thirty-four, far too long in the tooth to be a suitable bride for the duke. I shall, of course, apologize to him and confess how stupid and wrong I was. I must. But the two of us—no, that is long in the past."

"Really?"

"Yes. Really. Pray do not give me that disbelieving look. I am certain of this. You know that I am done with marriage. And even if I were not, it has been too long, and too much has happened between us. He could never forgive me for breaking it off with him—not to that extent. Rochford is a very proud man. And whatever feeling he might have had for me once, by now it is long dead. It has been fifteen years, after all. I do not still love him. Even less would he harbor any love for the woman who rejected him. Why, for ages he scarcely even spoke to me. It has only been in the past few years that we have been something like friends again."

"Well, if you are certain…?"

"I am."

Irene shrugged. "Then what do you intend to do?"

"I…ah! There is Lady Althea." Francesca had spotted her quarry standing beyond the dancers, chatting with another woman. "I shall start with her. I think that I may chat with her a bit, maybe plan an outing together. Then I can arrange it so that Rochford makes up one of our party."

"If that is your plan, it seems that fortune has smiled on you," Irene told her, nodding toward another part of the ballroom. "Rochford just walked in."

"He did?" Francesca's heart sped up a bit, and she turned to look in the direction her friend indicated.

It was Rochford, all right, effortlessly elegant in formal black and white, and easily the most handsome man in the room. His thick black hair was cut into an artfully casual style that many copied but few could achieve, and his lean, tall figure was perfectly suited for the close-fitting trousers and jacket that were the current fashion. There was nothing ostentatious about him— the only decoration he wore was a stickpin anchoring his cravat, the head of which was an onyx as dark as his eyes—yet no one, seeing him, would have thought him anything less than an aristocrat.

Francesca's hand tightened on her fan as she watched him glance about the room. Every time she had seen him lately, she had felt this same roiling mixture of emotions. It had been years since she had felt this way, so jittery and filled with trepidation, yet strangely excited, as well. Daphne's words, she reflected, had opened some sort of door on the past, letting in a whole host of feelings that she had thought time and experience had worn away.

It was entirely foolish, she realized. Knowing, as she

did now, that Rochford had not been unfaithful to her made no real difference in her life. Nothing had changed because of it, and nothing would. Yet she could not deny the little spurt of joy it aroused in her whenever she saw him. He had never belonged to Daphne; his firm, well-cut mouth had not kissed her, nor whispered in her ear. His hands had not caressed her or showered her with jewels. The mental pictures that had tortured her fifteen years ago had been entirely false, and she could not help but be glad of it.

Francesca turned away, suddenly busy with her gloves and fan, smoothing down the front of her skirt. "I must tell him," she said softly.

She knew that she could not be at ease around him again until she had revealed what she had learned and apologized for not trusting or believing him. And, clearly, she could not match him with a wife if she could not even be around him without going into a fit of nerves. She must tell him…but how?

"I think that you are about to get your chance," Irene told her dryly.

"What?" Francesca looked up.

And there, climbing the stairs toward them, was the Duke of Rochford.

CHAPTER TWO

FRANCESCA FROZE, aware of a craven impulse to flee. But she could not, of course. Rochford was looking straight at her. She could not turn away without being rude. Besides, Irene was right: this was her opportunity to explain everything to him.

So she stood her ground and smiled as the duke approached them.

"Lady Haughston. Lady Radbourne," he greeted them, sketching a bow.

"Rochford. How nice to see you," Francesca replied.

"It has been a long time. I have seen you at few parties."

She might have known that he would notice. Rochford rarely missed anything. "I…have been resting a bit since Callie's wedding."

"Have you been ill?" He frowned.

"Oh. No. No, not at all. Um…" Francesca sighed inwardly. Hardly two sentences spoken, and already she was floundering.

She found it the most difficult thing to lie to Rochford. Even the most innocuous social lie that she might blithely relate to anyone else seemed to curdle and die on her tongue when she was faced with his dark gaze. She felt sometimes as though his eyes could look deep inside her, see to the very depths of her soul.

She glanced away from those eyes now as she went on. "I was not ill, merely…tired. The Season can grow somewhat wearying, even to me."

She had the distinct feeling that he did not believe her. He studied her for one long moment more, then gracefully replied, "None would know it, I assure you. You are as radiant as always."

Francesca acknowledged his compliment with a gracious nod, and he turned toward Irene. "As do you, my lady. Marriage seems to suit you."

"It does," she admitted, sounding faintly surprised.

"Is Radbourne here this evening?" he asked. "I am surprised not to find him by your side."

"That is because Irene deserted him," Francesca put in, grinning.

"'Tis true," Irene agreed. "I abandoned him to Lady Pencully's clutches and fled like a coward for the stairs."

"Good Gad, is Aunt Odelia here?" he asked, casting an alarmed glance toward the ballroom below.

"Yes, but she will not climb the stairs," Francesca replied. "So long as you stay up here, you are safe."

"I would not be so sure. The woman seems to have become positively reinvigorated since her eightieth birthday ball," Rochford responded.

Irene glanced over at Francesca, then said lightly, "I suppose I had better play the good wife and go rescue Gideon before his patience grows too thin and he says something to her that he will later regret."

Francesca quelled the spurt of panic that rose in her at her friend's departure. She had conversed with the duke hundreds of times; it was absurd that it should suddenly seem so awkward.

"How is the duchess?" she asked once Irene had left, for want of anything better to say.

"Grandmother is well and enjoying Bath. She keeps threatening to come for at least a few weeks of the Season, but I think she will not. She is too relieved at no longer having to do her duty by chaperoning Callie."

Francesca nodded. That seemed to be the end of that topic. She shifted nervously and glanced out over the ballroom again. She had to tell him, she knew. She could not continue in this way, being shy and uncomfortable around him. Over the past few years, she had become accustomed to having him as something of a friend again. She looked forward to conversing with him at parties; it was always enlivening to bandy words with him, and his wit made even the most boring gathering tolerable. And she could count on him for a waltz, which meant that at least one dance of the evening would be effortless, like floating around the floor.

She had to make amends. She had to confess and ask his forgiveness, no matter how much the thought of it frightened her.

She glanced up and found him watching her, his dark eyes thoughtful. He knew, she thought; the man was simply too discerning. He knew that there was something wrong with her. With them.

"Perhaps you would care to take a stroll with me," he told her, offering her his arm. "I understand that the Whittingtons' gallery is quite enjoyable."

"Yes. Of course. That sounds quite pleasant."

Francesca placed her hand upon his arm and walked with him through the double doors into the long hallway running along one side of the Whittington mansion. The gallery was hung with portraits of ancestors and a variety of other subjects, including a favorite hunter or dog of one Whittington or another throughout the centuries. They strolled along, now and then glancing at the pictures, but with little real interest. There was no one else about, and their steps echoed hollowly on the polished parquet floor. Silence stretched between them, growing deeper and more awkward with each passing moment.

Finally Rochford said, "Have I offended you past remedying?"

"What?" Startled, Francesca's eyes flew to his face. "What do you mean?"

He stopped and turned to face her. His expression was solemn, his straight black eyebrows drawn together harshly. "I mean that while 'tis true that I have seen you at few parties in the past weeks, you have been at *some* of them—and whenever you saw me, you immediately turned and disappeared into the crowd. And if, by chance, you came upon me unexpectedly, with no way to avoid the encounter, you seized the first opportunity to make your excuses and leave. I can only assume that you have not forgiven me for what I said to you that day, when I found out that Bromwell had been courting Callie."

"No!" Francesca protested, laying a hand earnestly upon his arm. "That is not true. I did not blame you. Truly I did not. I… Perhaps you were a bit harsh. But you apologized. And, clearly, you had reason to be concerned. But I could not betray Callie's trust, and she had the right to choose her own future."

"Yes. I know. She is quite independent." He sighed. "I realize that you had little choice, and I had no reason to expect you to be able to control my sister. God knows, I had poor enough luck at it. And once I was over my anger, I knew I was in the wrong. I apologized, and I thought you had accepted my apology. But then you began hiding from me."

"No, truly…" Francesca told him. "I did accept your apology, and I am not angry with you about what you said. I have seen your temper a time or two before, you know."

"Then why are you upset with me?" he asked. "Even at Callie's wedding, I saw you but little." He stopped abruptly, then asked, "Was it because of that scene at the hunting lodge? Because I—" He hesitated.

"Because you knocked your sister's future husband

to the floor?" Francesca asked, a smile hovering at the corners of her lips. "Because the two of you were brawling through the parlour, knocking vases off tables and overturning chairs?"

Rochford started to protest, then stopped, his own mouth twitching into a small smile. "Well…yes. Because I was acting like a ruffian. And making a general fool of myself."

"My dear Duke," Francesca drawled, laughter glimmering in her eyes, "whyever should I have taken exception to that?"

He let out a short laugh. "Well, at least you have the good grace not to say that it is nothing unusual. Although I might point out that while I may have been a ruffian, at least I was not telling enormous clankers, as were some of us." He shot her a droll look.

"Clankers!" Francesca tapped his arm lightly with her fan, scarcely noticing that the awkwardness had fallen away from them and she was bantering with him once again in a carefree way. "You are most unjust, sir."

"Come, now, you cannot deny that you were…shall we say, most inventive that morning?"

"Someone had to bring that mess into some order," she shot back. "Else we would all have been in a pretty predicament."

"I know." His face sobered, and he reached out, surprising her, and took her hand. "I know how much you did for Callie that day. You earned my undying gratitude for your 'inventiveness.' And your kind heart.

Callie would have been embroiled in a serious scandal if it were not for you."

Francesca felt her cheeks growing warm under his steady regard, and she glanced away. "There is no need to thank me. Indeed, I am quite fond of Callie. She is much like a sister to me."

It occurred to her then that her words had been unfortunate, and she blushed even harder. Would Rochford think her presumptuous? Or assume that she was reminding him of the fact that they had nearly become man and wife?

Francesca turned and continued walking. Her hand was curled so tightly around her fan that the sticks were digging into her flesh. Rochford fell in beside her, and for a moment they walked in silence. She could feel him watching her. He knew something was wrong. She was only making it worse and prolonging her own anxiety.

"I have to apologize to you," she blurted out suddenly.

"Excuse me?" he asked, surprise clear in his voice.

She stopped and turned to him, steeling herself to look up into his face. "I wronged you. Fifteen years ago, when we—" She stopped, feeling as though her throat was closing up on her.

He stiffened slightly, the puzzlement on his face turning to a slight wariness. "When we were engaged?" he finished for her.

Francesca nodded. She found she could not hold his gaze, after all, and she glanced away. "I— At Callie's wedding, Lady Swithington told me—she said she lied about the two of you. That there was never anything between you."

When he said nothing, Francesca squared her shoulders and forced herself to look back up at him. His face was still, his gaze shuttered, and she knew no more of what he was thinking or feeling than she had when she was turned away from him.

She swallowed and went on. "I was wrong. I accused you unjustly. I should have listened to you, heard you out. And I—I wanted you to know that I am sorry for what I said to you, for what I did."

"Well…" He half turned from her, then swung back. "I see." He was silent for a moment longer, then said, "I am afraid I don't know what to say."

"I don't know that there is anything to say," Francesca admitted, and they turned and began to stroll back the way they had come. "There is nothing to be done. It is all long over. But I could not feel easy without telling you how wrong I was. I don't expect you to forgive me. But I wanted you to know that I learned the truth, and that I am sorry for misjudging you. I should have known your character better."

"You were very young," he replied mildly.

"Yes, but that is not an adequate excuse, surely."

"I daresay."

Francesca cast a sidelong glance at the duke. She had worried that when she told him, he would slice her with a cold, acerbic remark. Or that his eyes would light with fury, and he would storm at her or stalk away. She had not considered that her confession might render him speechless.

They walked through the double doors leading into the upper level of the ballroom and stopped, turning toward each other awkwardly. Francesca's heart hammered in her chest. She did not want to simply part from him this way, unsure of what he thought and felt, not knowing if he was seething inside or simply relieved to know that she no longer believed him a cad. She could not bear it, she thought, if her confession resulted in the ruination of the delicate friendship they had built over the years.

Impulsively, she asked, "Shall we dance?"

He smiled faintly. "Yes, why don't we?"

He extended his arm to her, and they started down the curving staircase.

A waltz struck up just as they reached the floor, and Rochford swept her into his arms and out to join the dancers. Something fluttered inside her, soft and insistent, and she was suddenly uncertain and nervous, yet almost giddy, as well. She had danced with the duke many times over the course of the past few years, but somehow, in this moment, it felt different, even new. It felt…almost as it had years before.

She was very aware of the strength of his arms encircling her, his warmth, the smell of his cologne mingled with that faint, indefinable scent that was his alone. She remembered how it had been that Boxing

Day, at the ball he had given at Dancy Park, when he had taken her into his arms for a waltz, and she had looked up at him and realized that the girlish infatuation she had felt for him for years was something much more. Gazing into the depths of his dark eyes, she had known that she was hopelessly, madly in love with the man. She had been dizzy with excitement, her entire body tingling with awareness of him. He had gazed back down at her and smiled, and in that moment, heat had burst inside her like a sun.

Staring up at him now, Francesca felt color rush to her cheeks at the memory. He looked so much the same; if anything, the years had only added to his handsomeness, the faint lines at the corners of his eyes softening the sharp planes and angles that could make his face appear cold. He had always looked a bit like a pirate, she thought, with his black eyes and black hair, and the high swooping line of his cheekbones. Or at least he appeared that way when his straight black brows drew together, or when he turned his level, icy stare on one. At those moments he seemed a trifle dangerous.

But when he smiled, it was a different matter altogether. His face lit up and his eyes warmed, and his mouth curved in a most inviting way. It was almost impossible not to smile back at him at such a moment, and, indeed, it made one want to do something to bring that smile out again.

She glanced away quickly, embarrassed at the direction of her thoughts. She hoped that he had not seen her blush or had any idea what had brought it about. It was absurd, of course, for her to be nervous or eager. And even more laughable for her thoughts to go skittering to juvenile maunderings about his good looks or appealing smile. She was long past such feelings—for Rochford or anyone else. Whatever girlish love she had felt for the man had died many years ago, burned away by long nights of sleepless anguish, drowned in a sea of tears.

She cast about for some topic to bridge the silence. "Have you heard from Callie?"

"I have had a letter from her. Very brief, I might add. 'Paris is beautiful. Bromwell is wonderful. Looking forward to Italy.'"

Francesca chuckled. "Surely 'twas not quite so short as that."

"Oh, no, there was a bit more description of Paris. But all in all, it was a model of brevity. Their plan is to return to London in another week—if, of course, they do not decide to extend the honeymoon."

"Well, at least it sounds as if she is happy."

"Yes. I believe she is. Against everything I would ever have thought, Bromwell apparently loves her."

"It must be lonely for you without her."

"The house is a trifle quiet," Rochford admitted with a faint smile. "But I have kept busy." He raised an eyebrow at her. "What about you?"

"Have I kept busy? Or have I been lonely without Callie?"

"Either. Both. She was with you more than she was at home the last two months before she married."

"That is true. And I have found that I miss her," Francesca admitted. "Callie is…well, her leaving creates a larger hole in one's life than I would have imagined."

"Perhaps you should take another young lady under your wing," Rochford suggested. "I have seen a number of women here tonight who could do with an application of your expert touch."

"Ah, but none of them has asked for my help. It is a bit rude, you know, to offer one's opinion, unasked, on how another can be improved."

"I suppose it would be. Although one cannot help but wish that you might say something to Lady Livermore."

Francesca stifled a giggle, following the direction of Rochford's eyes to where Lady Livermore was dancing with her cousin. She was wearing her favorite color, a strong puce that would show to advantage on very few women. Lady Livermore was not among them. The color would have been bad enough in itself, but Lady Livermore was of the opinion that if something was good, then more of it was even better. Ruffles festooned the neckline of her dress and the bottom of the skirt, billowing out beneath the scalloped hemline of her overdress. Even the short puffed sleeves carried two rows of ruffles. Silk rosettes marked the upward points of the scallops, each one centered by a pearl, with a swag of pearls stretching from point to point. A pearl-trimmed toque of matching color sat atop her head.

"Lady Livermore, I fear, is unlikely to change," Francesca told him. She paused for a moment, then said, "Do you know Lady Althea?"

Francesca could have bitten her tongue as soon as she said it. *How could she have blurted that out so clumsily?*

"Robart's daughter?" the duke asked in a surprised tone. "Do you think that she needs help finding a husband?"

"Oh, no! Goodness." Francesca let out a little laugh. "I am sure Lady Althea has no need for any help from me. I just saw her dancing with Sir Cornelius, that's all." She paused, then went on. "I am sure that she has no lack of suitors. She is quite attractive, don't you think?"

"Yes," Rochford answered. "I suppose she is."

"And accomplished, too. She plays the piano quite well."

"Yes, she does. I have heard her play."

"Have you? She is much admired, I understand."

"No doubt."

Francesca was aware of a distinct spurt of annoyance at his reply. She was not sure why the duke's agreeable admissions of Lady Althea's excellence irritated her. After all, her job would be much easier if Rochford already found the woman appealing. And surely she was not so vain herself that she could not bear to hear another woman praised. Still, she found it hard not to respond sharply, even though she herself had raised the subject.

She turned the conversation to something else, but later, when the music ended, she subtly maneuvered Rochford into walking off the dance floor in the direction that Lady Althea and her partner had taken. She was lucky enough that Sir Cornelius was taking his leave of the lady as they approached.

"Lady Althea," Francesca greeted her with apparent pleasure. "How nice to see you. It has been an age since we have met, I vow. You know the Duke of Rochford, do you not?"

Lady Althea offered them a measured smile. "Yes, of course. A pleasure to see you, sir."

Rochford bowed over her hand, assuring her politely that the pleasure was all his, as Francesca cast an assessing eye over the woman. Lady Althea was tall and slim, and her white silk ball gown was tasteful, if somewhat lacking in dash in Francesca's opinion. And if her lips were a bit too thin and her face a trifle long for real beauty, she did have a wealth of dark brown hair, and her brown eyes were large and lined with thick, dark lashes. Many men, Francesca was sure, would call her pretty.

She cast a sideways glance at Rochford, wondering if he numbered among those men.

Lady Althea inquired politely after Rochford's grandmother and Francesca's parents, then moved on to compliment Callie's wedding. It was the sort of polite chitchat in which Francesca had engaged for much of her life, as had Lady Althea and Rochford, and they were able to spend several minutes talking about almost nothing at all.

When they had finished praising Lady Whittington's ball—perhaps her finest, in Lady Althea's opinion—as well as commiserating over the sad state of Lady Althea's mother's nerves, which had kept her in bed tonight instead of attending this event, they moved on to the latest play at Drury Lane, which, as it turned out, none of them had actually seen.

"Why, we must go!" Francesca exclaimed, looking at Lady Althea.

The other woman seemed faintly surprised, but replied only, "Yes, certainly. That sounds quite pleasant."

Francesca beamed. "And we shall press the duke to take us." She turned toward Rochford expectantly.

His eyes, too, widened a trifle, but he said evenly, "Of course. It would be my privilege to escort two such lovely ladies to the theater."

"Wonderful." Francesca glanced back at Althea, who, she noticed, appeared more eager about the invitation now that the duke was attached to the expedition. "Let us set a night, then. Tuesday, shall we say?"

The other two agreed, and Francesca favored them with a smile. She had, she knew, ridden roughshod over them. She was customarily more deft in her maneuverings than she had been tonight. She was not sure why she had been clumsier than usual, but at least neither of the others looked disgruntled or suspicious.

She made a few more minutes of small talk, then slipped away, leaving Rochford with Althea. She made her way across the room, greeting some and pausing to chat with others. She should have felt a sense of triumph, she knew. She had finally set her plan in motion.

But, in truth, all she felt was the beginning of a headache.

She paused and glanced around her. She saw Irene in the distance, and a moment later she spotted Sir Lucien on the dance floor. She could make her way to Irene or wait for Sir Lucien—or, indeed, she could find half a dozen others to talk to, and there were any number of men who would doubtless ask her for a dance.

However, she found herself unwilling to do any of those things. Her temples were beginning to pound, and she felt bored and curiously deflated. All she really wanted, she reflected, was to go home.

Pleading a headache, which for once was real, she bade good-night to her hostess and went outside to her carriage. The vehicle was ten years old and growing somewhat shabby, but it felt good to be in it, snugly away from the music and lights, and the noise of a multitude of people chattering.

FENTON, HER BUTLER, was surprised to see her home so early, and immediately hovered over her solicitously. "Are you well, my lady? Have you caught a chill?"

The man had been her butler for over fourteen years;

she had hired him soon after she and Lord Haughston were married. He was intensely loyal, as all her servants were. There had been many times when she had been unable to pay their wages, but Fenton had never grumbled—and she felt sure he had made quick work of any servant who did.

Francesca smiled at the man now. "No. I am fine. Just a bit of a headache."

Upstairs, she faced the same quizzing from her maid, Maisie, who immediately took down Francesca's hair and brushed it out, whisked off her dress and helped her into her nightclothes, then bustled out of the room to fetch lavender water to ease her headache. Before long Francesca found herself ensconced in her bed, pillows fluffed behind her, a handkerchief soaked in lavender water stretched across her forehead and the kerosene lamp beside her bed turned to its lowest glow.

With a sigh, Francesca closed her eyes. She was not sleepy. The hour was far earlier than she was accustomed to retiring. And, in truth, the headache had eased as soon as she returned home and let down her hair. Unfortunately, the gloom that had touched her at the ball seemed to have settled in.

She was not a woman who dwelled upon her misfortunes. When her husband had died five years ago, leaving her with little but this town house in London, one of the few things that had not been entailed with his estate, she had not sat about twisting her hands and bemoaning her fate. She had done her best to marshal her resources and pay off his debts, reducing her own expenses to the bare minimum. She had closed off part of the house and reduced the staff, then proceeded to gradually sell her silver and gold plate, and even her own jewelry. She had also quickly learned to practice economy, turning and refurbishing her old gowns rather than buying new ones, and wearing her slippers until the soles wore through.

Even so, it had become apparent that such economies and her small jointure were not enough to support her and even a small staff for any length of time. Most women in her position would have sought a new husband, but after her experience with the first one, Francesca had been determined not to embark on that course again. Without a marriage to finance her, she knew, the expected course would be to retire to her father's house, now her brother's, to live as a dependent relative for the rest of her life.

Instead, she had cast about for some means of bringing in more income. There were no jobs for ladies, of course, except for something like a companion or a governess. Neither of those held the slightest appeal for Francesca, and, indeed, she was sure that no one would have hired her for either one. The skills she possessed— impeccable taste, an eye for the fashions that complemented one's looks rather than taking away from them, a thorough knowledge of the London social scene, the ability to flirt to exactly the right degree, as well as to enliven even the dullest party or most uncomfortable situation—were not the sorts of things that would make one money.

However, it occurred to her, after yet another society matron begged her help in bringing off an unpopular daughter's Season, that her skills were quite useful in the primary occupation of the mamas of the *ton*—securing a good marriage for their unmarried daughters. Few could better guide a naive young girl through the treacherous waters of the Season, and none were as adept in finding the perfect dress or accessory to flatter a figure or diminish a fault, or the most becoming hairstyle for any sort of face. Patience, tact and a ready sense of humor had helped her through an unhappy marriage, as well as fifteen years as one of the leaders of the *beau monde,* an always-perilous position. Surely those qualities could be used to successfully steer a young woman into a good marriage—even, if she was lucky, into love.

Francesca had been matchmaking for three years now—always under the genteel guise of doing a favor for a friend, of course—and she had managed, if not to live well, at least to get by. She was able to keep food on the table and pay a small staff, as well as heat the house in the winter—as long as she kept many of the larger, draftier rooms closed off. And given the amount of business she was able to bring dressmakers and millinery shops, she was often given a dress that had been ordered but not picked up, or allowed to buy a frock or hat at a considerable discount.

It was not the life she had dreamed of as a young girl,

certainly, and she spent far more time than she cared to think of worrying about whether she would be able to pay her bills. But at least she was able to live on her own, as independent as any lady could be if she hoped to be respectable. Her mother, she knew, would have been shocked if she had known about Francesca's secret occupation—as would a number of other members of society. Perhaps what she did was not genteel, but, frankly, she found it satisfying to take those without a sense of style and turn them into fashionable and attractive young ladies, and it was always pleasing to help a couple find each other.

All in all, she was quite content with her life. Or, at least, she had been. But over the last few weeks she had been aware of a feeling of dissatisfaction, a certain ennui. She had even at times been…well, lonely.

That was absurd, of course, because her social calendar was invariably full. She had invitations for every night of the week, often more than one a night. Every day brought a steady round of callers, both male and female. She never wanted for a dance partner or an escort. If she had been alone often during the past few weeks, that had been of her own accord. She had not really wanted to go out much or see anyone.

She missed Callie, she knew. She had grown quite accustomed to having the girl around, and the house seemed emptier without her, just as she had told the duke. And, she had to admit, she was also suffering remorse and guilt about the terrible mistake she had made so many years ago. She would have been less than human, she supposed, if she had not considered how different her life would have been if she had not broken off her engagement.

Certainly, if she had married Rochford, she would not now be spending her days worrying about how she was to keep food on the table or whether an old dress could be restyled yet again. But far more than the material benefits, she had to wonder if she might not have lived a happy life with him.

What if she had been married to a man of honor rather than a libertine? What might have happened if she had married the man she truly loved? She remembered the dizzying excitement she had felt when she was with Rochford back then, the glow that had filled her every time he smiled at her...the way she had tingled all over when he kissed her.

His behavior with her had been quite correct, and the few kisses he had given her had for the most part been chaste. Even so, she remembered, her heart had pounded at his nearness, and her senses had been filled with the sight and sound and scent of him. Once or twice, when he had laid his lips upon hers, she had felt heat surge in him, and he had pulled her close to him. His lips had dug into hers, opening her mouth before he pulled away abruptly, apologizing for his lack of decorum. Francesca had scarcely heard him. She had stared at him, lips open slightly, dazed by the new and strange sensations sizzling along her nerves, the fire exploding in her abdomen, and she had shivered, wanting more.

If she had married Rochford, she might now be surrounded by children, honored by her husband, perhaps even well-loved. She might have been happy.

A tear escaped from the corner of her eye and trickled down her cheek. She opened her eyes and reached up to dash away the wayward drop. What foolishness, she thought. She was no longer a girl of eighteen to be carried away by romantic notions.

The truth was that, though she might have had children, her marriage to Sinclair would probably have been equally unhappy.

When she had fluttered inside at Rochford's kisses, she had not realized what came after the kisses and embraces, or how those tantalizing sensations would die when she was confronted by the reality of the marital act. If she had married the duke, she told herself, the result would have been the same. The only difference would have been that she turned stiff and cold with Rochford, and it would have been he, not Andrew, who left her bed cursing and calling her Lady Ice—or, rather, the Duchess of Ice, she supposed.

A grim little smile curved her lips. The duke had been fond of her, but it was absurd to dream that she might have won his love over the years. He would have acted more honorably than Haughston, of course. He would not have harangued her or paraded his mistresses before her. But he would doubtless have enjoyed their marital bed as little as Andrew had. He, too, would have lost whatever feeling he had for her when she could not respond to him with ardor. And how much of her love for him would have remained as, night after night, she had had to endure having him thrust into her, hoping that this time it would not be painful, sighing with relief when the act was over and he left her bed?

There was no reason to think that any of that would have changed. She would not magically have become a passionate woman simply because she married a different man. It would have been worse, she thought, to have seen the disenchantment dawn on Rochford's face as he realized that his wife was cold in bed. And it would have been worse, surely, to have come to dread the nighttime visits of the man she loved.

No, it was better by far to have lived the life she had. Better to still have her happy memories of the love she had once felt. Rochford, too, would have been thankful that she had not married him if only he had known the sort of woman she was. He could still marry and have heirs.

Indeed, any of the women she had chosen would make an excellent wife and duchess for Rochford. He could easily fall in love with one of them. After all, Francesca had achieved a great deal of success in that regard with the matches she had helped to bring about. The rest of his life would be happier than it doubtless would have been if they had married. And such an outcome would make her happy, too. Very happy, she told herself.

So why, then, she wondered, did the thought of arranging his wedding to another leave her feeling so empty inside?

CHAPTER THREE

FRANCESCA WAS WALKING through the garden at Dancy Park. The sun was warm upon her back, and the air was redolent with the scent of roses. In the golden light, flowers bloomed in a riot of color: purple larkspur, white and yellow snapdragons, the huge pink and red bursts of peonies, and everywhere roses in all shades, climbing trellises and spilling over walls. A breeze ruffled the flowers, sending their heads nodding and petals floating on the air.

"Francesca."

She turned, and there was Rochford. The sun was behind him, and she could not see his features clearly, but she knew his voice, his form, the way he walked toward her. She smiled, emotion welling up in her.

"I saw you from my study," he went on, coming closer to her.

His face was all angles and planes; she wanted to trace her fingertips along them. In the sunlight, his dark eyes were lighter than they appeared indoors, the irises the color of warm chocolate surrounding the coal-black of the pupils. Her eyes went to his mouth, firm and well-defined. His lips, she thought, looked succulent, and at the idea, something twisted in her abdomen, hot and slow.

"Sinclair." His name was no more than a breath upon her lips. Her chest tightened, her throat closing up as it often did when he was near. He was as familiar to her as this garden or this house, and yet whenever she was around him these days, she was as skittish and eager, as thrumming with energy, as if she had never seen him before.

He raised his hand, cupping her cheek in his palm. His hand was hard, and warmer than even the sun's caress. His thumb smoothed its way across her cheek and brushed against her mouth. Featherlight, he traced the line of her lips, and the exquisitely sensitive flesh blazed to life beneath his touch.

Tendrils of heat twined through her body, tangling deep in her loins. A pulse sprang to life between her legs, surprising her, and she drew a quick breath.

She watched in anticipation as he lowered his head to hers, finally closing her eyes in sweet surrender as their lips joined. His hand upon her cheek was suddenly searing. He wrapped his other arm around her, pressing her into his body, his hard flesh sinking into her softness.

Francesca was aware of her heart thudding like a wild thing in her chest, and her insides seemed to be made of molten wax. His lips pressed against hers, opening her mouth. An unexpected, unknown hunger roared through her, and she squeezed her legs together against the ache that blossomed there. She trembled all over, heat surging in her, yearning for something that seemed just beyond her reach.

Her eyes flew open, and Francesca lay in the dark, staring blindly up at the tester above her bed. Her chest heaved, and her skin was damp with sweat. Her heart thundered within her, and there was a sweet, aching warmth between her legs. For a moment she was lost, unsure of where she was or what had happened.

Then she realized. She…had been dreaming.

A trifle shakily, she sat up, glancing around her as though to make certain that she was still in her bedroom at home. The dream had been so vivid, so real….

She shivered and pulled the covers up around her shoulders. The air was cool against her damp skin. She had dreamed of Rochford in his garden at Dancy Park before they came to London for her first Season. Had it been the youthful Rochford she had seen? She could not remember exactly how his face had looked.

She could remember quite clearly the sensations the dream had caused, however; they quivered in her still. She closed her eyes, drifting for a moment in the unaccustomed feelings. It was so odd, so unlike her, to have that sort of dream, drenched with heat and hunger. Again she shivered.

She felt, she thought, incomplete…aching for she knew not what, caught in a void between emptiness and wonder.

Was this, she thought, desire? Did it always leave a woman feeling this way—alone and unsure whether she wanted to smile or cry? She remembered the inchoate longing that had once kept her awake at night, thinking of Sinclair and his kisses, daydreaming about the day when she would belong to him.

She had known nothing then of what "belonging" to a man entailed. She had found that out on her wedding night as Andrew drunkenly pawed her, shoving up her nightgown and running his hands over her. Francesca remembered the humiliation of his looking at her naked body, the sudden fear that she had made a terrible mistake.

Her husband had leered down at her as he unbuttoned his breeches and shoved them down, his manhood springing from its restraint, red and pulsing. Horrified, she had closed her eyes as he pushed her legs apart and climbed between them. Then he had thrust into her, tearing her tender flesh, and she had cried out in pain. But he had been unheeding, continuing to shove himself into her again and again, until at last he collapsed on top of her, hot and damp with sweat.

It had taken her a moment to realize that he had fallen asleep that way, and she had needed to wriggle and squirm her way out from beneath him. Then she had pulled her nightdress back down over her naked body and turned away from him, curling up into a ball and giving way to sobs.

The next morning Andrew had apologized for causing her pain, assuring her that it was only the first time that hurt a woman. In the light of day, she had hoped that it would get better. Had not her mother hinted, in her tight-lipped way, about getting the worst out of the way on the wedding night? Francesca had not known what she meant, but clearly that must have been it. Besides, Andrew had been drunk from the wedding feast. Surely he would be more tender, more loving, when he had not been drinking. And now that she knew what was involved, it would not be so frightening or embarrassing.

She had been wrong, of course. It had not been as painful, that was true. But there had been none of the sweet eagerness, none of the glowing happiness, that she had once believed would await her in marriage. There had been only the same feeling of awkwardness and humiliation as he ran his hands over her, squeezing her breasts and shoving his fingers between her legs. She had endured the same harsh thrusting into her tender flesh, leaving her bruised and battered. And her tears had flowed the same afterwards—except that this time Andrew had been awake to hear her, and had wound up cursing and leaving her bed.

It had never improved in any real way. As time passed, it did not hurt as much—sometimes only a little and sometimes not at all. But it was always uncomfortable and humiliating. And, she found, Andrew was more often drunk than otherwise. She dreaded his coming to her bed, his breath stinking of port, his hands grabbing at her breasts and buttocks, his body invading hers in rough, jarring thrusts.

She had learned to close her eyes and turn her head away, to think of something else as she lay beneath him, and before long it would be over. Andrew would curse her for her lifelessness and call her cold as ice. The cheapest whore gave him a better ride than she did, he told her bitterly, and if she complained to him about his faithlessness, he reminded her that he would not have to turn to a mistress if she were a real woman.

Francesca wished that she could deny his words. But she suspected that he was right, that she was not like other women. She had heard other married women talk and giggle over what happened in bed or how virile their husbands were. She had heard whispers behind fans of the prowess of a certain man and murmurs praising the form of this fellow or that, speculations regarding some lord's performance beneath the sheets. Other women, apparently, enjoyed the marital bed rather than dreading it.

She had wondered if something had died within her when Rochford broke her heart. However, she also could not help but wonder if Rochford had perhaps sensed the coldness that dwelt within her, even before they married, and that it had been her lack of passion that had driven him into Daphne's arms. She had assumed that it was gentlemanly restraint that had kept him from trying to sneak into some corner to kiss and caress her. But what if he had not done so simply because he realized that she was as cold as a fish?

At least she would get children out of it all, she had told herself, but even there, she had been wrong. Six months into their marriage, she had gotten pregnant. Four months later, as she and Andrew had been arguing about his gambling losses, he had grabbed her arm as she stormed away from him. She had jerked herself free and stumbled backward, crashing into the railing at the top of the stairs and falling down several steps. Within hours, she had miscarried, and her doctor, frowning, had warned her that she might not be able to have children.

He had been right. She had not conceived again. Those had been the darkest days of her life, knowing that she had lost all chance at the family she had once thought she would have. She was not sure if she had ever really loved her husband; certainly, whatever love she had felt for him had died since they became man and wife. And now she knew that she would not have the joy of children, either.

It had been a relief when Andrew came less and less frequently to her bed, and, frankly, she had not even really cared that he stayed away from their home more, as well, spending his time wenching and drinking. She had not bothered to remonstrate with him over anything but his gambling, which further endangered their always precarious finances.

When he died falling from his horse in a drunken stupor, she had not been able to summon up a single tear for him. What she had felt, really, had been a blessed sense of freedom. However great a struggle it had been to keep her head above water since, at least she had been her own person for the last five years. At least she no longer had to worry that Andrew might come stumbling in and once more lay claim to her body.

Nothing, she thought, would ever bring her to put herself in that position again. She had no interest in marrying. There were men far better than Lord Haughston had been, of course, but none, she felt sure, would welcome a wife who did not want to share his bed. And she had no desire to subject herself to the duties of marriage even with a nice man. Perhaps she was freakish in her lack of passion, as Andrew had told her. But she knew that she was unlikely to change at this age. She simply was not touched by desire.

It was that fact that made the dream she had just had so startling. What was that jangling heated yearning she had felt? And what did it mean? From whence had it come?

She supposed that the dream had grown out of the memories that had invaded her mind tonight—thoughts and emotions from fifteen years ago, when she had been in love with Rochford. It had been those girlish hopes and inexperienced feelings that had somehow entwined themselves in her dreams. Those feelings meant nothing about the barren husk of a woman that she had become.

Nothing at all.

TWO DAYS LATER, Francesca was upstairs consulting with her maid, Maisie, on the possibilities of freshening up one of her gowns, when her butler came to the door to announce that Sir Alan Sherbourne had come to call on her.

"Sir Alan?" she repeated blankly. "Do I know him, Fenton?"

"I do not believe so, my lady," he replied gravely.

"And do you think I should receive him?"

"He seems quite unexceptionable. A gentleman who spends most of his time in the country, is my opinion."

"I see. Well, my curiosity is piqued. Show him into the drawing room."

When Francesca entered the drawing room a few moments later, she saw at once that her butler's description of Sir Alan was perfectly apt. Of medium height, with a pleasant face that was neither handsome nor unattractive, the man was not particularly noticeable, but was also not lacking in any regard. His carriage, speech and demeanor were clearly those of a man raised a gentleman, but there was no arrogance about him. And though his clothes were of a good quality and cut, they were not in the most up-to-date fashion, indicating, as Fenton had remarked, that he was not a man of the city, an impression reinforced by the plainness and open quality of his manner.

"Sir Alan?" Francesca asked a trifle questioningly as she stepped into the room.

He turned from his contemplation of the portrait above the mantel, and his eyes widened expressively. "Lady Haughston. Beg pardon…I did not realize…" He stopped, a faint line of color forming on his cheeks. "Excuse me. I am not usually so inarticulate. I am afraid I was unprepared to find that Lady Haughston was someone as young and radiant as you."

Francesca could not refrain from smiling. It was always pleasant to hear a compliment, particularly when it appeared as spontaneous and surprised as this one.

"Oh, dear," she replied, her tone teasing. "Has someone been painting me as old and haggard?"

The color in his cheeks deepened as he stammered out, "No. Oh, no, my lady. No one said anything like that. It is simply that everything I have heard about your influence and your considerable social skills led me to envision someone much older than yourself. A matriarch…a—" He stopped short. "I am making a hash of it, clearly."

Francesca chuckled. "Do not fret. I promise you, I am not offended. Please, sit down, sir." She gestured toward the sofa as she took a seat on the chair that lay at a right angle to it.

"Thank you." He accepted her invitation, sitting down and turning toward her. "I hope you will forgive my intrusion. It is presumptuous of me, I know, not being acquainted with you, but a friend told me that you might be willing to help me."

"Really? Well, certainly, if I can."

"It is about my daughter. Harriet. She made her debut this year."

"I see." His mission here was becoming clearer to Francesca. She tried to remember a girl named Harriet Sherbourne, but she could not picture her. Of course, that was probably the problem: Harriet was not making an impression in her first Season.

"I am a widower," her visitor went on. "It's been just Harriet and me for six years now. She is a good, sweet girl. She's been a wonderful companion to me, and she would make any man a good wife. Why, she has more or less run my household since she was fourteen. But she, well, she just doesn't seem to be 'taking.'" He frowned, obviously puzzled.

"It can be difficult for a young girl when she first comes to London," Francesca assured him.

"It's not that I am anxious to see her married," he went on quickly. "Quite frankly, I know I shall be quite lonely when she's gone." He gave her a small smile. "But I hate to see Harriet not enjoying her time here. And how can she, always sitting against the wall and not dancing?"

"Exactly right."

"Someone told me that you were known to work wonders with young girls who had been, well, left behind in the social race, so to speak. I know you have no reason to help me, not knowing us, but I hoped that you might consider favoring me with some advice. I was told you were most generous in that regard."

"Of course I should be happy to help you," Francesca assured the man.

She liked her first impression of Sir Alan, and, in any case, she could scarcely turn down an opportunity that had happened along so fortuitously. She should have been combing the ranks of the new marriageable girls, looking for those who could benefit from her expertise—and were willing to open their purses, of course, to achieve results.

"I am not sure exactly what it is that you *can* do," her guest continued a little uncertainly.

"Nor am I," Francesca admitted. "It would help, no doubt, if I were to meet your daughter."

"Yes, of course. If it would be acceptable for us to call on you, I should be most happy to bring her to visit you."

"That sounds like just the thing. Why don't the two of you come to see me tomorrow afternoon? Lady Harriet and I can become acquainted, and I can get a better idea of the problem."

"Excellent," Sir Alan responded, beaming. "You are very kind, Lady Haughston."

"In the meantime, perhaps you might tell me a bit about what you, um, would like to happen for Lady Harriet this Season."

He looked puzzled. "What do you mean?"

"Well, I find that parents often have different expectations. Some hope for their daughter to make a quick match, others a highly advantageous one."

"Oh." His face cleared. "I have no expectations of marriage, my lady. I mean, if Harriet were to meet a suitable young man whom she wished to marry, that would be very nice, of course. But she is still young, and I have not heard her express a great interest in marrying. I wish only for her to have a pleasant Season. She never complains, but the past few years she has had to take on more responsibility than a girl her age should. She is entitled to a little fun. That is why we came here for the Season. But, truthfully…well, I believe she is bored at these parties. She would like to dance and converse. My mother has been sponsoring Harriet, but she is getting up in years. It is a burden to her to take the girl about. And I sometimes wonder if the parties she attends are really, well, entertaining to Harriet."

Francesca nodded, the picture growing clearer for her. "Of course."

Sir Alan seemed a kind and pleasant man, one who wanted only the best for his daughter, which was certainly a refreshing change from many of the parents who had come to her. Most of them seemed more interested in an advantageous marriage than a happy one, and few expressed, as this man had, an interest in their daughter enjoying her come-out.

Of course, kindness did not necessarily translate into a willingness to spend money to accomplish his goals. There had been far too many parents who had expected her to work wonders for their daughter without purchasing different clothes, or to purchase an adequate wardrobe on a cheeseparing budget.

"I have found that bringing a girl out properly often demands adjustments to her wardrobe, entailing further expenses," Francesca said, probing delicately.

He nodded agreeably. "Of course, if that is what you think is best. I would leave that matter entirely in your hands. I fear that my mother was not, perhaps, the best person to choose my daughter's frocks for the Season."

"And doubtless you will need to host a party yourself." At the man's dismayed expression, she hastily added, "Or we can hold it here. I can take care of the preparations."

"Yes." His face cleared. "Oh, yes, that would be just the thing, if you would be so kind. Just direct the bills to me."

"Certainly." Francesca smiled. It was always a pleasure to work with an openhanded parent, especially one who was happy to put all the decisions and arrangements into her hands.

Sir Alan beamed back, clearly quite pleased with the arrangement. "I don't know how to thank you, Lady Haughston. Harriet will be so pleased, I'm sure. I should not take up any more of your time. I have already imposed on you more than enough."

He took his leave, giving her a polite bow, and Francesca went back upstairs, feeling a good bit more cheerful. Taking Harriet Sherbourne in hand would give her something to do, as well as provide her with some much-needed coin in the coming weeks. Given the quality of the last few meals her cook had prepared, she knew that Fenton must have run out of the money the duke's man of business had sent them for Callie's upkeep while she was living with Francesca. The butler and her cook had, of course, worked their usual economic magic with the cash, managing to apportion the money so that it lasted several weeks longer than the time Callie had been there.

The household was still solvent and would remain so for the rest of the Season, due to the gift that Callie's grandmother, the dowager duchess, had sent. When Callie had left Francesca's household, she had given Francesca a cameo left to her by her mother, a gift so sweet and instantly dear to Francesca that she had been unable to part with it, even for the money it would have brought. However, shortly thereafter, the duchess had sent her a lovely silver vanity set as her own thanks for taking the burden of arrangements for the wedding ceremony off the duchess's hands. Francesca hated to give up the engraved tray and its set of small boxes, pots and perfume bottles, simply because it was so beautifully done, but yesterday she had turned it over to Maisie to take to the jeweler's and sell.

Still, the cash the set would bring would not last forever, and after the Season ended, there would be the long stretch of fall and winter, in which there were few opportunities to make any more income. Whatever she could earn by helping Sir Alan's daughter would be very welcome. Besides, life always seemed better when she had a project to work on. Two projects, therefore, should utterly banish the fit of the blue devils she had suffered the other evening.

Her spirits were further buoyed by the fact that, in her absence, Maisie had recalled some silver lace that she had salvaged from a ruined ball gown last fall, and which would, the maid was sure, be just the thing to spruce up Francesca's dove-gray evening gown for her visit to the theater.

The two women spent the rest of the afternoon happily remaking the ball gown in question, replacing its overskirt with one of silver voile taken from another gown, and adding a row of the silver lace around the hem, neckline and short, puffed sleeves. It took only a bit of work on the seams and the addition of a sash of silver ribbon, and the dress seemed entirely new and shimmery, not at all like the same gray evening dress she had worn a year ago. Francesca thought that she would look quite acceptable—and not at all like a woman fast approaching her thirty-fourth birthday.

When Tuesday evening came, bringing with it the trip to the theater that Francesca had arranged, the duke arrived, unsurprisingly, before his appointed time. It was much more unusual that Francesca, too, was ready early. However, when Fenton informed her of Rochford's presence downstairs, she dawdled a few minutes before going down to greet him. It would never do, after all, for a lady to appear eager, even if the man in question was a friend, not a suitor.

The butler had placed Rochford in the formal drawing room, and he was standing before the fireplace, studying the portrait of Francesca that hung over it. The painting had been done at the time of her marriage to Lord Haughston, and it had hung there so long that she never noticed it anymore, regarding it as one of the familiar pieces of furniture.

She cast a glance at it now, however, and wondered if, indeed, her skin had been that wondrously glowing and velvety, or if it was just an example of the painter's art.

Rochford glanced over his shoulder at the sound of her footsteps, and for an instant there was something in his face that brought her up short. But then the moment passed. He smiled, and Francesca could not work out exactly what it was she had seen in that brief glimpse.... Whatever it was, it had left her heart beating a trifle faster than was customary.

"Rochford," she greeted him, walking forward with her hand extended to shake his.

He turned around fully, and she saw that he held a bouquet of creamy white roses in his hand. She stopped again, her hand coming up to her chest in pleased surprise. "How beautiful! Thank you."

She came forward and took them from him, her cheeks becomingly flushed with pleasure.

"I am a day early, I know, but I thought that by the

time we parted this evening, it would be your birthday," he told her.

"Oh!" The smile that flashed across her face was brilliant, her eyes glowing. "You remembered."

"Of course."

Francesca buried her face in the roses, inhaling their scent, but she knew that her action was as much to hide the rush of gratification on her face as to smell the intoxicating odor.

"Thank you," she told him again, looking back up at him. She could not have said why it brought her so much pleasure to know that he had remembered her birthday—and had bothered to bring flowers to commemorate it. But she felt unaccountably lighter than she had for the past week.

"You are very welcome." His eyes were dark and unfathomable in the dim light of the candles.

She wondered what he was thinking. Did he recall how she had looked fifteen years ago? Did he find her much changed?

Embarrassed at the direction of her thoughts, she turned away, going to the bell pull to summon the butler. Fenton, efficient as always and having seen the flowers when the duke entered, bustled in a moment later, a water-filled vase in hand. He set it on the low table in front of the sofa, and Francesca busied herself for a few moments with arranging the flowers.

"I do hope, however," she went on lightly, watching the flowers rather than Rochford's face, "that your memory is kind enough not to recall the number of years that I have gained as well as it remembered the date of my birth."

"Your secret is safe with me," he told her with mock gravity. "Though I can assure you that if I were to reveal your age, there are none who would believe it, given the way you look."

"A very pretty lie," Francesca retorted, the dimple flashing in her cheek as she grinned at him.

"No falsehood," he protested. "I was just looking at your portrait and thinking how remarkably the same you look."

She was about to toss back a rejoinder when suddenly, unbidden, the memory of her dream the night before came back to her. She stared at him, feeling as though her breath had been stolen from her, and all she could think about was the look in his eyes as he had gazed into her face and the velvet touch of his lips as they met hers.

She blushed deeply, and something in his face changed, his eyes darkening almost imperceptibly. He was about to kiss her, she thought, and her body suddenly shimmered with anticipation.

CHAPTER FOUR

BUT, OF COURSE, he did not kiss her. Instead, he took a step back, and she saw that his face was set in its usual cool reserve, not at all the expression that she had thought she glimpsed for an instant. It was a trick of the light, she decided, some shifting of shadows. No doubt Fenton, conserving money, had not lit enough candles.

"I am surprised that you are not holding a party to celebrate the occasion," Rochford said somewhat stiffly.

Francesca turned away, struggling to quiet the tumult of butterflies in her stomach. She would *not* think about that ridiculous dream. It had meant nothing. And Rochford had no inkling of it, in any case. There was no reason to feel awkward and unsettled.

"Don't be absurd," she told him tartly, sitting down and gesturing for him to do the same. "I have reached the age where one does not want to draw attention to growing older."

"But you deprive everyone of the opportunity to celebrate your presence here among us ordinary mortals."

She cast him a dry look. "Doing it a bit too brown, aren't we?"

He gave her a wry smile. "My dear Francesca, surely you are accustomed to being called divine."

"Not by a man well-known all over the city for adhering to the truth."

He let out a chuckle. "I yield. Clearly I am outmatched. I am well aware that it is an impossibility to have the last word when contesting wits with you."

"'Tis nice to hear you admit it," she replied with a smile. "Now…I believe that Lady Althea is awaiting us?"

"Yes, of course." He did not look as interested in the prospect as Francesca would have hoped.

But then, she reminded herself, she had known that this would be a long and doubtless uphill battle with Rochford. He was not a man known for his changeability; it would take some time and effort to reverse the course he had pursued for years. Besides, she was not entirely certain herself whether Lady Althea would be the right wife for Rochford.

She could not help but remember the comment Irene had made the other night. Althea Robart was, frankly, a trifle snobbish, and while that was not really a problem for a duchess, Francesca could not help but wonder if such a person would really make Rochford happy. Rochford was certainly capable of assuming his "duke face," as his sister Callie called it, when it suited him, but he was not a man who took himself too seriously most of the time. He was quite capable of conversing with almost anyone of any social level, and Francesca could not remember a single occasion when he had been too careful of his dignity to listen to or help someone.

Francesca glanced over at him as they left her house and approached his elegant town carriage. This carriage, for instance, was an example of his lack of overweening pride. Though well-made and obviously expensive, there was no ducal crest stamped on the side. Rochford had never sought the admiration of the general crowd, nor did he feel a need to announce his name or station to the world.

He handed her up into the carriage and settled across from her. She leaned back into the luxurious leather seat, the soft squabs cushioning her head. It was dark and close in the carriage, somehow much more intimate than sitting this near to one another in the chairs in her drawing room.

She could not remember when she had ever ridden in a carriage entirely alone with Rochford. He had never been one of her escorts, at least not since that brief time when they had been engaged, and then she had been a young, unmarried female, so there had always been a chaperone accompanying them—her mother or his grandmother. Francesca looked down at her gloved hands in her lap, feeling unaccustomedly uncertain.

It was ridiculous, of course. She knew that she was a woman who was counted upon to keep a conversation running, yet here she was, unable to think of anything to say—and with a man whom she had known all her life. But she could not seem to keep her mind from turning to that dream she had had the night before, a vision that quickly dried up any words that came to her lips and set her heart knocking foolishly in her chest. Besides, she could not escape the feeling that Rochford was *looking* at her. Of course, there was no reason why he should *not* be looking at her. They were seated across from each other, their knees only a few inches apart. And there was certainly no reason why his gaze should make her nervous…yet she could not help but feel unsettled by it.

It was a relief that the trip to Lady Althea's residence took only a few minutes. Francesca waited in the carriage while Rochford went in to escort Althea. It did not take him long, Francesca noted, so clearly the two of them had spent little time chatting. She supposed she could not fault Althea, given that she had just spent the last few minutes in the carriage with Rochford feeling quite tongue-tied herself. Still, it seemed to her that the woman could have made a little more of a push.

As they paused outside the carriage while the footman opened the door and set down a stool for Althea to step up on, Francesca heard Althea say in some disappointment, "Oh. Then you did not bring the ducal carriage?"

Rochford's glance flickered over to Francesca, who sat watching them out the carriage window, and he arched one eyebrow sardonically. Francesca had to raise her hand to her mouth to cover the smile that sprang up there.

"No, my lady, I am afraid only my grandmother uses the carriage with the crest. Still, one could say that this is the ducal carriage, being that it belongs to me."

Lady Althea gave him a slightly puzzled glance. "Yes, of course, but how is one to know it?"

Francesca suppressed a sigh. Lady Althea appeared to have little lightness or humor in her.

"Very true," the duke murmured, extending his hand to help her up into the vehicle.

Althea sat down beside Francesca, favoring her with an unsmiling nod. "Good evening, Lady Haughston."

"Good evening." Francesca smiled. "How lovely you look."

"Thank you."

It nettled her only a little that Lady Althea did not return the compliment. It was more annoying that after her brief answer, Althea made no effort to say anything else to move the conversation along.

"I trust your parents are well," Francesca went on gamely.

"Yes, quite, thank you. Father is rarely ill. It is always so with the Robarts, of course."

"Indeed?" Francesca noted the amusement that briefly danced in the duke's dark eyes. Althea, she thought with a flash of irritation, was doing little to make a positive impression. "And is Lady Robart enjoying the Season? I confess, I have seen her only rarely this summer."

"She is frequently at my godmother's side," Althea commented. "Lady Ernesta Davenport. Lord Rodney Ashenham's sister, you know."

"Ah." Francesca knew Ashenham and his sister, both rather priggish sorts. As she remembered, Lady Davenport had once told her that a true lady did not laugh aloud—that only the common sort were given to braying—when Francesca had burst into a fit of giggles over some mishap or other during her first Season.

"They grew up together, you see," Althea went on. "They are first cousins, as well."

"I see."

Althea apparently took this mild statement as an expression of interest, for she spent some time exploring the family tree of the Ashenhams, who had, apparently, ties to most of the major families of England.

Francesca, keeping her face fixed in the courteous expression of listening that had been ingrained in her as a child, mentally began to go through her slippers, trying to find a pair that would suit the sea-green evening gown of voile over silk that she had seen in Mlle. du Plessis' store last week. The modiste had told her that it was waiting for a buyer, hostage to that woman's final payment on a bill that had been too long outstanding. Mlle. du Plessis had admitted to grave doubts that the buyer would ever return, and she had agreed to sell it to Francesca at only a third of its original cost if the woman had not paid her bill within a week.

The dress was too long, but that was a trifling matter that Maisie could take care of easily enough, and Francesca knew that she was desperately in need of a new gown. There were only so many times that one could redo a gown to look fresh, and it would not do to appear in the same ball gown too often. Pride was a sin, Francesca knew, but she could not bear for people to know how close she skated to the edge of penury.

The problem, however, was the slippers to go with it. No matter how careful she tried to be with them, the thin soles of dancing slippers wore through incredibly quickly, and they were not the sort of thing on which one could normally work a bargain. Therefore, she did her best to stick to plain colors that would go with many different frocks. What would really look marvelous with the dress, of course, would be a pair of silver sandals, but that would be too extravagant a purchase. But perhaps… There were several other dresses they would suit, after all.

Maybe she could go into the attic and dig about in the trunks again. Some valuable trifle that she could sell might turn up.

"Lady Haughston?"

Francesca glanced up quickly, aware that she had become entirely too lost in her thoughts. "What? I'm sorry. I must have been woolgathering."

"We are here," Althea told her somewhat stiffly.

"Ah, yes, so we are." Francesca glanced out the window to see the familiar form of the Royal Theater.

She suspected that she had put Althea's nose out of joint a bit by drifting off like that. But, really, the girl should learn that analyzing one's family tree was scarcely the way to capture anyone's attention. She would have to think of some way to tutor the girl in the art of conversation if she was to have a chance of winning Rochford's favor. Of course, that was *if* she decided Lady Althea was the woman she wanted to win his favor. Francesca was, quite frankly, beginning to have her doubts.

Rochford climbed out with alacrity and reached back up to hand the women down. Francesca managed to hang back a bit as they strolled into the theater so that Rochford was walking beside Althea alone. She must, after all, give him a chance to get to know the woman better. Perhaps Althea had been a trifle nervous about the situation; Rochford's presence sometimes had that effect. Nerves frequently made people chatter on about the most inconsequential things.

Francesca cast a glance at them, walking slightly ahead of her. Rochford's dark head was bent a little toward Althea as he listened to her. Perhaps he had not minded Althea's conversation earlier. She had seen husbands who were quite content with the most ninny-hammered of wives. And Althea *was* attractive.

It occurred to her that perhaps she ought to drop by someone's box during intermission; that would give the couple a chance to be alone together without it being improper, given that there was an entire theater of people around them. She would have to look around the place before the play began to see if she could spot an acquaintance.

She turned to glance around at the other people walking into the theater. Startled, she felt a touch beneath her elbow and turned to find Rochford gazing quizzically at her. He and Lady Althea had dropped back beside her.

"Woolgathering again, Lady Haughston?" he asked with a faint smile.

"Oh, um…" Francesca felt a flush rising in her cheeks. "I beg your pardon. I am afraid I must be a trifle distracted this evening."

They continued into the theater, with the duke now by Francesca's side, Lady Althea in front of them. However, when they reached the duke's luxurious box, Francesca managed to neatly maneuver things so that she was against the wall, and Althea was between her and Rochford. Again separating herself from their conversation, Francesca scooted forward in her seat and raised her opera glasses to inspect the other occupants of the theater.

There was Mrs. Everson, with her husband and two daughters. Francesca supposed she could visit with them later, though the prospect was not inviting. She lowered her glasses and nodded to them, just in case, then resumed her search. She wished she had urged Sir

Lucien to attend with someone tonight, for then she could have visited with him and been assured of a lively conversation.

As she looked, she became aware of that odd, indefinable sensation of being watched. She lowered her glasses and swept her eyes around the large room, taking in the tiers of boxes, then glanced down at the floor below.

She let out a low exclamation as her eyes fell on a man standing in the aisle, staring up at her. Her hand tightened involuntarily on her fan.

"Francesca? What is it?" she heard Rochford say, leaning forward and following her gaze.

"The devil!" he exclaimed under his breath. "Perkins."

The man, seeing that he had gained Francesca's attention, swept her a mocking bow. Francesca looked away without even a nod, sitting back in her seat.

"What is he doing here?" she asked with disgust.

"Who?" Lady Althea asked, glancing toward the crowd below.

"Galen Perkins," Rochford answered.

"I don't believe I recognize the name."

"There is no reason for you to," Francesca assured her. "He has been out of the country for years."

"He is a thorough rogue," Rochford added, shooting a quick sideways glance at Francesca.

He knew, Francesca thought, that Perkins had been one of her late husband's cronies. Though he came from a minor branch of a good family, he had done all

he could to tarnish their name. He had been a gambler
and drinker, accompanying Lord Haughston on many
of his wilder ventures. He had even, Francesca recalled,
with a tightening of her stomach, been so low as to
make advances to her despite his friendship with her
husband.

"What is he doing back in London?" Francesca
asked. She explained in an aside to Althea, "He had to
flee to the Continent several years ago because he killed
a man in a duel."

Althea's eyes widened. "Oh, my. Who?"

"Avery Bagshaw, Sir Gerald's son," the duke told
her. "As Sir Gerald died not long ago, I presume Perkins
has decided that it is safe to return. Without Sir Gerald
to push the authorities to arrest him, it is doubtful that
anything will be done now. It has been seven or eight
years, and they are apt to turn a blind eye to such things,
anyway."

"Well, I am sure he will not be received anywhere,"
Althea said decisively, delivering what was for her, apparently, the greatest punishment.

"No. I am sure not," Francesca agreed. It was terrible
that he was once again able to live here freely, given
what he had done. But at least she would not have to
be around the man. With Andrew gone, he would not
be coming to her house, and Althea was right in saying
that he would not be received by polite society, so he
would not be at any parties.

She pulled her mind away from the thought of Galen

Perkins, turning her attention back to her companions. Conversation had lagged while she had been scouting the theater, and Rochford and Althea fell silent again once the topic of Galen Perkins had been dropped.

Gamely, Francesca took up the conversational baton again, saying, "Have you read the newest book?"

"Lady Rumor?" Rochford tossed back, a smile quirking at the corner of his lips.

"Who?" Althea asked, looking confused. "Lady who?"

"Rumor. It's a *nom de plume,*" she explained. "No one knows who it is. It is said that she is a member of the *ton.*"

Althea looked at her blankly. "Why would a member of the *ton* wish to write a book?"

"It is supposed to be full of scandals and rumors— thinly disguised, of course. Everyone is said to be quaking for fear they will be in it," Francesca went on.

"Ah, but how slighted they will feel if they are left out," Rochford added.

Francesca chuckled. "True enough."

"But that's absurd," Althea said, frowning. "No one would wish to be included in a book about scandal. Who would wish for a blot upon one's name?"

It occurred to Francesca that Althea Robart truly was entirely lacking in a sense of humor. She glanced at Rochford and saw his dark eyes dancing in amusement.

"You are right, of course, Lady Althea," he said

smoothly. "I cannot fathom why I should have thought such a thing." He cast a droll glance at Francesca, and she had to turn away to hide a smile.

But that would not do, she knew. Clearly, the light social conversation in which she was wont to engage was not the sort of thing at which Lady Althea shone. Therefore, it was incumbent upon her to turn the conversation in the other woman's direction, to introduce a topic upon which Lady Althea could expound. She cast about for such a subject. The problem was that she did not know Lady Althea well.

"Lady Symington's ball will be coming up soon," she said after a moment. "Will you be attending, Lady Althea?"

"Oh, yes. She is second cousin to my father, you know."

Francesca suppressed a groan. Indeed, she *had* managed to hit on a topic the woman enjoyed—family.

"Ah, look, the lights are going down," Rochford spoke up. "The play is about to begin."

"Why, yes, so it is." With relief, Francesca turned her attention to the stage.

She was not really interested in the action that was occurring there, however. She was too much occupied with her plans. She seemed to be failing at every turn to bring Althea into any interesting conversation. It would be best, she thought, if she followed up on her idea to visit someone else during intermission, leaving Althea and Rochford alone in the box.

It would have been better if she could have found

someone more engaging than the Eversons, of course. Mr. Everson was the sort who thought himself an expert on almost any topic and was more than happy to give his opinion, whether one wished it or not. Mrs. Everson, on the other hand, was given to conversing about her ailments, which seemed to be legion, but which never appeared to keep her from attending all social functions. The girls, at least, had little to say—though it was not hard to see why, given that both of their parents strove to dominate any conversation.

However, Francesca knew that she had little choice. She was growing more certain that Althea Robart was not the wife for Rochford, but still, she ought to give it one more push. Perhaps, if she was alone with Rochford, Althea would unexpectedly blossom in some way.

Therefore, as soon as the curtain fell and the lights came on, Francesca stood up, turning to the others. Rochford, however, had been faster than she. He, too, had risen, and before she could speak, he began, "Ladies, shall I bring you some refreshments? A glass of ratafia, perhaps?"

"How kind of you," Francesca replied quickly before Althea could say anything. "Not for me, thank you. I believe that I shall slip around to see Mrs. Everson. But perhaps Lady Althea would like a glass."

Rochford stared at her, his eyebrows rising. "Mrs. Everson?"

"Yes. I saw her across the way." Francesca gestured vaguely about the theater.

"Yes. So did I." Rochford looked at her oddly. "Well, then…pray allow me to escort you."

"What?" Now it was Francesca's turn to stare at him. "You?"

She was well aware that the duke had avoided Mr. Everson like the plague ever since the man had tried to inveigle Rochford into some investment scheme in India. Why, just a few weeks ago Callie had related, laughing, the way Rochford had spent an entire weekend at Lord Kimbrough's country house dodging Mr. Everson. Why would he be volunteering to enter the man's presence now?

"Yes," Rochford returned her gaze blandly. "I."

"But I— That is—"

"Yes?" He cocked an eyebrow in that maddening way he had.

Francesca swallowed. "Of course. How nice." She turned to the other woman with a smile. "Lady Althea, would you like to accompany us?"

Althea blinked and cast a glance across the theater— no doubt wondering, Francesca thought caustically, what was so interesting about the Eversons.

"Yes, all right," she said after a moment, also rising to her feet.

Rochford stepped aside to let the women pass in front of him, but before Francesca was halfway to the door, there came a knock, and then it opened.

Galen Perkins stood framed in the doorway.

Francesca stopped abruptly, and for a long moment

there was nothing but silence in the small room. Then Perkins bowed and stepped inside.

"Lady Haughston. You look lovelier than ever. I would have thought eight years would have aged you, but clearly you have found some magic potion."

"Mr. Perkins," Francesca answered through tight lips, thinking that she could not say the same about him. She had never liked the man, but he had once been attractive. Years of dissipation, however, had padded his once-lithe frame and blurred the lines of his face. His golden curls, though still artfully tousled, had lost much of their glimmer and were growing thinner, and there was a jaded look in his pale blue eyes.

"Please accept my condolences on your loss," he went on. "Lord Haughston was a good friend to me. I was very sorry that I was out of the country when he passed away."

"Thank you."

Rochford stepped past the women, placing himself in front of Francesca. "Perkins."

"Rochford," the other man replied, looking faintly amused at the duke's gesture.

"I am surprised to see you here," Rochford went on flatly.

"Indeed? I wished to speak to Lady Haughston. I could not ignore the presence of an old friend."

"We were never friends," Francesca told him.

"Such harsh words," Perkins responded, the small, disdainful smile never leaving his lips. "After all the years that we have known each other, I would not have thought you could be so unkind."

"I did not mean that I was surprised to see you here in this box," Rochford explained sharply, "though it is somewhat presumptuous, given your lack of invitation. What I *meant* was that I would not have thought to see you in London after your precipitous departure eight years ago."

"That is all in the past."

"A man's life can scarcely be shrugged aside so easily," Rochford retorted.

"I can see that you have not changed," Perkins drawled. "You always were a sanctimonious sort." He turned toward Francesca, adding, "Setting your sights higher this time, my dear? I wonder what poor Andrew would think."

Francesca stiffened. It had slipped her mind over the years how thoroughly she disliked this man.

But the duke spoke before she could open her mouth to deliver a set-down. "I think it is time you took your leave, Mr. Perkins."

Perkins' lips tightened, and for a moment Francesca thought he was going to shoot back an angry retort—or worse—but then he visibly relaxed. "Of course, Your Grace." The honorific sounded like an insult on his lips. Perkins bowed toward Francesca and Althea. "Ladies."

He turned and left the box. For a moment no one spoke. Then Althea said, "Really. What an obnoxious creature. Do not tell me you actually associated with him, Lady Haughston."

"No, of course I did not," Francesca returned irritably. "He was an acquaintance of my late husband's, that is all."

"Very bad form, his coming here," Lady Althea commented.

"I don't believe that Mr. Perkins worries overmuch about 'form,'" Rochford said dryly.

"Well, there is scarcely time now to pay the Eversons a visit," Francesca announced. "Come, let us sit down again, Lady Althea."

She tucked her arm through Althea's, guiding her back to their chairs, so that Althea would once again be between Francesca and Rochford.

Throughout the next act, Francesca kept glancing over at Rochford, trying to see whether he ever even glanced at Althea. His eyes were always on the stage, except once, when she found him gazing at *her*. She blushed up to her hairline, grateful for the concealing darkness. She hoped she had not been too obvious. Rochford had always been annoyingly quick to notice things, and if he realized what she was about, he might very well order her to cease.

Deciding that the ploy of visiting another box had been a dismal failure, she remained seated during the next intermission and made a last attempt to engage Althea and Rochford in conversation. As it turned out, it was she and Rochford who did most of the talking, though she did her best to turn the discussion in Althea's direction whenever she could. When Rochford brought up a composer, Francesca asked Althea what she thought of him. When he mentioned going to his manor house in Cornwall, Francesca sought Althea's opinion of the loveliness of the area. And when Francesca and Rochford drifted off into a conversation about Francesca's old bay at Redfields, she turned to Althea and inquired whether she liked to ride.

It was a wearing way to conduct a conversation, and, frankly, Francesca could not tell that it did any good. Althea answered her questions, but her contributions were not particularly enlivening, and as a result the conversation did not flow naturally, but bumped and shuddered along.

Francesca could not imagine that Rochford felt any particular inclination to seek out Lady Althea's company in the future, but she was determined that if he did, he would be entirely on his own in the matter. She had no desire to spend another evening trying to milk an enjoyable conversation out of the woman.

When the play was over, Rochford escorted the women home, politely walking Althea to her door, then returning to the carriage to see Francesca back to her house. The butler answered the door, and then, with a bow, took himself off to bed. Francesca turned to Rochford.

She was suddenly, excruciatingly, aware of the dark silence of the house around them. They were alone for the first time that she could remember—not really alone, of course, but as much so as anyone could possibly be. The servants were all upstairs in their beds asleep. A candelabra set on the table in the hallway provided the only light.

The silence was profound, almost a presence in itself, and darkness hovered at the edges of the candlelight. She looked up into Rochford's face, feeling again the odd tingling of awareness that had affected her the night of the dance.

Her stomach plummeted, however, when she saw his expression. His brow was knitted in a frown, and his mouth was a straight line. His dark eyes glittered in the dim light.

"What the devil do you think you are doing?"

CHAPTER FIVE

FRANCESCA BLINKED, for a moment too taken aback to think. Then she lifted her chin and responded in a glacial tone, "I beg your pardon? I am sure I haven't the slightest notion what you are talking about."

"Please. That innocent expression may work with others, but not with someone who's known you since you were in short skirts. I am talking about your little performance tonight."

"Performance? Don't you think you are being a trifle dramatic?"

"No. What else would you call it? First you contrived for the three of us to attend the theater tonight—even though you are not friends with her."

"How can you know that?"

Rochford shot a level look at her. "Francesca... really, give me a bit more credit than that. Then, when we got to the theater, it was 'What do you think about this, Lady Althea?' and 'How do you like that composer, Lady Althea?' Not to mention your plan to leave the two of us together while you went to call on the Eversons. Admit it. You were practically throwing

Althea Robart at me this evening. I must say, it isn't like you to be so ham-fisted."

"Yes, well, if the woman had even an inkling how to carry on a conversation with a man, I wouldn't have had to be," Francesca retorted in an aggrieved tone.

"Why? Don't tell me that she has set her cap for me. I cannot imagine her unbending enough to pursue anyone. Nor can I envision her mother seeking anyone else's help, either."

"No. No one asked me to. Althea is not trying to catch you. I think that should be clear."

"Again I ask, why?"

Francesca simply looked at him for a long moment, wondering whether there was any good way out of this situation. At her delay, Rochford crossed his arms and cocked a brow at her.

"Don't bother to think up a lie. We both know I shan't believe it."

She grimaced. "I daresay not. Can you not accept that I was simply trying to do you a favor?"

"By saddling me with a woman who can recite her entire family tree for five generations back?" he retorted.

"I did not realize she was so boring," Francesca admitted. "I am not well acquainted with the woman."

"Yet you thought she was the perfect woman for me?"

"No. I thought she was only one of a number of candidates."

He stared, seemingly bereft of speech. Finally, speaking each word with great care, he said, "Why would you have *any* candidates?"

"Well, really, Rochford, it is time that you married. You are thirty-eight, after all, and as the Duke of Rochford, you have a duty to—"

"I am well aware of my age, thank you," he ground out. "As well as of my many duties as the Duke of Rochford. What I fail to understand is why you thought I was seeking a wife. Or why *you* should be the one to provide me with prospects!"

"Rochford!" Francesca cast a glance up the staircase. "Shh. The servants will hear."

She turned and picked up the candelabra, then slipped into the drawing room, motioning for him to follow her. She set the candelabra down on the nearest table and closed the door behind her.

"Very well." She faced him, squaring her shoulders. "I will tell you, since you are so insistent."

"Please do." Rochford watched her grimly, his entire body taut as wire.

"I did it to help you," Francesca began a trifle nervously. "I looked around and found several women whom I thought would be…qualified to be your duchess. I wasn't trying to push any particular one upon you. But I thought that if you were around them, you might come to realize that you had an affinity for one or the other."

"You still have not explained why you felt compelled to do this."

"Because of what I did to you!" Francesca exclaimed, feeling tears rising and battling them back down. She took a deep breath and went on more calmly. "Because I believed Daphne instead of you. Because I did not trust you. I broke our engagement. I wanted to make up for the mistake I made fifteen years ago."

Rochford looked at her for a long moment. His face was set and his voice deadly quiet as he said, "You broke our engagement, and when you found out you were wrong, this was your response? To find me a wife to replace the one I lost?"

"No. Of course not," she protested. "You make it sound quite horrid."

"How else is it supposed to sound?"

"I was not offering her as a replacement for me. That is absurd. I just thought— I know that you have not married all these years. And I feared that I— Well, that what I did to you must have influenced you against marriage. That I made you feel that women were not to be trusted, that we would all fail you. I felt responsible."

"Not marrying was my choice, Francesca."

"I cannot help but feel that if it had not been for me and what I did, you would have married long ago," she insisted. "I was concerned about you. And I thought that this is a skill I apparently have, bringing couples together. I did not mean to upset you, truly. I was trying to help. I mean, obviously you must marry."

He grimaced. "Now you sound like my grandmother." He swung away, pacing a few steps, then whirled back to face her. "Do you think that I am so incapable of wooing a woman that you must do it for me? So lacking in charm? Do you think that I will frighten off any prospective bride if I am left to my own devices?"

Francesca's eyes widened. "I—I—"

He stalked back to her, anger fairly crackling off him. "Am I so clumsy? Tell me, you are the one who would know. Was my courtship that dreadful?"

He stopped, looming over her, and she stared up at him, stunned. His anger was overwhelming. He seemed so huge, so close, his eyes lit with an inner fire.

"Was my kiss that unappealing?" he went on, his voice so low she could barely hear it. "Was my touch that repulsive to you?"

Then, astonishing her even more, he grabbed her by the arms and pulled her to him, his mouth coming down to seize hers in a hard, thorough kiss.

Francesca felt rooted to the spot, every thought in her head flying off into the atmosphere. She was aware of nothing except the fierce grip of his fingers upon her upper arms and the hot, hard pressure of his lips upon hers. A flame shot to life inside her, and she trembled, astonished as much by her own reaction as by what Rochford had done.

He moved his mouth against hers insistently, opening her to him, and his tongue swept inside. Heat washed through her, and her skin prickled. She felt strangely giddy and weak, as if she might tumble to the ground if his hands were not clutching her arms, holding her up.

Just as suddenly as he had kissed her, he pulled back. His eyes were wide, the light in them fierce. He let out an oath and pulled his hands away from her. Then he turned and strode out the door.

For a long moment Francesca stood where she was, staring after him. Her heart thundered in her chest, and her breath came hard and quick in her throat. She felt dazed, bombarded by a hundred different emotions.

His words had twisted her heart, and tears welled in her eyes. She had wounded him unknowingly. She wanted to run after him, to cry and beg him to stay and hear her out. Hurting him had been the furthest thing from her mind. Somehow she must make him believe that. She must make him see that she had meant nothing unkind by what she had done.

How could it have turned into such a disaster? She had thought he might be a bit annoyed at her machinations, but it had never occurred to her that he would be so furious. Now, however, she feared that she might have lost Rochford entirely, that she might no longer even have him as a friend. The thought of that made her cold all through.

And why had he kissed her? His kiss could hardly be considered an expression of feeling—or, at least, not an expression of any good sort of feeling. His mouth had been hard and brutal, seizing her lips, not asking or seducing. There had been more anger than passion in the way he had grabbed her and pressed his mouth to hers. It had almost been as if he were punishing her.

But what she had felt had been anything but punishment.

Francesca raised her fingertips to her lips, laying them gently against the tingling, sensitive flesh. She could still feel his lips on hers, the taste of his mouth. And deep in her abdomen there was a molten heat. Everything inside her was now jangling and alive in a way she had never felt before…or at least not in years and years.

She wanted to fling herself on her bed and indulge in a good cry. She wanted to curl up and float in the memory of that kiss all over again. Indeed, she was not sure what she wanted at all.

Shaken and confused, Francesca turned and, picking up the candelabra, made her way up to bed.

THE DUKE OF ROCHFORD strode through the front door of White's, looking neither left nor right. He wasn't sure why he was there. He certainly had no desire for company right now, but neither had he been able to face the prospect of going back to the huge empty Lilles House.

All he wanted, he thought, was to settle down with a bottle of port and drink himself into oblivion. With that purpose in mind, he gestured toward Timmons, the maitre d', and flung himself down in a chair across the room, in an area unoccupied by anyone else.

He leaned his head back, closing his eyes as he struggled to restore himself to some semblance of calm. *How the devil did she manage to get him twisted around like this, after all these years?* He knew that he was generally regarded as an even-tempered sort—calm in a crisis and slow to anger. It was only with Francesca that he found himself on the edge of exploding.

Footsteps stopped beside his chair. Rochford kept his eyes closed in the hopes that the person would decide to pass him by. But there was no sound of anyone moving on, and after a moment he let out a little sigh and opened his eyes.

"Gideon!" He didn't know who he had expected his visitor to be—perhaps one of the chaps who were always determined to speak to a duke, seemingly impervious to set-downs or hints—but he certainly had not thought he would see the man who was now standing beside his chair. "What are you doing here?"

"I belong to this club," the other man answered, a faint smile tugging at the corners of his lips. "Perhaps you remember—you put me forth for membership."

Rochford grimaced. "I am quite aware of that. It is just that you are so rarely here—particularly not at this time of the evening." He gestured vaguely toward the chair sitting at a right angle to him. "Sit. Please."

"One might say the same about you." Gideon, Lord Radbourne, sat down in the chair Rochford indicated.

Gideon was a cousin of sorts to the duke, another grandnephew of the much-feared Lady Odelia Pencully, and there was a faint hint of family resemblance between them. Both were tall, with thick, dark hair, but Gideon was somewhat shorter, broader of chest and shoulders, and his hair was a shade lighter. It was not that which set him apart, though, so much as the way he carried himself and the harder, warier set to his face. Though an earl, Lord Radbourne had grown up on the hard streets of the East End of London, unaware that he was actually the son of the Earl of Radbourne. It had been only a year or so ago that the truth of his existence had been made known, but in that time he and Rochford had grown into a kind of friendship that had less to do with blood than with their essential natures.

The duke shrugged now, saying, "I admit I am not much one for clubs. I fear I am a boring sort. However, I do drop by now and then for a tipple before bed. But I do not have a beautiful wife waiting for me at home." He looked significantly at the other man.

"Neither do I," Gideon returned. "Irene has gone, along with her mother, to visit Lady Wyngate, her brother's wife. 'Tis almost time for Lady Wyngate's lying-in, you see."

"Ah." Rochford nodded sagely. "And she wants Irene there for the event."

Gideon's normally saturnine face lightened with a grin. "I sincerely doubt it. Maura and Irene get along like oil and water—and that is when they are feeling pleasant. No, 'tis Irene's mother whose presence is requested. Irene is merely traveling with her. Her mother will doubtless be there several weeks, but Irene, I am sure, will be back within a sennight, if she can bear it that long. But for the moment, I am at loose ends."

"And not enjoying it, I'll warrant," Rochford replied. His cousin's deep attachment to his new bride was well known throughout the *ton*. There were even those who called him henpecked—though none dared do so to his face, of course.

"No." Gideon frowned. "I don't understand it. I was well content by myself before I met Irene. 'Tis strange how empty my house seems without her now."

Rochford shrugged. "I fear that is a subject beyond this bachelor's understanding."

Timmons arrived with the bottle of port and, observant man that he was, two glasses. They spent a few minutes pouring and sipping in companionable silence.

Then Radbourne, with a glance at his companion, began, "I wasn't certain whether you were desirous of company. You looked as though…I'm not sure…perhaps as though you might be in need of a second."

The duke let out a short laugh. "No. Nothing so dire as a duel. Only…Lady Haughston." He finished his drink and poured another.

Gideon did not appear to be particularly enlightened by this explanation. "You are…at odds with the lady?"

"She is the most infuriating, most difficult, most… *impossible* woman I have ever known!" Rochford burst out.

Gideon blinked. "I—I see."

"No, I am sure that you do not," the duke retorted. "You have not spent the last fifteen years trying to deal with the woman."

Gideon made a noncommittal murmur.

"Tonight is just the latest of her many—do you know what she is doing?" The duke fixed him with a black stare. "Do you know what latest idiocy she is trying to foist on me?"

"Indeed not."

"She wants to find me a wife." Rochford's mouth twisted on the word, as if it tasted too bitter to bear. "She has set out to choose the woman she thinks will make the best Duchess of Rochford."

"I presume that you did not ask her to," Gideon ventured.

"Indeed not. She thinks that if she finds me a wife, it will somehow make up for—for something that happened long ago." He paused and glanced at Gideon. "Oh, devil take it! The truth is, she broke off our engagement."

Gideon gaped at him. "Engagement? You and Lady Haughston are engaged?"

The duke sighed. "We were, long ago. She was not Lady Haughston then. It was fifteen years past, and she was only Lady Francesca, the daughter of the Earl of Selbrooke."

"But how have I never heard this? I mean, of course I would not have known it at the time, but since I've been returned to my family... I cannot imagine why

Aunt Odelia or my grandmother or someone has never brought it up."

"They never knew about it, either," Rochford replied. "It was a secret engagement." He sighed, and suddenly he looked older, weary. "Francesca had just turned eighteen. I'd known her practically all her life, of course. Selbrooke's estate, Redfields, bordered on my lands at Dancy Park. But that last winter, when she was seventeen, and I saw her…" A faint smile lifted one corner of his mouth. "It was as if the scales fell from my eyes. It was Boxing Day, and we held a ball. There she was, wearing long skirts at last, with a blue ribbon in her hair that matched her eyes. I was stunned." He glanced at his companion ruefully.

"I know the feeling," Gideon assured him in a dry tone.

"Yes, I imagine you do, at that. So…I fell in love with her. I tried not to. I told myself she was too young. She seemed to return the feeling, but I knew that she had not even made her debut yet. She had not been to London parties, only country things. She knew few men, beyond her relatives and the locals. How was she to truly know her heart?"

Rochford was silent for a moment as he took a drink, then gazed reflectively into his glass. When he looked up again, his face was set, all emotion carefully absent from it. "Finally, I could not bring myself to wait until she had had her first Season. I feared that if I stood back, some other man would move in and sweep her off her feet."

"So you compromised by making the engagement secret," Gideon said.

"Exactly. I could see the stars in her eyes. I knew that she thought she loved me. But I feared that she was simply dazzled by her first romance. I could not bear to set her free, with no knowledge of my regard for her, my hopes for the two of us. But I did not want her irrevocably bound to me by a public engagement. If she changed her mind or if she realized that she did not love me as much as she had thought she did, then she would be able to break it off without being subjected to the scandal."

"I see." Gideon had not been raised among his peers, but he had learned enough about the society in which he now lived to know that a broken engagement was an enormous scandal that could haunt a woman, in particular, for the rest of her life. As a result, both parties rarely cried off, even if one or the other began to have doubts about the upcoming marriage.

"Unfortunately, in the end I proved to be right. She did not love me enough."

"What happened?"

The duke shrugged. "She was deceived. She was made to believe that I was having an affair with another woman. I tried to tell her what had really happened, but she would not believe me. She refused to see me. By the end of the Season, she had become engaged to Lord Haughston. And that was the end of it."

"Until now."

Rochford nodded. "Until now." He polished off the

liquor in his glass and reached out to pour another drink. "Recently she discovered that she had been lied to, that the woman in question had arranged for Francesca to find the two of us apparently *in flagrante delicto*. She realized that I had told her the truth and that she had been wrong, that she had treated me unfairly." He raised the glass toward Gideon in a kind of salute, saying, "So she decided to make it up to me by finding me a wife."

Gideon watched silently as the other man downed the drink. He had never seen Rochford consume liquor at quite the pace he was drinking it now. Of course, neither had he ever seen him looking quite so...off balance. The duke was one of the most self-contained men he had ever met, rare to show anger or even irritation. But tonight, clearly, he was disturbed, fury bubbling just below the surface, seemingly ready to jump out at any moment, and it was clear that he was having to hold it in with some effort.

"Why the devil did she take it into her head to do that?" Rochford exclaimed as he set his glass down with a thud on the small table between them. "God, and to think for a little while I was fool enough to believe—"

When he did not go on, Gideon prodded quietly, "To believe what?"

Rochford shook his head and made a dismissive gesture with his hand. "It doesn't matter. It's nothing." He paused, then went on. "She told me what she had found out, and she apologized. And then she maneuvered it so that I agreed to escort her and Lady Althea Robart to a play. I thought…"

"That she wanted to go back to—"

"No!" Rochford replied quickly. "Good Gad, no. There's no question of that, of course. But I thought, perhaps, she hoped we could be better friends now. Then she started throwing Lady Althea at me. Lady Althea, of all people!"

"I don't know her."

"You don't want to," the duke told him bluntly. "She is pretty enough, but too high in the instep for me. Not to mention that after ten minutes of her conversation, one is ready to go to sleep."

"Do you still love Lady Haughston?"

Rochford glanced at him, then quickly away, saying gruffly, "Nonsense. Of course not. That is, well, of course I have some degree of feeling for the woman. We are old…not exactly friends, of course, but, in a way she is almost family."

Gideon cocked a skeptical eyebrow at that description, but refrained from saying anything.

"I have not been nursing an unrequited love for her all these years," the duke went on firmly. "We could never go back to what we were, what we felt. It has been fifteen years, after all. We both lost those feelings long ago. I'm not angry because I hoped the two of us might— No, it's just Francesca's absolute gall in deciding to take over my life. Everyone lets her manage things. She is terribly good at it, maneuvering and arranging."

A smile lifted the other man's lips. "I have had experience."

"But that she should decide to do it for *me!*" Rochford's dark eyes snapped. "That she thinks she is better able to choose a wife than I am. That I need her help in getting a woman to marry me!" A muscle in his jaw jumped as he clenched his teeth.

Rochford poured himself a fourth drink and took a healthy slug of it. "Then she has the nerve to preach duty to me. To me! As if I were some young fool who flits about indulging my whims, with no concern for my name or family. As if I had not devoted my life to the title and the estate since I was eighteen years old. To top it off, she implies that I am getting past the age of marrying. As if I must seize some silly girl and father children as fast as I can before I am no longer capable of reproducing!"

Gideon smothered a smile. "I feel sure she did not mean to imply that."

The duke made a disgruntled noise and sipped his drink.

"Pardon me if I am prying—you know my manners are not polished," Gideon began. "But do you mean not to marry?"

"Of course not. I will marry. I must. Eventually."

"You do not sound eager."

Rochford shrugged. "I have simply not found anyone I want to marry. Everyone reminds me of my duty to have progeny, and I suppose they are right. The line must go on. And my cousin Bertram has no desire to inherit all the work and responsibility that go with being a duke. But surely there is time yet. I am not quite ready to 'shuffle off this mortal coil.'" He swirled the brandy around in the bottom of the snifter, watching the dark liquid broodingly. "I will find a wife someday. And I will do it in my own way, without any help from Lady Haughston."

"I must say, she did rather well for me," Gideon pointed out mildly, watching his cousin. "I cannot imagine a mate better suited for me than Irene." He paused, then added, "You might let her try."

Rochford snorted. "It would serve her right if I did."

This thought seemed to arrest him, for he stopped speaking and stared off into space for a long moment. Finally a slow smile curved his lips, and he thoughtfully took another drink.

"Maybe I should," he murmured. "Let Lady Haughston see just how much she enjoys finding me the proper duchess."

CHAPTER SIX

Sir Alan came to call on Francesca the following afternoon, bringing his daughter with him. Francesca was relieved to see them. She had felt dispirited all day, fearing that she had lost Rochford's friendship forever. She had stopped and started several tasks, unable to concentrate on anything, for her thoughts kept returning to Rochford's anger. It seemed terribly unfair, she thought, that he had been so angry at her when all she had done was try to help him. Perhaps she had been a trifle clumsier than she normally was about such matters, but surely he could see that she had bore him no ill will in the matter.

If he had just allowed her to explain, she was sure that she could have made him understand—or at least kept him from becoming enraged. It was not like him to be quick to anger or disinclined to listen to reason. But Francesca was becoming aware that she apparently had that effect upon him. It was, she suspected, her frivolous nature that had grated on him. Rochford had always been serious—well, not serious, exactly, for he had a quick sense of humor and a wonderful laugh. And, of course, when he smiled, the room seemed to light up. He was not one of those dreadfully boring sorts who was always grim.

But he was so responsible, so dedicated to his duty, so careful and well-planned in everything he did. He was well-read, even scholarly, and his interests ranged over a wide variety of subjects. He corresponded with scientists and scholars in many different fields. She knew that he must consider her far too flighty and shallow, a woman interested only in clothes and hats and gossip. It was for that reason, when they had been engaged, that Francesca had feared he would one day grow tired of her or, worse yet, come to view her as an annoyance.

Now he obviously did view her that way, since his infatuation with her was long gone. Still, she was surprised that his reaction had been so extreme. She wished that she had been smoother in her dealings with him and Althea, and she spent much of the day going over and over what she could have done differently.

When Sir Alan arrived, she met him with cordiality, glad to turn her attention to someone else. Sir Alan smiled when she greeted him, and she saw again in his eyes a certain masculine appreciation. She would have to be careful in dealing with him, she thought; she certainly did not want to encourage any romantic inclinations.

Francesca turned quickly to say hello to his daughter, then rang for tea and settled down for a chat, studying Harriet covertly as they talked.

The girl was pretty enough, with nice brown eyes, a snub nose and thick brown hair. Her skin was too brown; she obviously was not careful about wearing a hat in the country. But at least she was not spotty or freckled. She had a frank, open face and a friendly smile—not the cool, aristocratic look that was deemed correct by society mavens. But Francesca had never found that that particular look attracted a man, anyway.

A different style for her hair would work wonders, as would a lesson in plucking her eyebrows. And her dress did not suit her at all. It was dowdy and prim— and Francesca had no difficulty in believing that Sir Alan's mother had picked out the girl's clothes.

"Your father tells me that you are interested in making a bit of a splash this Season," Francesca began in a friendly tone.

Harriet grinned back at her. "Oh, I would not aim so high as a 'splash,' Lady Haughston. I think mere notice would be an improvement."

Francesca smiled, liking the girl's forthright response. Of course, she would have to school some of that out of her if Harriet hoped to be a success. "I think we can do better than that—if we put our minds to it."

"I am willing," Harriet replied. She cast a smile at her father as she went on. "I fear Papa has wasted his money so far. I would hate for it all to have been for naught."

"Now, Harry," her father protested fondly. "You needn't worry about things like that."

"I know you do not mind," she responded. "But I despise waste in any form."

"Then you are, um, willing to be guided by me in

these matters?" Francesca inquired. There was nothing worse than a recalcitrant student.

"I put myself entirely in your hands," Miss Sherbourne assured her. "I know that I haven't sufficient town bronze. I can tell that sometimes the things I say make people look at me askance. But I am a quick learner, and I'm willing to change in whatever way I have to—at least for the length of a Season."

"I think that a shopping expedition is the place to start," Francesca said, with a quick glance at Harriet's father. He nodded agreeably, and she continued. "I also think it would be a good idea, Sir Alan, if we put on some sort of party. We could invite some of the people whom I think would be helpful in getting your daughter noticed. Now, the other day, you mentioned that you would prefer that I—"

"Oh, yes, Lady Haughston," Sir Alan jumped in eagerly. "If you would—my mother, you see, is not in the best of health. Nor does she move about in Society that much. I think it might be too much for her. Not, of course, that she wouldn't be willing." The expression on his face put the lie to that last sentence.

"I could easily have a small soiree or a dinner here," Francesca suggested.

The man heaved a sigh of relief. "Just the thing, I'm sure. It is a great deal to ask of you, I know, but I am certain that you would handle everything so much better. Just direct all the bills to me—as you must do with the dresses, of course."

"I shall be happy to play hostess," Francesca assured him honestly. She enjoyed arranging parties, and it was much more fun to do so when she was not limited by her own financial situation.

Harriet and her father rose to leave not long afterwards. As Francesca and Harriet stood making arrangements for the shopping expedition the following day, the butler appeared in the doorway to announce another visitor.

"His Grace, the Duke of Rochford, my lady," Fenton intoned.

Francesca turned toward the door, startled to see Rochford standing in the hallway behind her butler. Her stomach tightened, and she could feel a blush rising up her throat. She hardly knew what to say or think as memories of the evening before flooded in on her. In the space of a single instant she veered from embarrassment at the thought of his kiss to pain from the angry words he had thrown at her to an answering anger of her own.

"Rochford. I—I did not expect you. I—oh, forgive me." Belatedly, she remembered her other guests. "Pray allow me to introduce you to Sir Alan Sherbourne and his daughter, Miss Harriet Sherbourne. Sir Alan, the Duke of Rochford."

To her surprise, Sir Alan smiled and said, "Thank you, Lady Haughston, but the duke and I have met. Good to see you again."

"Sir Alan." The duke nodded to the other man, explaining to Francesca, "Sir Alan and I met the other day at Tattersall's." The horse sales were conducted every Monday, and had become a favorite congregating place for men of all ranks.

"Yes, and his Grace was kind enough to advise me against buying a certain hunter that I had my eye on."

"I had knowledge of him, you see. Good-looking animal, but no go in him." The duke turned toward Harriet, saying, "But until now I have not had the pleasure of meeting your daughter, Sir Alan." He nodded. "Miss Sherbourne."

Harriet, who was rather goggling at the duke, hastily curtsied, a blush spreading along her cheeks. "An honor, Your Grace."

Sir Alan and Harriet then took their leave, with Sir Alan once again expressing his gratitude to Francesca. After they were gone, the duke turned back to her.

"One of your projects?" he asked her, raising an eyebrow.

"I have decided to take an interest in Miss Sherbourne, yes," Francesca replied a little stiffly, not sure how to respond to him.

It seemed unlikely that he would have come to expound on his dislike of her actions, but neither was it reasonable that he would have abandoned his anger this quickly. Even if he had, Francesca thought, she was not inclined to ignore the way he had railed at her just the night before.

"I came to apologize," he told her now, coming

straight to the point. "I have no excuse for how I acted last night. I can only hope that your good nature will lead you to forgive me."

"Some would say that appealing to my better nature would fall on deaf ears," Francesca retorted crisply, but she could not help but be disarmed by his apology.

He smiled. "Anyone who could say that obviously does not know you."

"I did not mean to upset you, you know," she told him. "I wanted to make up for my mistakes, not commit a new one."

"You are not to blame for my reaction." He shrugged. "I fear that I am a trifle sensitive on the subject of marrying. My grandmother has taken me to task for it far too many times, as has Aunt Odelia."

"Oh, dear. I hate to hear that I am behaving like a grandmother or great-aunt." She had no interest in staying angry with Rochford. And she certainly did not want to get into the matter of his kiss! No, better to gracefully let go of the whole matter.

"I hope that you will accept a ride through the park as an adequate peace offering," he went on. "It is a lovely May day out."

He had surprised her again. Francesca could not remember when she had ridden out alone with Rochford—well, yes, she could. It had been when they were engaged so long ago. But better not to think of that.

"Yes," she told him with a smile. "That sounds delightful."

A few minutes later he was handing her up into his high perch phaeton, a fashionable vehicle with a seat so far from the ground that Francesca would have felt alarmed had any less notable a whip than Rochford been handling the horses.

He climbed up beside her and took the reins, and they set off. She could not deny an unaccustomed bubbling of excitement inside her. Though she was used to being admired by many gentlemen and was not averse to a little light flirtation, she rarely accepted any man's invitation to ride through the park. It was her practice not to allow even so small a step toward courtship.

It was a rather heady experience to be sitting up this high, and there was a certain added fillip of danger without any need to be scared. There was no one better at handling a team than Rochford.

They did not talk much as they made their way through the city streets, for the traffic made it necessary for him to concentrate on keeping his powerful team in hand. Francesca did not mind. Frankly, it was taking her a bit of time to adjust to the feelings that were running through her.

She and Rochford had often driven through Hyde Park when they were engaged. When she had come to London for her first Season, she had missed him terribly, for she had been accustomed to seeing him almost every day in the country. They had ridden together, and strolled in the gardens at Redfields and Dancy Park, and gone on long rambles through the countryside. When he had come to call on her at Red-fields, no one had watched them too closely, and it had been easy enough to talk together and to exchange glances, perhaps even for his hand to brush against hers.

But once they were in London, all that had changed. They were surrounded by people everywhere. There were always callers in Francesca's drawing room and crowds of people at parties, other men vying for the opportunity to dance with her or escort her to the opera. She had felt alone and frustrated, and she had looked forward to the times when the duke took her for a drive.

Of course, they had had to be circumspect about the number of times they went to the park and the length of time they stayed. Any excessive attention on Roch-ford's part would have been fuel for rumors. But Fran-cesca had felt happier on those rides than at any other time during that Season.

Memories of those long ago moments rushed in upon her now, nearly taking her breath away. It was the same time of year, with the same feel in the air, the same caress of the sun on their backs. Francesca could not help but remember how excitement had surged up in her on those drives, the breathless joy she had felt just sit-ting beside Rochford.

He was just as close to her now. She had only to reach out a hand and she could touch him. She remem-bered how much she had longed to do just that fifteen years ago, worried that he would be disapproving of her boldness, afraid that someone else might see.

The breeze caressed her cheek and tugged at a lock of hair beneath her hat. Everything around her seemed brighter, the leaves glossier, the shade beneath the trees deeper and more inviting. The faint scent of the duke's cologne teased at her nostrils, and she was very aware of him beside her. She thought of his kiss the night before, of the way his hard body had pressed into hers, his arms tight and strong around her. His lips sinking into hers…his mouth velvety and inviting, hot with desire.

Francesca swallowed and turned her face to look off to the side, hoping that the sudden flush in her cheeks would cool down before he glanced at her. How could she be thinking this way about that kiss—her flesh tingling, her muscles tightening, heat coiling in her stomach?

She wished that she could deny the effect his kiss had on her, but she knew that she could not. Even the other night, in her dream, she had thrilled to his kiss, her whole body melting against him, her mouth opening to his seeking tongue.

"I thought a great deal last night about what you said," Rochford began when they had reached Hyde Park and he no longer had to focus on the reins to such a degree.

Francesca, lost in her thoughts, started. "Oh?" She hoped he did not notice how breathily her voice came out.

"Yes. When I calmed down, I realized not only that I had been appallingly rude, but also that you had been quite correct in what you said. And my grandmother, as well."

"Really?" Francesca stared at him in some astonishment. "Do you mean—"

He nodded. "Yes. It is time that I married. Past time."

"Oh. I see. Well…" Francesca was aware of an odd feeling in her stomach, a faintly queasy sensation reminiscent of the way she felt when she looked down from a great height.

"I decided you were right—it is time I started looking for a bride. I doubt I shall suddenly develop any interest in marrying. I should simply set myself to the task and do it."

"Being resigned hardly seems a good foundation for marriage," Francesca blurted out. She was, she realized, perversely disheartened by the duke's words.

Rochford quirked an eyebrow at her. "I thought that was what you wanted."

"No! I didn't want you to drag yourself to the altar. I—I wanted to make you happy."

As soon as she said the words, she realized that they sounded all wrong. She glanced away, hoping that she did not appear as flushed as she felt.

"What I mean," she continued, "is that I hoped that marrying would provide you with happiness. That it would change your life for the better."

Quietly he asked, "Did marriage make you happier?"

Francesca shot a flashing look at him, then turned away. Tears clogged her throat. She would not, *could* not, talk to him about *that*. Swallowing hard, she gave a shrug and turned a bright smile toward Rochford.

"Ah, but we are discussing you and your happiness, not me." Quickly, she moved on. "What are you planning to do, now that you have decided on marriage?"

"I have already taken the first step," he informed her, his eyes steady on her face. "I came to you."

Francesca stared at him speechlessly for a moment. "I—I beg your pardon?"

"What better person to guide me through this project than the woman who has brought about so many successful matches?" Rochford asked. "I thought that you could help me find my bride."

"But I—" She felt blank and strangely weak. Whatever she had thought Rochford might say when he arrived at her house today, this certainly had not been it. "I fear that my accomplishments have been greatly exaggerated."

"If even half of what people say you have done is true, then you must be quite skilled in the matter," Rochford protested. "Certainly you did well by my cousin. I don't know when I have seen a more happily married man. And your brother and his wife are quite happy. I saw them only recently, and they are obviously still as much in love as the day they married—perhaps even more so."

"Those are unusual cases. And I cannot take credit for—for the love that they have found."

"But for you, none of them would be together today," he pointed out. "Nor my sister and Bromwell."

"You cannot be pleased about that."

"As long as Callie is happy, I am well pleased." He paused, then went on. "In any case, you have already done a great deal of the work. If I understood you correctly last night, you have come up with several prospective brides for me."

"You are not shamming?" Francesca studied his face earnestly. "Do you really want me to help you?"

"That is why I am here."

She gazed at him for another long moment, then gave a little nod. "All right, then. I will help you."

"Excellent."

A barouche was approaching from the opposite direction, and when it pulled close, they could see that the open carriage held Lady Whittington and her bosom friend Mrs. Wychfield. Since the Whittington barouche stopped beside them, Rochford could not pass with only a polite nod, but had to stop and exchange a greeting. Naturally, they must then spend a few minutes commenting on Lady Whittington's ball, how splendid it had been and how much everyone had enjoyed it, followed by polite inquiries as to the other members of everyone's families.

Francesca could feel the women's eyes fixed on her speculatively, and she knew that soon the news that she had been riding through the park in the duke's phaeton would be circulating throughout the *ton*. Even though everyone knew that they were well-acquainted, it did not take more than a change in the routine, such as this, to set the gossips' tongues wagging.

Finally they were able to take their leave, and the duke set his team in motion, taking up their conversation again. "Tell me, how many candidates have you found for me?"

"What? Oh. Well, I had narrowed it down to three young women."

"As few as that?" He cast her an amused glance. "Am I so unpopular?"

Francesca rolled her eyes. "You know it is exactly the opposite. There are scores of women who would love to be chosen as your fiancée. But I had to be rather choosey."

"And what were your criteria, if I may ask?"

"Naturally, they must be pleasing in face and form."

"I am fortunate that you took that into account."

Francesca cast him a speaking glance and continued. "They must come from excellent families, though I did not think that wealth would be a matter of concern for you."

He nodded. "You are correct, as always."

"I also thought that it would be good if they were intelligent enough to converse with you and your friends, although I do not imagine that you would expect them to be as learned as your scholarly circle. They should also have the social skills necessary to be a hostess at the sorts of dinners and parties that a duchess must give. They have to be able to converse with important guests. And they must have the knowledge and ability to oversee a large staff of servants—indeed, the staffs of several houses. Then there are the other duties that are expected of a duchess, such as dealing with your tenants' families and the local gentry at your various estates. And, of course, they must be pleasing to you personally."

"I had wondered if that entered into your equations," he murmured.

"Really, Rochford, don't be absurd. That is the most important thing. She must not be vain and self-centered. She must not be unkind or flighty or frequently sick."

The duke chuckled. "I am beginning to understand why you came up with so few prospects."

Francesca laughed with him. "I know that your standards are high."

"Yes, they always have been," he agreed.

The implication of his words hit her—he was implying, was he not, that *she* had met his high standards—and she cast a quick glance up at him. She found his gaze on hers, and she blushed, feeling foolishly pleased and a little flustered.

She cleared her throat and looked away, suddenly unsure what else to say.

"Your first pick, obviously, was Althea Robart," he said, breaking the awkwardness of the moment. "One has to wonder why."

"She is quite attractive," Francesca pointed out, defending her selection. "Also, her father is the Earl of Bridcombe, and her sister is married to Lord Howard. Her family is quite good, and she doubtless has an understanding of the tasks she would have to perform as the Duchess of Rochford."

"Rather arrogant, though," he commented, casting her a droll look.

"I assumed that would suit a duchess well enough," Francesca retorted.

"Mmm, but perhaps it would not suit the duke."

Francesca could not keep her lips from curling up into a smile. "All right. I will admit that Lady Althea was a poor choice."

"Yes. I suggest that we leave her out of any future considerations. Or perhaps hold her in reserve, if I should become desperate." He paused for a moment, then added, "No, I fear not even then. I do not think that even my sense of duty to my heirs could compel me to endure a lifetime of Lady Althea."

"Consider Lady Althea crossed off the list. What about Damaris Burke? She is intelligent and competent. Her mother is dead, so Lady Damaris has been acting as Lord Burke's hostess for the past two years. As he is in government, she is accustomed to handling important people and putting on important parties."

"Hmm. I have met Lady Damaris."

"What did you think of her?"

"I'm not sure. I had not really looked at her with an

eye to her being my duchess, you see. I did not dislike her, as I recall."

"All right, then we shall consider her. Agreed?"

He nodded.

"The last one is Lady Caroline Wyatt."

The duke frowned, thinking. "I do not believe I am acquainted with her."

"This is her first year out."

Rochford looked at her, surprise and doubt mingling in his face. "A girl fresh from the schoolroom?"

"She is a trifle young," Francesca admitted. "But her family is actually the best of all three. Her father is only a baronet, but her mother is the youngest of the Duke of Bellingham's daughters, and her grandmother on her father's side was a Moreland."

"Impressive."

"I have been around the girl, and she does not seem to be a giddy or silly sort. I have not once heard her giggle or fly into raptures."

"Very well. I will consider her." He paused for a moment. "But I must say, it does seem that you have chosen rather young women for me. I am, if you will remember, thirty-eight years old."

Francesca pulled a face at him. "Indeed, yes. You are near decrepit, I am sure."

"Are any of them over twenty-one?"

"Lady Damaris is twenty-three, and Althea is twenty-one."

He quirked an eyebrow at her.

"Well, it is harder to find the best prospects among women who are older," Francesca defended herself. "If they are lovely and accomplished and all that one could want, they are often already married."

"There are widows who are nearer my age," he pointed out.

"Yes, but—I did not consider any widows as prospective brides for you."

"Why not? Some widows are the most beautiful women in the *ton*."

Francesca flushed. Did he mean her? If this were any other man, she would have been certain that he was flirting with her. But Rochford did not flirt—certainly not with her.

And yet…she could remember a time when he *had* flirted with her—in a very understated Rochford style, of course. Still, he had looked at her in a certain way as he teased her, a way that made her feel warm and excited inside—very much the way she felt right now.

She hoped she did not appear as flustered as she felt. "Surely it is important to a man that his wife not have been married before. That she be…" Francesca blushed even harder. It was beyond embarrassing to have to speak to Rochford, of all people, about such things. Finally she finished in a low voice, "That she be untouched."

He did not respond, and she rushed on. "Besides, there is the matter of children. A younger woman, after all, has more—more time…" She limped to a halt.

"Ah, yes, the all-important heir," he said dryly. "I had forgotten. We are choosing a broodmare, not a companion for me."

"No! Sinclair!" Francesca turned to him, concern overcoming her embarrassment. "'Tis not like that."

"Is it not?" His smile was wry. "At least I wrung a 'Sinclair' from your lips."

She glanced away again, unable to hold his gaze. Why did she feel so disconcerted around him today? One would have thought she was a schoolgirl, the way she was acting. "It *is* your name," she pointed out a little breathlessly.

"Yes, but I have not heard it on your lips in many years."

There was a tone in his voice that made her heart flutter in her chest. She raised her eyes to his and found herself caught by their dark depths. She remembered another time when she had looked up at him, feeling as if she might drown in his eyes. She had uttered his given name then, too, had whispered "Sinclair" as if it were a prayer, and he had kissed her, pulling her hard against him and seizing her lips like a man starved. The memory of that kiss sent a stroke of heat through her, and her pulse began to pound in her throat.

Francesca tore her eyes away from his. Struggling to keep her voice even, she said, "There are— I did consider two more women. They are both older than the others."

"Indeed?" The odd note was missing from his voice

now; he spoke in his usual dry, faintly amused tone. "And who are these ancients?"

"Lady Mary Calderwood, Lord Calderwood's eldest daughter. She is, I think, somewhere in her midtwenties. And Lady Edwina de Winter, Lord de Winter's widow. She is a trifle older than that. Lady Mary is quite intelligent, I believe, though a bit shy. It is for that reason that I did not include her earlier."

"I will be happy to meet both of them," he told her. "Now, tell me, how do you propose I interview these candidates? Do you plan to stage a house party for all of them, as you did with Gideon? It is rather handy, I must say, collecting them all in one spot. Though I am not so sure that I should want to have to make my choice at the end of the two weeks."

"No, I see no need for that. There were special circumstances, as you know, with Lord Radbourne, which hardly apply in this case. It is not necessary, anyway. It is the Season, after all, and everyone is here in London. I am sure it will not be difficult to arrange for you to meet them while you are out and about. Although…" She paused, thinking. "Why don't you come to the party that I am holding for Sir Alan's daughter next week? Your presence there would help establish Harriet in Society, and at the same time you would have a chance to talk with Lady Damaris and the others."

"Very efficient of you."

Francesca shot him a wary glance, not sure what his dry tone indicated. But he only smiled at her and added,

"I will put myself in your hands. I am sure that you will come up with the perfect woman for me."

"I shall do my best," she answered.

"Good. Then let us move on to more amusing topics. Have you heard about Sir Hugo Walden's challenge to Lord Berry's youngest?"

"To race their curricles?" Francesca chuckled. "I had indeed. I was told it ended with Sir Hugo landing in a henhouse."

Rochford laughed. "No, no, that was some poor parson who got caught between them on the road. Sir Hugo wound up in the duck pond, I believe."

The rest of the drive passed in cheerful conversation, talking of the latest gossip and dissecting the political news, then moving on to the changes that Francesca's brother was instituting at Redfields. The awkwardness that had cropped up during their earlier conversation fled entirely, and Francesca found herself laughing and chatting freely.

It had been a long time, she thought, since she had spoken with Rochford with such a lack of restraint. In her earlier years, he had been not only the man she loved, but also a close friend. It had been the absence of his companionship as much as her shattered heart that had darkened the first years without him. She did not know that she had ever felt the same closeness and affection with anyone else.

Perhaps they could be friends again now, she thought, when he had returned her to her house. She went to the window of the drawing room, which looked out onto the street, and watched him climb back up onto the high seat of the phaeton. She found her eyes lingering on his long, leanly muscled legs and on his strong hands, masterfully taking up the reins again.

There could be more afternoons like this, more conversation and laughter, now that the barriers of the past had fallen. She no longer carried the hurt of his betrayal, and he—well, he must have lost most of his anger, coming back to her and apologizing as he had done today.

They could work together on finding him a wife, she told herself. And when she had done that, she would have rid herself of the guilt she felt. She would have helped him find happiness. He would have a wife and children. And she would have his friendship.

Then why, she wondered, as she watched him drive away, did she feel such a strange emptiness inside?

CHAPTER SEVEN

FRANCESCA WAS VERY busy during the course of the next week, helping Harriet with her wardrobe and planning for the party. She had decided to throw a small soiree. Nothing too grand, where everyone would get lost in the crowd, nor too elegant, where everyone would feel stiff. The guest list was the major consideration. She must invite women important enough to ease Harriet's way in Society, but none so rigid that they would disapprove of the girl's frank and open manner. The party itself, of course, must be both enjoyable and memorable, not only for Harriet's sake, but also for her own reputation as a hostess. On the other hand, she could not allow it to overshadow Harriet.

As far as Rochford went, at least, little would be required. She had no doubt that anyone she invited would attend, and no eligible young woman would balk at being put in the duke's company.

The following day Francesca threw off the odd, rather unsettling sense of sadness that had befallen her the evening before. She was in her element planning a party, and it was doubly enjoyable when there was no need to consider the expense. She was soon ensconced at her desk, making lists and menus.

She broke off that afternoon to go shopping with Harriet, another occupation that was among her favorites. Having been given free rein by Sir Alan, she was able to plunge into the search for clothes without any qualms.

They spent much of the afternoon at her favorite modiste's, and by the time they left, Harriet had acquired three new evening gowns, four day dresses and a walking dress, as well as a charming new pelisse. And since Mlle. du Plessis, her eyes shining with delight at the large order, suggested to Francesca that she might have the sea-green gown she had been considering for an even lower price, Francesca had been unable to resist purchasing the evening gown for herself, as well.

She did, however, refrain from buying a new bonnet when they visited the millinery shop, even though she found a delightful chip straw hat with a blue lining that brought out the dark blue of her eyes. Her maid had redecorated her bonnet from last year with a different satin ribbon and a clump of bright red cherries, and it would do well enough for this summer. Still, she could not keep from casting a last wistful look back at the hat as they left the store.

However, it was almost as much fun to shop for another as for herself, and Francesca threw herself into acquiring the remainder of the items necessary for Harriet's transformation. Next stop was the shoemaker's, for the slippers necessary for two of Harriet's new evening gowns, as well as a pair of half boots. They followed their shoe purchases with a trip to Grafton's, where they could acquire a new kerseymere shawl to replace the rather outdated one given Harriet by her grandmother, as well as other such necessary items as handkerchiefs, gloves and accessories for the girl's hair. Francesca was also pleased to find a satin band precisely the same color as the sea-green gown she had just purchased, which would make a perfect fillet for her hair. She might even, she thought, add a few false pearls to it.

They finished up their expedition with a trip to Gunter's for a lemon ice before they returned, weary and well-pleased with themselves, to Francesca's house, the boxes from Grafton's and the milliner's piled onto the seats of the carriage. The shoes and dresses, of course, would not be ready for several days, though Mlle. du Plessis had promised that one of Harriet's evening gowns would be given utmost priority, so she could have it by the day of Francesca's party the next week.

"I hope your father will not mind the bills when they arrive," Francesca commented, a trifle worried that perhaps she had been too extravagant on Harriet's behalf. Sir Alan had seemed quite unconcerned about the cost, but she was not entirely sure that a gentleman accustomed to living in the country was fully aware of the sort of expenses they would be running up.

"Oh, no," Harriet assured her. "He isn't at all close-fisted. Particularly about the expenses for my Season. He did not turn a hair at what Grandmama spent, even though I must say I thought the dresses were vastly overpriced, considering the way they looked. They seemed dowdy to me, and when I saw the other girls at the parties, I knew that I had the right of it."

"I am sure your grandmother is accustomed to an older style."

Harriet nodded. "I don't mean to speak badly of her, my lady. She is good-hearted. But she tires easily, and she finds shopping and parties exhausting. Also, I fear the mantua-maker she uses is simply not as talented as Mademoiselle du Plessis. And more expensive, as well. I could tell that even Papa was a bit disappointed in how I looked in my wardrobe—though, of course, he is far too good to say anything."

"I think he will be pleased when he sees these dresses on you."

Harriet smiled. "Good. I should enjoy not feeling like such a wallflower. Do you think it is possible that I will get asked to dance next time when we go to a ball? *Will* we go to a ball?"

"Of course. A number of them. There are several weeks left in the Season. And once my friends Sir Lucien and the Duke of Rochford have asked you to dance, I do not think that you will remain a wallflower."

"The duke!" Harriet exclaimed, paling, her eyes opening wide. "You think the duke will dance with me?"

"I shall make sure that he does."

"Oh, no, my lady, I daren't dance with someone like him. I shall be sure to trip or step on his foot, and then I shall just drop from embarrassment."

"Nonsense. The duke is an excellent dancer. He will make certain you do not."

"It is not him I am worried about," the girl told her earnestly. "What If I make a fool of myself? I haven't the least idea how to speak to a duke. I would be in jitters, I am sure."

"You will have a chance to converse with him at my party, and after that he will not seem so fearsome."

Harriet looked unconvinced. "He is so well-bred. I've never seen any man who looked half as elegant, no matter what he wore."

"That is true," Francesca allowed. Even in a jacket of blue superfine and fawn trousers, Rochford would outshine any man in a formal black coat and breeches. There was simply something about the way he carried himself.

"And he's dreadfully handsome," Harriet went on. "Like Lucifer himself, I thought, with that black hair and those black eyes. Don't you think so, Lady Haughston?"

"Yes. He is a very attractive man."

"And a *duke*… I am sure he is not accustomed to listening to someone like me."

"But he isn't at all high in the instep," Francesca assured her. "He treats everyone with respect. I have seen him talk to his tenants and servants with great civility. He is not arrogant or unkind. Ask your father."

"Papa thinks him an admirable gentleman. He told me so when he came back from Tattersall's that day. It was the duke who recommended to Papa that he come see you."

"Really?" Francesca turned, startled. "He did not mention that to me."

"Oh, yes. Papa could not believe how generous he was, especially given that he had only just met him."

"The duke is quite generous—and he is an excellent judge of character. I am sure he took your father's measure instantly and decided that he was worthy of his friendship."

Despite her words of assurance to Harriet, Francesca could not help but be taken aback by the duke's directing Sir Alan her way. She supposed Sir Alan must have brought up the matter of his daughter's lack of success, although it seemed a rather peculiar topic for two gentlemen at Tattersall's. But even if they were discussing the matter, she was surprised that the duke would even think to tell the man to ask her for her help.

She was glad he had, of course—but she could not rid herself of the notion that it almost seemed as though Rochford had been going out of his way to help her in her endeavors.

But no, surely not. He did not know about her financial straits. No one did. She had done her utmost to hide her struggles with money all these years. Besides, even if Rochford had somehow guessed that she was skirting the edge of poverty and had also realized that she was using her skills to stave off that threat, there was no reason for him to try to help her.

No. The idea was absurd. It must be that Sir Alan had raised the subject in some manner, and Rochford had simply mentioned her because of what she had done for his cousin Gideon. No more than that.

To change the subject from the vaguely disquieting one of Rochford, Francesca asked, "What do you hope to achieve this Season?"

"I'm not sure what you mean." Harriet frowned. "I would like to enjoy it. And I would like for Papa to be happy. He so wants me to have a good Season."

"Are you hoping to find a husband?" Sir Alan had told her that marriage was not the goal of their efforts, but Francesca was not sure that the father knew the extent of his daughter's wishes in the matter.

A blush stained the girl's cheekbones. "Oh, no, Lady Haughston. I do not care— That is…well, I do not think I am the sort to marry a lord or anyone like that. I have no desire to live in London or to—to participate in the social whirl of the *ton*. I am a country girl at heart. I enjoy the Assemblies and calling on the people I know there. Taking baskets to Papa's tenants when they are sick. Asking after people's children and grandchildren. That is the sort of life I like. It is what I am suited for. I have little desire to leave Papa. And…" She hesitated, her blush deepening. "There is a boy—the squire's son. They live not far away. I know Papa likes him, although he tells me I could look higher."

"Ah, I see." Francesca nodded. "But you don't wish to look higher."

Harriet nodded, grateful for the sophisticated woman's understanding. "That is it, exactly. His name is Tom, and I have known him all my life. He used to be—oh, such a nuisance, teasing me and telling ghost stories to frighten me. But last year, the first time I went to the Assembly, we danced—and it was entirely different. He is ever so much nicer, and when he comes to call, we talk about all sorts of things, and I cannot wait until the next time he comes. It is so odd. I know him well, and yet he is like someone I've just met. Do you know what I mean?"

"Yes," Francesca told her, and her smile was bitter-sweet. "I know just what you mean."

FRANCESCA WAS AT her desk in the morning room the next day, planning the decorations for her soiree, when her butler stepped into the room. He carried a small silver tray, and on it rested a white calling card.

"There is a…person to see you, my lady," he began, and Francesca knew immediately from his carefully blank face and the choice of his words that the visitor was not someone of whom the butler approved. "Mr. Galen Perkins."

"Perkins!" *Whatever was he doing here?* "Tell him I am not receiving."

"What? You would treat an old friend like that?" Perkins stepped into view behind the butler.

Francesca rose to her feet, her back straight. "I do not believe that we were ever friends, Mr. Perkins."

Fenton cast a look of dislike at the man and turned back to Francesca, his tone frosty as he asked, "Shall I escort Mr. Perkins to the door, my lady?"

Perkins flashed a wicked grin of amusement. "I should like to see you try."

"No, it's all right, Fenton." Francesca had little doubt that Perkins would not go willingly, and she feared he might hurt the old man. "I will talk to Mr. Perkins."

"Very well." Fenton executed a little bow, adding, "I shall be right outside, if you need me."

The butler stepped around Perkins and ostentatiously took up a position in the hallway opposite the door.

Perkins sauntered into the room, remarking, "What a faithful knight you have, dear lady. No doubt he protects you from all dangers."

"Why are you here, Mr. Perkins?" Francesca asked crisply. "What do you hope to accomplish by forcing your way in to see me?"

"Why, surely it is appropriate to offer my respects to the widow of my old friend," Perkins commented, the amused smirk lingering on his face.

"You offered your condolences the other night at the theater," Francesca reminded him. "So I scarcely think a visit is necessary."

He came around the side of the desk. He was closer

than Francesca would have liked, but she refused to back up, for she knew that he would take the gesture as fear. He ran his pale eyes insolently down her.

"A man can hardly be blamed for wanting to renew his acquaintance with so lovely as woman as yourself," he told her.

Francesca's fingers curled into her palm. She would have liked very much to slap him, so insolent and insinuating was his tone.

"It must get very lonely," he went on, "being a widow. Living alone as you do."

"I would never be lonely enough to seek your company," she assured him.

He shrugged. "Very well, then. Let us get down to business."

"Business?" Francesca looked at him in surprise. "What business? I have no business with you."

"I am afraid that I must differ." He smiled in the same annoyingly amused way, the lines of dissipation crinkling around his eyes.

Reaching into his jacket, he pulled out a piece of paper, which he unfolded. "Andrew and I played cards a short while before I had to leave for the Continent—"

"You mean before you killed a man."

He shrugged, his flat gaze showing no remorse. "A man must defend his honor."

"If he has any."

"Your husband lost heavily," Perkins continued, ignoring her remark. "As he so often did, I'm afraid. He ran out of funds, and he'd already thrown in his cuff links and stickpin. I could hardly take a voucher from him, as he so rarely paid them. So, on the final hand, he threw in his house. Sad to say, but not unexpectedly, he lost."

Francesca stared at him blankly. Her stomach felt as if it had dropped to the floor, and for a moment she could not move, could not speak. Finally she said, her voice rasping a little, "What do you mean? What house? Haughston Hall? It is entailed."

"I am aware of that," he replied, watching her. "I'm not a fool, whatever the company I kept. That is why I told him that it must be this house that he wagered."

Her insides turned to ice, but she struggled to keep her face from dissolving into fear. "You are lying."

"Am I?" He extended the paper, holding it out to her so that she could read it. "Do you really think Andrew was not capable of such a thing?"

Francesca's eyes flew over the words, taking in the formal terms of sale and, at the bottom, the faded but dreadfully familiar handwriting: Andrew, Lord Haughston. Her lungs felt squeezed together, and for a moment she feared that she might faint. *This couldn't be true. It simply could not. Surely Andrew, even Andrew, had not done this to her!* But, of course, she knew that he certainly could have. Andrew rarely thought of consequences, especially in terms of what might happen to her.

She swallowed hard and raised her eyes to meet his, a saving anger boiling up in her. "Get out of my house."

Again that faintly amused, taunting smile curved his lips. "*My* house, I am afraid, my lady."

"Did you think that I would meekly turn it over to you?" Francesca asked. "Let me assure you that I will not. I am not some weak reed who will break at the slightest blow. I am not without friends. People of influence and power. For all I know, you have forged that document. I saw no witnesses upon it."

He took a step forward so that he loomed over her, his pale eyes gleaming with a cold light. "Nor am *I* a weak reed, my lady." He made the formal address a sneer of contempt. "There were witnesses. Two other men playing cards with us, not to mention the whores and the madam of the brothel. I will take you to court if you do not turn over this house to me. And they will all come forward as witnesses to the deed." He raised his eyebrows, adding silkily, "If that is what you want."

His words struck her like a blow, as he had intended. If she fought him for the house, he would expose her late husband's scandalous behavior to the world. She would be dragged through the mud of gossip; everyone would whisper avidly about Andrew and his profligate ways, his drunkenness and gambling, his lightskirts.

But she kept her back straight and looked him in the eye as she repeated grimly, "I will not leave this house."

He studied her for a moment longer, then stepped

back, saying easily, "Of course, I could make you the same offer I gave to Andrew at that time. I told him if he came up with the money in lieu of which he put up the house, I would tear up the deed."

Francesca relaxed fractionally. Perhaps there was a way out of this, after all. The man just wanted money. "What was the sum?"

"Five thousand pounds."

She felt the blood drain out of her face, and she grasped the edge of her desk to steady herself. He might as well have said the moon. There was no way that she could come by £5000.

"I gave him two weeks to come up with the sum, but then, unfortunately, I had to leave the country because of the…incident with Bagshaw."

"Incident? Is that what you term murder?"

As if she had not spoken, he said smoothly, "Oddly enough, though, Haughston never saw fit to send me the money he owed me." He shook his head, as though despairing over the lack of loyalty among friends. "Still, I am willing to extend the same courtesy to you. In two weeks, you can pay me the money and we will tear up the note."

She knew that she could not come up with that sum if he had given her a lifetime to redeem the note, but still she exclaimed, "Two weeks! You cannot possibly expect me to gather so much together in that length of time. Haughston had far more resources than I. I must…write my parents and…and others. I have to speak to my man of business. Surely you can see that it is not enough time. Give me a few months."

"A few months!" he scoffed. "I have been waiting to take possession of this house for nigh seven years. Why would I wait still longer to obtain it?"

"It will be far easier, surely, if I were to give you the money," Francesca argued desperately. "What does a single gentleman need with a house? And I cannot obtain that much money so quickly. Please. Just two months."

He gazed at her for a long moment, then said shortly, "Very well. I will give you three weeks."

It was scarcely any better, but she nodded, glad for any delay. "Very well."

He smiled, sending a shiver through her, and sketched her a bow. "'Til then, my dear Lady Haughston."

He walked out of the room. In the hallway, Fenton turned and followed him, intent on showing him the door.

Francesca sank down into her chair as soon as he was out of sight. It was a wonder, she thought, that her legs had held her up this long. Setting her elbows on the desk, she dropped her face to her hands. Terror gripped her.

How could she possibly come up with such an amount of money? She was barely able to get by as it was; and she had very little left to sell. Her carriage was old, and her horses, too; they would bring very little. She had no jewelry that was not paste, except for the bracelet and earrings the duke had given her, and the cameo from his sister Callie. All of those things would not amount to a tenth of what Perkins said she owed him. Indeed, even if she stripped the house of every last piece of furniture and silver plate, it would not be enough.

The only thing she owned that would bring in any amount of money would be the house itself. Of course, if she sold the house and paid Perkins the money, it would still leave her without a place to live. She might be able to sell the place for more than the amount Perkins claimed she owed him and have enough to pay for a smaller home in a less fashionable area. However, selling a house would require a great deal more time than the three weeks Perkins had given her, and she did not think that she would be able to talk him into any extra time. Indeed, if he knew that she was trying to sell the house, she suspected that he would take her to court to block the sale.

Nor could she go to her father. He had already run his estate into the ground and been forced to turn it over to her brother Dominic to manage. Dominic would help her if he could, she knew, but he was struggling to return the estate to solvency. He had even sold his own manor house, an inheritance from their uncle, to pay off some of the estate's debts and make the improvements necessary to get the place on solid financial footing again. She could not ask him to endanger those efforts by creating a new load of debt to pay for her house. She would never be able to give him back the money.

She could think of nowhere else to turn. She could scarcely ask her friends for such a large sum of money, and she had no other family. Nor was she close to Lord Haughston's cousin, who had inherited the estate—not that even he had that much available money. Andrew had bled the estate as dry as he could, along with everything else.

She could fight Perkins to the bitter end. She could refuse to leave the house. Perhaps he would not really take her to court—though he had certainly seemed confident in that regard. Even if he did, it was always possible that the document was a forgery. While she did not doubt that Andrew would have thrown away his house on a hand of cards, neither did she doubt that Galen Perkins was capable of forging the document.

If she did force him to go to court to obtain the house, though, she had little doubt that he would make good his threat of dragging her husband's low acquaintances into court and exposing her to public humiliation. Even if the document was a false one and there had been no witnesses, she felt sure that he could find two men and a few prostitutes who would willingly testify, for a few gold coins, that Lord Haughston had indeed signed away his house in front of them.

Francesca could not bear to think of living through the scandal, of having her name spread through the newspapers, whispered about by all of London, from the highest lord to the lowliest chambermaid. And in the end, she would probably lose the house anyway. The signature on the deed had looked very much like Andrew's.

What was she to do if she lost this house? Where would she go? To Redfields, where she would have to live out the rest of her life on her brother's generosity? She had no doubt that Dom and his wife, Constance, would welcome her with never a word of complaint. But she dreaded the thought of being a burden to them just as much as she dreaded the idea of having nothing of her own anymore. And living the entire year away from London seemed like exile.

Perhaps the pittance her jointure provided would allow her to eke out a life in London, renting a room somewhere. But what sort of life would that be? Without a house, without servants or the money to buy clothes, and with everyone in the *ton* knowing that she was utterly penurious, she could scarcely maintain her position as one of the shining lights of the *beau monde*. It would be impossible for her to continue to supplement her income by guiding girls through their Seasons.

No, she thought bleakly, fighting back the tears, the truth was, she was facing ruination. If she could not somehow stave off Perkins, it would be virtually the end of her world.

CHAPTER EIGHT

FRANCESCA AWAKENED THE next morning with a heavy sense of dread. She had cried herself to sleep the night before, thinking about her situation, and her night had been filled with vague, frightening dreams about which she could remember nothing but her fear.

A little shakily, she sat down to the tea and toast that Maisie had brought her, and as she nibbled halfheartedly at the bit of breakfast, her mind raced. If only there were someone whose advice she could ask, but she could think of no one. Her brother was the closest person to her and would be the most understanding of her problem, but she knew that if she brought the matter up with him, he would try to help her buy her way out of the note, even if it meant ruining his own finances. Therefore, she could not tell him.

Sir Lucien had always been her good friend, and though they did not actually discuss it, he was aware of her money problems. However, he had money problems of his own, equal in severity to hers, and she knew there would be no help from that quarter. Moreover,

Lucien was not one who understood money matters; he would be as stumped for a solution as she.

She had grown quite close to Irene, who was an intelligent woman, and suspected that Irene had at least an inkling of the sort of financial straits in which she lived. She would be the person most likely to have an idea, as well as the one most likely to be able to help, given that her husband, Gideon, was one of the wealthiest men in London. But everything inside Francesca recoiled at the thought of asking Irene for help.

She could not impose on a friend in that way. There was no one, really, to whom she felt close enough, except her family. Or...

Sinclair.

Unbidden, the duke's name came to her, but Francesca closed her mind to the thought, crossing her arms over her chest as though to further bar the idea.

She could not go running to the duke. She would not presume on their past relationship or impose on his kindness. She was nothing to him now, and she refused to try to put some sort of obligation on him. She could not deny that it would be a great relief to turn her problem over to him, but it would also be far too humiliating. And, anyway, the man owed her nothing.

No. She had to solve this herself.

Putting aside her breakfast tray, Francesca rose and went to her jewelry box. Opening it, she went through her baubles, separating the paste from those things that had some value. The pile of valuables was, she thought with a sigh, pitifully small: the necklace of pearls her parents had given her on her eighteenth birthday, the cameo given her by Callie, the sapphire earrings from the duke upon the occasion of their engagement and the sapphire bracelet she had won last summer in a wager with him. Her wedding ring and whatever jewels she had gotten from her husband were long since gone to pay for her daily living. What was left was what was too dear to her to give up.

She was not sure she could give them up even now. *But did she have any choice?*

When Maisie returned to take her tray, Francesca told her, "I have some items to sell to the jeweler."

Maisie faced her in some surprise. "You do? I did not realize." She frowned, obviously thinking about the usual signs of impending financial disaster, which were not present at the moment.

"I need to sell everything I possibly can. As soon as I am dressed, I shall inspect the silver in the butler's pantry. I think we must get rid of all of it."

Maisie's jaw dropped. "All, my lady?"

Francesca nodded. "How much will it fetch, do you think? Can we sell the crystal glasses, as well? And what about furniture? How much of that do you think we could get money for?"

Maisie shook her head. "But, my lady, what will you use? You cannot get rid of all your silverware and dishes."

"Most of it," Francesca said inexorably. "I shall—I

shall simply have to hold small dinners from now on, that is all. And I am sure that we could sell most of the silver candelabras, as well. After we go through the butler's pantry, I must scour the attic. And I should speak to the coachman about selling the brougham and the horses."

"Sell your carriage! My lady, what has happened?" Maisie cried. "You will have nothing! What will you do?"

"I have to do this." Francesca thought of the future before her, and her resolution wavered. What use would it be to her to save the house if she had to give up her entire way of life in order to do so?

She steeled herself and went on. "I am sending for my man of business."

"You're not going to sell out the Funds, are you?" Maisie asked, even more alarmed, if that was possible.

Francesca shook her head. "No. I cannot leave myself with absolutely nothing. But I need to see about selling the house."

Despite her maid's shocked protests, Francesca was adamant, and she spent the rest of the day going through the house and taking note of everything that she would try to sell. The agent who handled her business matters, minor as they were, called on her late in the day, and they remained closeted in her sitting room for close to an hour.

By the time he left, she was spent, and she sat for a long time simply staring out at the dying afternoon. Everything she had done was useless, she thought, utterly pointless.

Even if she sold all her personal possessions, they would not bring anywhere near the sum that she needed. If she sold out of her Funds, she would be close, but it still would not be enough, and she would not have anything left to live on except what she could scrape up by helping girls find husbands.

Only selling the house would provide adequate money, but as she had known last night when she had asked Mr. Perkins for more time, it would take a good while to find a purchaser, certainly more than the three weeks he had given her. Her agent had agreed to try to sell it, but he had been quite set against the idea. Better to lease it out during the Season if she needed to raise money, he had told her. But, of course, that would not answer her needs at all. And she could not bring herself to explain to him why she needed the money so desperately and so quickly.

Still, she thought, she must set Maisie to selling off whatever she could. She would, after all, need money to pay a solicitor if she decided to fight Perkins in court.

She went back to the jewelry box and took out the earrings and bracelet again. Everything else, she thought, but not these.

All through the week, as she prepared for Harriet's party, Francesca's worries gnawed at the back of her mind. But no matter how much she thought about the matter or how many tears she shed at night in the privacy of her bedroom, she could not come up with any solution.

She tried to put the matter of Perkins and the house out of her mind, going on about the business of creating a successful soiree. To her gratification, replies to her invitation were quickly returned, all but a very few happy to attend. The assembly room, one of the rooms in the east wing that she kept permanently closed off and now largely unfurnished, was opened up and received a thorough cleaning, requiring the hiring of two extra maids and a footman. Once that was accomplished, the task of decorating that room and the front hallway began. Wines were selected, and the final menu for the food and beverage tables chosen.

There were, moreover, the sessions she had set herself with Harriet, instructing the girl in the niceties of conversation, strategic flirting and other skills that would help her navigate her way through the Season. Harriet knew how to dance, at least, and she was amenable to applying the daily lotions Francesca recommended to lighten her sun-kissed complexion. But getting her to restrain her tongue was another matter. It was not that she was rebellious; she simply did not understand why the straightforward way she spoke was too blunt, or why some of the topics she brought up would cause many a matron to look at her askance.

Still, no matter how busily Francesca flung herself into her tasks, she could not keep Perkins and his threats out of her head. Even if she managed to outrun them during the day, every night, when she lay down to bed, they were there again, tormenting her: What was she going to do? How was she to live?

She could think of no answer, but neither could she find ease. Her thoughts ran round and round, covering the same ground with the same lack of success. She tossed and turned in her bed, often getting up to wrap her dressing gown about her and sit at the bow window of her bedroom, staring down at the empty street below.

In the mornings, she deeply regretted her nighttime vigils. Her head ached, and there were blue circles growing beneath her eyes. If she did not get more sleep, she would look like a hag, she told herself. But there seemed nothing she could do to stop her worrying.

In only a little over a week, she would have to decide. Would she stay in her home and make Perkins fight her in court, facing the scandal that would ensue? Or would she give up her house and take refuge at Redfields? Neither option seemed bearable.

The night of the party finally came. It was a soft summer evening, with no prospect of rain to keep anyone away. Francesca, dressed in her new light green silk, a silver tissue wrap about her bare arms, greeted her guests with a merry smile. For tonight, at least, she was determined to keep all worrisome thoughts at bay. It was the only party she had given this Season, and she meant to enjoy it.

In fact, as it turned out, she had little time to enjoy it. She was far too busy making sure that Harriet—who was quite pretty in her new white ball gown and with her hair done up in charming ringlets by Francesca's maid—was introduced to each of the young men Francesca had invited, as well as to the women who could ease the girl's path through the *ton*. An invitation to Almack's might be too much to hope for, Francesca knew, but she thought that she could get Harriet invited to a number of entertaining parties.

When she was not busy with Harriet, of course, there was her other goal to be attended to: introducing Rochford to the young women she had chosen for him. She was gratified to see that every one of the four candidates had come to the party, and she skillfully maneuvered each of them into a conversation with the duke at some point in the evening.

Throughout the party, whatever she was doing, Francesca kept an eye on the duke. She was pleased to see that he made an effort to talk for some time to each of the women.

Once, when she looked over, she saw him conversing with Lady Damaris, and as she watched, Rochford smiled, then laughed, his face lighting up in that way it did. Something pierced her chest, sharp and painful, and for an instant Francesca wanted to cry.

Silly, of course, she told herself. Of course Sinclair would enjoy talking to Lady Damaris. She was intelligent and sophisticated, adept at conversation. Nor was she unattractive, with a short but pleasingly rounded form, and soft brown curls and lively hazel eyes. She was, in Francesca's opinion, the most likely of the young women to appeal to the duke.

Lady Edwina de Morgan, on the other hand, was the prettiest of the women, with black hair and vivid green eyes, though her features were a bit too sharp, Francesca thought.

She feared that Lady Mary would prove too shy to talk to him, given her retiring, bookish nature. She was gratified to see him talking to the girl, for she imagined that it took some effort to get Mary to say anything. Somewhat surprisingly, when she glanced over a few minutes later, she saw that the two of them were still in conversation, and Lady Mary was even talking rather animatedly.

Francesca smiled to herself. Trust Rochford to manage that feat. He was nothing if not patient. And kind. And charming. He was, in short, the quintessential gentleman—or, at least, what a gentleman should be. She had to wonder if any of the women she had chosen were actually good enough for him.

But that, too, was foolish—almost as much as the pang of loss she had felt earlier when she watched him with Damaris Burke. Of course he would be happy with any of these women. She had researched them carefully, and while none were perfect, she was not likely to find one who was. Neither was the duke, for that matter.

Indeed, he could be impossibly stubborn. He was maddeningly sure of himself. And there was that way he had of quirking his eyebrow at one sardonically, a most irritating habit—all the more so because when he did it, the recipient of the quirked brow was usually in the wrong.

The evening was not entirely given over to work. Francesca managed to spend a few minutes chatting with Sir Alan, whose pleasant, affable nature she found calming. Sir Lucien was there, as well, of course, as were Lord and Lady Radbourne.

Irene set Francesca laughing with an account of her recent visit to her brother and sister-in-law. "Impending-motherhood has brought not the slightest improvement to Lady Maura's temperament. Thank heavens it is Mother staying with her and not I. I would doubtless wring her neck before she delivers. One moment she is too hot, the next she is too cold. Pillows have to be adjusted behind her back, then taken away. And someone has to help her up from her chair, because she has grown so terribly fat."

Irene paused, looking thoughtful. "I suppose it's wrong of me to find that fact amusing, but I do. Maura claims that it is because Humphrey's heir is such a large, strong boy, but my opinion is that it has more to do with the plentiful servings of roast and potatoes she eats at supper—not to mention the box of chocolates that is always by her side."

Francesca chuckled. "You are unkind."

"Yes, I am," Irene admitted unrepentently. "I suppose I shall be as large as she is before long."

Francesca stared at her friend. "Irene! Are you—? Do you mean—?"

Irene smiled a little secretively. "Yes. I am. No one knows besides you and Mother. I am not three months along yet, and Mother says that is the most dangerous time. We don't want to let Gideon's family know about it until we are more assured that I will carry the child to full term. You can imagine how Lady Odelia will seize upon it."

"Goodness, yes. Oh, Irene." Francesca beamed at her friend, and reached out to take her hand and squeeze it. "I am so happy for you. I am sure that Gideon must be up in the boughs about it."

"No more than I," Irene admitted a little shame-facedly. "You know that I was never one of those women to gush about babies and motherhood. But these past few weeks—oh, Francesca, I have never been so filled with hope and happiness, even though I spend half the morning being sick. I am scarce like myself. I hardly ever argue with Gideon. I think he believes it is because of how ill I feel—and he is so careful around me, so solicitous, that I actually cried, I was so touched by his behavior. Which, of course, convinced him even more that I am exceedingly ill. But the truth is I am just so happy that I cannot bring myself to disagree with anyone. Well, anyone but Maura."

"And *I* am so happy *for* you," Francesca said honestly. "First Constance, and now you—soon there will be infants crawling all over."

"You must promise to be his godmother—or hers," Irene said. "I am sure that Constance has already claimed you for the honor, but I insist that you stand for my baby, as well."

Tears came unbidden to Francesca's eyes. She hoped that her friend believed that they were simply tears of joy. She *was* enormously happy for Irene and Gideon, just as she had been for her brother and his wife when Constance had written with the news of her impending pregnancy. But Francesca also knew that deep down inside, her happiness was laced with pain and grief for her own lost child. Part of her cried not for joy, but for the knowledge that she would never herself know motherhood.

"Of course I will. I shall be the most doting godmother you have ever known," she promised.

"There you are!" A familiar voice came from a few feet to their left, and both women whirled around to see a black-haired beauty in a stunning peacock-blue dress walking toward them, her hand on the arm of a tall, handsome man.

"Callie!" Francesca cried, jumping to her feet and hurrying over to her friend. "Oh, my goodness! I am so surprised to see you! I did not know you were in town yet. Your brother did not say a word about it."

Francesca reached out and pulled Rochford's sister into a hug. Callie squeezed her tightly, laughing. "I made him swear not to. I wanted to surprise you. Brom and I arrived just before Sinclair left for your soiree, and I told him that I had to come see you, even if we were not invited. Since we first had to clean up and dress, I made him promise not to tell you before I got here."

"You are always invited," Francesca assured her, stepping back to gaze at her friend. "You know that. You look beautiful."

"'Tis the gown." Callie's dark eyes danced merrily. "I bought it in Paris."

"It is not the gown," Francesca told her firmly.

"Then perhaps it is married life." Callie cast a fond look over at her husband.

Tall and broad-shouldered, with a leanly muscled build, Bromwell was one of the best-looking men in the *ton*. Indeed, only the duke could be said to be more handsome than he. His thick hair was the color of mahogany, and his eyes were a vivid blue. In looks, one could see the resemblance to his striking sister Daphne, but fortunately his character was a far cry from that woman's.

Because of his sister's lies, Bromwell had hated the duke for many years, and when he had begun courting Callie, he had acted more out of a desire to upset Rochford than anything else. In the end, though, he had come to realize that nothing else mattered but Callie and the way he felt about her. Even he and the duke had become reconciled to one another after Bromwell learned of his sister's lies. Of course, that had not happened until after a dustup between the two men, but somehow, in that peculiar way men had, the incident had actually seemed to increase their regard for one another.

The Earl of Bromwell bowed to them in greeting.

"Lady Haughston. Lady Radbourne. 'Tis good to see you both looking well."

"And you, sir," Francesca greeted the earl warmly. Early in the pair's relationship, she had feared that Bromwell meant to harm her friend, and she had watched him like a hawk. But clearly the two of them were meant for each other, and Callie was a very happy woman.

"I am pleased to see you again," Irene added. "I hope that you enjoyed your trip."

"I think I have seen every cathedral in France and Italy," Bromwell told them in mock complaint. "I had not realized my wife was so fond of churches."

"It isn't the churches, although they are lovely. It is the art," Callie explained.

The four of them chatted for a few minutes about the sights the couple had seen on their honeymoon. Then Irene led the earl away to say hello to Gideon, and Francesca pulled Callie over to the chairs where she and Irene had been talking earlier.

"You are happy, aren't you?" Francesca asked, her eyes searching her friend's face.

"Incredibly, wonderfully happy," Callie replied. "If I had known how very much I would enjoy married life, I would have wed years ago."

"I think this particular husband might have had something to do with it."

Callie beamed. "I love him, Francesca. More than I even realized. Or maybe it is just that it grows every day. I did not think it possible to love him any more than I did the day we married, but I do, somehow."

"I am so happy for you, my dear."

She had always been fond of Calandra, whom she had known since the girl was in leading strings, but over the last few months, the two of them had grown very close. Callie had once said that she felt almost as if Francesca were her sister, and Francesca knew that her own feelings about Callie were much the same.

"Tell me the latest news," Callie urged. "I feel as though I have been gone forever—although it also seems as if the time simply rushed by."

Francesca began by recounting the latest bits of gossip. There seemed oddly few of them, and she added a little apologetically, "I fear that I have not been to as many parties as usual. I am probably not up on a great deal of the news."

"Have you been feeling ill?" Callie turned concerned eyes on her.

Francesca's gaze fell before Callie's searching one. She was suddenly afraid that Callie would realize how troubled she had been lately. "No, of course not. I am a little tired—I have been so busy with this party."

"It's lovely." Callie glanced around. "Of course, that goes without saying. You have such an elegant touch. Sinclair said your party was for Harriet Sherbourne. Do I know her?"

"No, she is recently up from the country. She is over there, talking to Oscar Coventry."

"Oh, yes. Pretty girl. Another one you are polishing up?"

"A little."

Callie's roving gaze stopped. "Who is the girl to whom my brother is talking?"

Francesca turned to where Callie's gaze was directed. Rochford was standing beside a pretty young blonde, who was gazing at him raptly.

"That is Lady Caroline Wyatt. She just made her come-out this year. She is Sir Averill Wyatt's daughter."

"Sir Averill…" Callie frowned, then her face cleared. "Oh, she is Lady Beatrice's daughter?"

"Exactly. Bellingham's granddaughter."

"Goodness, I can scarce believe that Sinclair is talking to her as long as he is. Usually young girls bore him to tears. Do you think he is interested in her?"

"Perhaps. She is quite pretty," Francesca pointed out. Rochford did seem to be talking to the girl for a long time. The girl was saying very little, just nodding, and now and then smiling prettily or wafting her fan to cool her face.

They continued to watch the couple. Rochford continued to talk; Lady Caroline continued to smile.

"I must say," Francesca commented with some asperity, "she does not seem to talk much. I should not think Rochford would find her very entertaining."

It occurred to her as soon as the words came out of her mouth that they sounded harsh. She glanced over at Callie, wondering if her friend had noticed.

Trying for a pleasanter tone, she added, "Of course, I suppose many men prefer that sort of woman."

She found herself hoping that Rochford was not one of them. Why had she even included the girl? She was not sure, but suddenly it seemed almost unbearable to think that Rochford might fall in love with the dewy-faced young woman.

That, of course, was utterly absurd. It should not matter to her which of the women he chose. She had tried to find ladies who would appeal to him. The whole point was for him to fall in love, wasn't it? Why should it be worse if he chose a blond girl almost young enough to be his daughter? After all, Francesca herself had been a fresh-faced blond girl once.

"I would not think my brother is of that opinion," Callie commented, which warmed Francesca's heart.

There was the sound of masculine voices raised in the hallway, and Francesca pulled her gaze away from Rochford and Lady Caroline to look. As she watched, Galen Perkins strolled into sight, Francesca's butler at his side, remonstrating.

"Oh, dear." Francesca's stomach twisted into knots. Was Perkins going to ruin her party, as well? She could easily imagine him declaring to one and all that this house was not really hers. "Excuse me," she murmured to Callie, as she stood up and made her way to the open double doors.

"Ah, Lady Haughston." Perkins smiled at her in an

obnoxiously smug way. "I am glad to see you. Pray tell your servant that I am welcome at your little party."

"What are you doing here?" Francesca asked in a low voice, ignoring his request. "I did not invite you."

"I am sure you merely overlooked it," he told her. "You would not have wanted to exclude an old friend of your husband's."

"Please leave." *What would she do if he made a scene?* "You told me it would be three weeks—"

He leered at her, his grin growing broader. "Three weeks 'til what, my lady?" As always, the title sounded like an insult on his lips.

"Mr. Perkins, please…"

"Lady Haughston." The duke's cool, modulated tones sounded behind her.

Francesca turned to him in relief. "Rochford…"

"May I be of some assistance?" His gaze went to Perkins, and there was a flat, hard look in his eyes that took Francesca aback. "What are you doing here?"

"Why, I am a guest of the lady's. The late Lord Haughston and I were good friends." His eyes cut toward Francesca. "I shall be happy to tell people about our friendship, should anyone question my being here."

"Shall I toss him out for you?" the duke asked, his gaze never leaving Perkins.

Perkins sneered. "As if you could."

The duke said nothing, simply gave him a long, level look. Perkins was the first to turn his eyes away. Then Rochford looked at Francesca questioningly.

"No," Francesca said hastily, reaching out to put her hand on the duke's arm. The last thing she wanted was for Rochford to haul Perkins out of the room, with the man screaming out imprecations, shouting that her house actually belonged to him now. "Pray don't. I—I do not want a scene to ruin Lady Harriet's party. It would be much too bad."

Rochford frowned. It was obvious that he did not approve of her letting the man stay. She sent him a pleading look. "Rochford, please…"

"Of course." He gave in gracefully. "As you wish. Have a care, Perkins. I shall keep my eye on you."

"It's a wonder I shan't die of fright," Perkins retorted.

"Come in. Why don't you partake of something to eat?" Francesca gestured vaguely toward the refreshments table.

She could only hope that the man would not reveal anything damaging if she allowed him to stay. At least the party was nearing its end. She would not have to endure his presence for more than another hour or so. Unfortunately, where Perkins was concerned, that time could seem like an eternity.

Callie came up beside Francesca, linking her arm through hers. "Come, introduce me to Miss Sherbourne. I should so like to meet her."

"Of course." Francesca turned gratefully to her friend, and they walked away from Perkins.

"Who is that man?" Callie asked. "Sinclair looked like thunder when he saw him."

"No one. He—he was an acquaintance of my late husband. A low sort of man. But I could not ruin Harriet's party by letting Rochford throw him out."

"Of course not," Callie agreed. "But don't worry, Sinclair will take care of him if he does grow unruly. And Brom, too, I should imagine. Do you know that the two of them have become almost friendly? Men are the oddest creatures."

Francesca chuckled. It was hard not to relax around Callie. "Very true."

The rest of the evening passed well enough. Francesca circulated among her guests, now and then glancing around the room for Perkins. She spotted him by the refreshments table and later just strolling around the room, nodding to this or that man. The men invariably appeared a trifle nervous at the sight of him, and Francesca wondered if they knew him from the gaming tables. Perhaps they, too, were wary of what he might reveal.

It was sometime later when she looked around for Perkins again and noticed that he was gone. She made another slow circuit of the room with her eyes and still did not see him. It seemed odd to her. He was not the sort of person to slip quietly out into the night.

She began to wend her way through the crowd, searching for him. By the time she returned to her starting place, she was certain that he was not in the room. She had also noticed that another person was missing: Rochford.

Her stomach clenched. Had Rochford somehow managed to quietly maneuver Perkins out of the house? She could not help but be glad for that, but she dreaded to think what might have happened after they left. Rochford was the sort of man who could take care of himself, of course. Lean and athletic, he was one of the aristocrats who followed the "fancy," as the sport of pugilism was known. She had even heard that he had been seen sparring at Gentleman Jackson's club with Jackson himself, an honor not given to just anyone. She did not doubt his abilities, having witnessed him brawling with Lord Bromwell three months earlier.

In a normal situation, she would not worry about him. But Perkins was a different matter. Francesca felt sure that he was not the kind who followed any gentlemanly rules when it came to fighting. If Rochford took him on, there was no telling what Perkins might do. Frowning a little, she glanced around again, wondering if she should approach Gideon, or perhaps even Lord Bromwell, for help.

It was then that it struck her that she had not seen the other two men, either. Had the three of them taken it upon themselves to usher Perkins out? For a moment, she relaxed. Rochford would be in no danger if that was the case.

However, her relief did not last long. Perkins would be furious if they had done so. She hated to think what he might .do if he was enraged enough. What if he blurted out his story to them? Francesca's cheeks burned. She hated to think of Rochford knowing the full depths of Haughston's behavior.

She set out to find Callie, and was somewhat surprised when she located her talking to Lady Wyatt and her daughter Caroline. When Francesca walked up, however, Callie excused herself with a smile and came up to Francesca's side.

"I am so glad to see you," Callie murmured. "I felt as if we were on an island. No one had come close to us in fifteen minutes at least. I thought I would be marooned there, listening to Lady Wyatt go on about her youngest sister's lying-in for the rest of the evening. Just because I am now a married woman does not mean that I want to hear terrifying stories of childbirth."

"I should think not," Francesca agreed. "I would have come sooner if I had but known. I was looking for your husband."

Callie smiled. "Forgive me. I fear it still makes me a trifle giddy, hearing him called that. I am not sure where he is." She glanced around. "The last time I saw him, he had gone off with Lord Radbourne to chat with Sinclair. I think perhaps they were conspiring to sneak off and enjoy a cigar out in the garden."

"I see." So they *were* all together. But perhaps it was true that they were only enjoying a smoke and some masculine companionship.

"There they are," Callie said, looking toward the doors.

Francesca turned to see Lord Radbourne and Lord Bromwell stroll into the room. Of Rochford, however, there was no sign. Had she been wrong, then? Was Rochford dealing with Perkins by himself? Or had Rochford simply left and Perkins had done the same, and she was making up worries for no reason?

"Shall we join him?" Callie asked. "Did you wish to talk to him about something?"

"What? Oh. No. That is, well, it wasn't important, really." Francesca knew her friend must think she was acting peculiarly, and indeed, she felt rather foolish. But she could think of no easy way to ask Bromwell what she wanted to know. If he had helped get rid of Perkins, he was not likely to tell her, and if he had not, it would only raise questions in him and Callie.

Fortunately, at that moment she noticed a couple making their way toward her and Callie, so she was able to say truthfully, "Oh, there are Lord and Lady Hampton. No doubt they are ready to make their goodbyes. Have you ever noticed how they are invariably the first to leave?"

She slipped away from her friend to meet the others. After that, other guests began to leave gradually. Francesca took up a station nearer the doors into the hallway so that she might more easily say farewell to her guests.

Before long, everyone had left, and the servants came in to begin cleaning up. Francesca climbed the stairs to her bedroom, and since Maisie was busy downstairs with the others, she struggled to unhook her dress without her maid's help and took down her own hair. Then, wrapping herself in her dressing gown, she sat down on the window seat and began to brush out her hair. One window stood open a little to let in the night breeze, and it felt good after the heat of the crowded party.

She had just finished brushing out her hair when a man's figure appeared at the end of the block. She leaned forward, squinting. It was too dark to make out his features, but she was certain, looking at his form, his walk, that it was Rochford.

He stopped in front of her house and looked up. Her room was dark, for she had set her candle down just inside the door, on the other side of the room from the windows. He hesitated, glancing at her front door.

Quickly Francesca leaned forward and rapped on one of the panes. His head snapped up, his eyes searching the upper floor. She bent down to the open window.

"Rochford," she whispered loudly.

When he saw her, he whipped off his hat and sent her an elegant bow. She pointed down at the front door, then slipped off the window seat and, grabbing her candle, hurried out of her room.

CHAPTER NINE

HE WAS WAITING on the front stoop when she unlocked the heavy door and opened it. Mindful of the servants finishing up their cleaning in the assembly room, she held a finger up to her lips for quiet. It would be just as well that the servants not see her letting a man into the house this late at night, even one of such character as the Duke of Rochford. Her own servants were discreet, but she did not know the ones whom Fenton had hired to help with the party.

Rochford raised his brows at her gesture but obediently did not speak, merely stepped inside. Francesca cast another glance over at the lighted room, then gestured for him to follow her and slipped off down the hall.

She led him to the morning room at the back, which was her favorite spot—and was also the farthest from the room where the servants were cleaning. When he stepped inside, she closed the door behind him and walked over to light a lamp.

Turning back to him, she crossed her arms and fixed him with a severe look. "All right. Confess."

"Gladly," he responded lightly. "To what would you like me to confess?"

"I saw that Mr. Perkins was soon suspiciously absent from the party."

"Perhaps he grew bored. I doubt he was well received by any of your guests."

Francesca quirked a brow. "I also noticed that you and your cohorts were gone at the same time."

He grinned. "My cohorts? Pray, tell me, who are my 'cohorts'?"

"Lord Radbourne and Lord Bromwell. What did you do?"

"We simply suggested to Perkins that he would be happier elsewhere…and then we went with him to make sure that he arrived safely."

"Sinclair! Did you hurt him?"

"Really, Francesca, what sort of ruffian do you take me for?" He idly picked a speck of lint from the arm of his immaculate black jacket.

"I would have said no ruffian at all, until I saw you trying to bash in your future brother-in-law's head."

"He was not my future brother-in-law at the time," he pointed out mildly. "Besides, I had a good deal more basis for hitting Bromwell. I thought he was trying to ruin my sister's reputation. Perkins was merely…bothersome."

"So you only talked to him?" Francesca asked.

He shrugged. "Yes. Gideon was in favor of throwing him in the Thames—" At Francesca's horrified gasp, a smile hovered at the corners of his mouth, and he went on in a confidential tone. "Gideon's upbringing, you know. Bromwell and I dissuaded him, though I may have intimated to Perkins that his fate would be worse if he bothered you again."

"What did he…did he say anything untoward?"

"He said a number of things I cannot repeat to a lady. Nothing of any significance." He studied at her, puzzled. "Tell me, why are you so concerned about the miserable villain? Surely you did not actually invite him tonight."

"No, of course not. I don't care about him. Well, I do care, but not in a good way. He is a wicked man. I was worried that he might have hurt you, if you must know." She turned away, crossing the room. "Though clearly I need not have been concerned."

He took a step after her, his expression softening, then stopped. "No, you need not. Perkins is no threat."

"He might retaliate," she pointed out as she opened the door of a walnut cabinet and reached inside.

"I can handle him."

"Very well. Brandy?" Without waiting for his reply, she pulled out a bottle of brandy and poured each of them a glass. Brandy was not considered a woman's drink, and she usually did not partake, keeping it on hand more for her friend Sir Lucien than for any other reason. But tonight, she thought, a brandy seemed just the thing.

Rochford watched her as she poured. He wondered

if she had even thought about the fact that she had answered the door in her dressing gown, her unbound hair flowing in a golden cascade down her back. Once he had dreamed of being with her this way—of course, in those daydreams he would have had the right to go to her and take her in his arms, to glide his hand down the silken fall of her hair.

He turned away abruptly and sat down on a chair. "Why did you permit him to stay tonight?"

Francesca sighed. "It seemed the easiest course. I did not want a scene, and I feared that Perkins was precisely the sort of man who would cause one. Besides, he was Andrew's friend. I—I hated to be openly rude to him."

She handed the duke a snifter of brandy and sat down on the sofa across from him. Rochford took a sip.

"I would have thought that it would be quite easy to be rude to most of Haughston's friends."

Francesca could not hold back a grin, but she tried to cover it by taking a quick drink of the brandy. It slid down her esophagus like velvet fire, igniting her stomach and sending soft tendrils of relaxation creeping through her. She let out a sigh, then took another sip and curled her feet up on the sofa beside her, like a child.

She looked across at Rochford. He was so strong, so capable. Of course Perkins would not worry him. He would brush the man off like an insect.

For an instant she thought of telling Rochford about Perkins and his threat, of putting the whole mess in his competent hands. Quickly she turned her gaze back to her drink, swirling the amber liquid around in the glass. She could not do such a thing, of course. She had no hold on Rochford, no claim. It would be unthinkably forward of her to tell him of her problems. Like the gentleman he was, he might try to solve the matter for her, but obviously that would be wrong.

Besides, it would be utterly humiliating to reveal to the man she had not married what a horrible, foolish mistake she had made in the man she *had* chosen. To let him see how close she lived to the edge of poverty, how she had to scrabble for money to pay for food and clothing and servants. Besides, he might think she was asking him for the money to pay off Perkins, which would sink her with shame. Quickly, she took another sip of her drink.

Rochford's eyes went to the front of her dressing gown, where her lapels gaped a little, showing the shadowed tops of her breasts and the dark valley of demarcation between them. He could not help but wonder what she wore beneath the robe. If it was a nightrail, it must be low-necked. Or perhaps she had thrown the robe on over her undergarments, so that only a flimsy chemise and pantalets lay under the dressing gown.

He started to speak and was startled by the hoarseness of his voice. He cleared his throat and started again. "I thought we might discuss the, ah, ladies we were considering."

"Yes, of course." Francesca was happy to divert her thoughts from their course. "How did you like Lady Damaris?"

"She seems quite competent, as you said. Adept at conversation." He paused.

"Then, um, was she your favorite?" His words seemed cool praise to her, but then, Rochford was a very sensible man.

"Not especially. I am not sure I had a favorite, really."

"You talked to Lady Mary quite a bit. I was surprised. She has usually seemed rather shy when I have been around her."

His lips twitched slightly. "I rather think that she thought me too old to be frightening. I believe she puts me in the category of her father and his friends."

"Old!" Francesca gaped at him, then burst into laughter. "Oh, my."

"Well you may laugh," he retorted. "I might remind you, my dear, that you are not that many years behind me."

"No, of course not. I am an old crone, as well, no doubt." She grinned wickedly at him. "Perhaps you can steal in beneath her defenses. I have no doubt that later you would be able to convince her that you are not entirely doddering yet."

"It seems quite an effort," he mused.

"What of Lady Caroline?" She remembered the pang she had felt, watching him with the young girl. Envy, she supposed, at the girl's youth. But she could not let that influence her—or cause her to try to influence him.

His mouth tightened. "Bloody hell, Francesca! What possessed you to saddle me with that chit? A more boring girl I hope never to meet."

Francesca pressed her lips together tightly to suppress a laugh. She should not feel so elated to hear that he had disliked the girl, but she could not quell the amusement rising up in her like a bubble.

"She was unable to talk about anything," he went on with some bitterness. "And if she had an opinion on something, I was unable to discover it. Every time I asked her a question, she responded by asking what I thought of it. Where is the sense in that? I already knew what *I* thought."

Francesca swallowed her chuckle. "Perhaps you should give Lady Caroline another chance. She is young, after all, and mayhap she is shy around someone like you."

"Someone like me?" he repeated, fixing her with his black gaze. "What do you mean? Are you implying that I am intimidating? Stiff and unyielding? Or perhaps it is my advanced age to which you are referring."

She could not repress a laugh at that. "You can be a trifle…overwhelming. You are a duke, after all, and when you get that look on your face—you know, as if a muddy pup had just put his paws on your best boots…"

"I beg your pardon. I am never unkind to puppies." With an effort, he controlled the quiver at the corner of his mouth. "And I must say, I have never noticed that you seemed to be in the least in awe of my being a duke. Not even when you were fourteen."

"It is difficult to be in awe of someone when you have seen him sliding down the roof of a barn into a haystack," Francesca shot back.

Rochford let out a hoot of laughter. "When was that?"

"At Dancy Park, when I was eight and you were thirteen. You and Dom and I had been riding, and we stopped at Jamie Evans' farm. The groom tried to stop us, but it was no use. There was a great pile of hay, and Dom jumped off a fence rail into it and dared me to jump into it, too."

"And you said, 'I'll go off the roof!' Of course. How could I have forgotten that? You were incorrigible."

"Well, I only did it because you told Dom that I was much too small to do such a thing, so I had to prove to you that I wasn't. And then you *ordered* me not to."

"Ah, yes. Of course that would have set you to it immediately. I was less wise at thirteen."

"Then *you* jumped off the roof, as well."

"I could hardly refrain if you were daring enough to do it."

"If that isn't just like you!" Francesca exclaimed in mock exasperation. "Putting the blame on me."

"That is precisely where it belonged most of the time. You were a mischievous imp."

"And you were entirely too full of yourself."

His smile broadened. "One has to wonder, then, why you chose to tag about after me."

"I did not do any such thing," Francesca retorted, adding with great dignity, "You and Dom simply happened to go where I wanted to."

He chuckled, his dark eyes alight, and rose from his seat. "Another brandy?"

"I better not. I am feeling quite pleasant. Any more and I would be absolutely tiddly." She took a last sip of her drink and stood up. "Would you like another?"

"No. I am fine."

She took his glass and crossed over to the cabinet to set the snifters down beside the decanter. Not looking at him, she said casually, "Do you have a preference, then?"

"A preference? What do you mean?"

"For one of the girls." She turned back. "Are you more in favor of one than another?"

He looked at her for a moment, then replied blandly, "Yes, I prefer one."

"Who?" Francesca walked back to him. The question seemed suddenly very important. Which of the women had caught his eye? Did he plan to pursue her?

"Not Lady Caroline," he told her dryly. He took a step closer to her. His voice was low as he went on, "Tell me, my dear, do you plan to oversee my courtship, as well?"

Standing this close to him, looking up into his face, stirred an odd feeling in Francesca, something warm and yet a trifle frightening, as well. She remembered that time on the roof of the barn, when she had stared down at the haystack below her, and her heart had hammered madly inside her ribs with fear, yet she'd been oddly drawn to jump, as well. She felt something like that now, as she gazed into his black eyes.

She pulled her gaze away, turning her head to the side as she said, her voice a little breathless, "I am sure that you will be able to handle that well enough on your own."

"I would not be so sure, if I were you," Rochford replied. "After all, look at my past attempts at wooing women. Obviously I have not been terribly successful." He paused, then went on, "Perhaps you should give me instructions in wooing."

"Indeed?" Francesca tilted her chin up challengingly. "I hardly think that is necessary. I am sure that you know well enough how to compliment a woman."

Her breath was coming much too rapidly, she knew. It was absurd to feel this way—warm and loose, yet tingling with barely suppressed anticipation.

"Such as telling her that her hair shimmers like gold in the candlelight?" he asked, his eyes going to her hair. "Or that her eyes glow like sapphires?"

"You must not do it too brown," she retorted, striving for a light tone.

He reached up and touched her hair lightly with the back of his hand. "It is only the truth."

His husky voice reverberated through her.

"I—I'm not sure the truth is ever a good idea when one is describing a woman."

"Not even when her skin is soft and smooth?" he asked, as his knuckles brushed down her cheek. "Or when her lips are perfectly shaped?" He traced his forefinger along the line of her upper lip. "Just waiting to be kissed."

"You seem quite skilled at this," Francesca breathed, her eyes fluttering closed. Tendrils of heat were stealing through her, awakening nerve endings all through her body.

"What should I do next?" He lowered his head, so close now that she could feel his warm breath against her cheek, and the delicate touch made her shiver.

"A kiss on the hand is never amiss."

He took her hand in his and raised it to his lips, pressing his mouth gently against the back of her hand. Then he turned it over and laid another kiss in her palm. His mouth was warm and soft upon her flesh, and at the touch, the strands of heat that were curling through her tangled and pooled deep in her abdomen.

Still holding her hand, Rochford kissed each fingertip in turn. He looked up at her again, and his dark eyes smoldered. "Would that be pleasing?"

Flooded by new and startling sensations, Francesca could do nothing but stare back at him, her eyes wide and lambent.

He moved closer to her, raising his hand to brush his knuckles down her face again. "Or perhaps this," he murmured, as he bent and touched his lips to her cheek.

He kissed the ridge of her jaw, and then moved on

to the tender skin of her throat. His hand went to her arm, sliding down it, and Francesca was aware of a vague wish that her dressing gown did not lie between her skin and his touch.

Nuzzling her neck, he moved lower, inch by inch, until he reached the collar of her dressing gown. Francesca trembled. Her knees were suddenly weak, and she feared that they might give way at any moment, and she would sink to the ground. She barely held back a soft animal moan as his mouth found the shallow hollow of her throat. Then his tongue crept out and traced the bony ridge around the hollow, and she could not restrain the tiny gasp of surprise and pleasure.

"They say," he went on, leaving her neck and moving up to hover near her ear, "that some women prefer something like this." He kissed her ear, then gently closed his teeth around the lobe and worried it.

Francesca swallowed, and involuntarily her hands came up to his chest, clutching the lapels of his coat, holding tightly as her world trembled around her. "Sinclair…"

His tongue traced the whorls of her ear, sending bright shivers of delight through her. She felt her nipples tightening almost painfully, and a pulse started between her legs. She had never felt anything like this before, this eager, thrumming surge of hunger that was spreading through her loins.

Then his hands were at the sash of her dressing gown, untying it, and one hand slid beneath the robe.

She felt his palm laid flat against her stomach, only the thin cloth of her chemise separating skin from skin. He slipped his hand up her body until he cupped her breast in his palm.

"A woman might wish something more…like this." His voice was thick and low; it pulled at her like a physical sensation.

His fingers played across her breast, caressing the nipple so that it turned tauter and harder. Francesca made a soft, inarticulate noise deep in her throat.

"Though no doubt some would hold it far too bold." His fingers slipped beneath the edge of her chemise and brushed across her bare skin.

Francesca feared that if she had not been holding onto his coat, her knees would have buckled and sent her to the floor.

"Mayhap it would be better…" Sinclair gently guided her to turn so that her back was to him, and he lifted the heavy mass of her hair in one hand, holding it up and away from her neck. He bent and kissed the back of her neck, making his way up the knobbed ridge of her spine, his mouth hot and featherlight, teasing at the sensitive skin.

A shudder shot through her, and Francesca sagged back weakly against his hard chest. His other hand went around her, splaying out over her stomach and pressing her into him. As he kissed the side of her neck, his hand slowly roamed her body, curving over her breasts, then drifting down onto her abdomen, moving ever closer to the seat of her yearning.

She drew in her breath softly, anticipating his touch, imagining his fingers sliding in between her legs. But instead he was turning her back around. She felt as limp and unresisting as a rag doll in his hands.

"Still, all in all," he murmured as he kissed first one cheek and then the other, "this would be the best thing to do."

His lips brushed hers, once, twice, and finally settled in. Francesca melted into him, her arms going up around his neck and her mouth opening to the pressure of his lips. His own mouth rocked against hers, pressure and heat increasing, and his tongue moved into her mouth to boldly claim it.

It was the way he had kissed her the other night, and like that other kiss, this one set her body aflame. Her skin felt taut and stretched, tingling all over with a new awareness. Their bodies were pressed together, nothing separating them but their clothes, and she found herself wishing that there was not even that. She wanted to feel his skin upon hers. She wanted, she realized wildly, to rub her body against him.

His arms wrapped around her, and he crushed her to him, his mouth avid on hers. Francesca clung to him, her heart leaping like a mad thing. She was lost in the experience, her senses so bombarded that she could not even name all she felt. She yearned and ached in an inchoate way, filled with a hunger she did not recognize.

He broke from her with a groan, burying his face in

her neck. "Francesca. My…" He bit off the rest of his words, and for a moment, there was no sound but that of their ragged breathing.

At last he said, somewhat unevenly, "I think this lesson is best ended."

Francesca nodded, too dazed to put together any words.

He put his hands on either side of her face and kissed her forehead briefly. Then he turned and left, striding rapidly through the door and down the hallway.

Francesca hurried to the door and stood, watching, as he opened the front door and walked out. The house was dark around her. She realized that the servants had finished in the assembly room and gone up to bed.

Slowly she turned and walked back to the sofa, collapsing onto it in a heap.

What had just happened?

She was weak and limp, yet at the same time wide-awake and thrumming with energy. She wanted to run after Sinclair and call him back. She wanted to throw herself into his arms and beg him to kiss her like that again. She wanted—sweet heaven, she didn't know what she wanted. All she was sure of was that she had never felt this way before.

Long, long ago, when she had been engaged to Rochford, there had been sparks of heat and desire, hints of feelings that lay buried deep inside. But never had she experienced this leaping, throbbing fire within her. Never had it seemed as if her skin was crackling with sensations. Her heart had not hammered 'til she thought it would burst from her chest, nor had she longed, desperately longed, to feel more.

Was this what others felt? Was this what made married women giggle among themselves and exchange droll looks as they talked about their husbands? Did they look forward to nighttime and their husbands' presence in their beds, knowing that a shimmering heat and pleasure awaited them?

She closed her eyes, sinking back upon the velvet cushions of the couch. If Sinclair had not stopped and stepped away, would she have ended up in bed with him? Would she have found herself enjoying a lusty coupling?

The thought brought fire to her cheeks. She rose and began to pace the room, running her hands up and down her arms as though she could rub away the strange feelings that had touched her.

She was being absurd, she knew. A few kisses were not the same as lying in bed with a man. Just because everything inside her had soared in response to Sinclair's touch, it did not mean that she would enjoy anything that came afterwards. After all, she had been entranced when she first knew Andrew. Her pulse had fluttered around him, and she had felt drunk on his honeyed, whispered avowals of love.

But then it had all turned to bitter disappointment when they finally engaged in the marital act. Tender looks and sweet kisses had given way to a sweaty, grunting rutting.

It would be the same with Rochford. It would be foolish to hope otherwise. A man did not want merely kisses and caresses. He wanted to be in bed, stripping her clothes away and thrusting himself into her. She would regret it, would despise it, as she always had with Andrew, and she would turn wooden and cold beneath his touch.

And then Sinclair would look at her with disappointment, even disgust, as Andrew had.

Francesca shook her head. That would be worse than the way it had been in her marriage—to have her sweet memories of the love she and Sinclair had once shared destroyed by the reality of her coldness in bed. She would rather almost anything than to have Sinclair look at her as Andrew had.

With a sigh, she left the room and made her way back up the stairs to her empty bed.

CHAPTER TEN

FRANCESCA DID NOT see the duke over the course of the next few days. It was only to be expected, she told herself. Her part in the campaign to find him a bride was largely done. It was up to him now to carry on a courtship.

Of course she would be interested to see which of the women he chose, but she could not really expect to be further involved in the process in any way.

She felt a bit at loose ends, which was also to be expected. The search for the right woman, the planning, the party—all had occupied a good deal of her time. It was no wonder if her life suddenly seemed a trifle empty, even flat.

There was still Harriet Sherbourne to be dealt with, but even she would now require less effort on Francesca's part. She was planning to attend the opera with Sir Alan and Harriet later in the week, and she would take the girl with her to a musicale tomorrow night and to several parties in the future.

But the real work was past. Francesca felt sure that the girl would receive invitations from the ladies to whom she had introduced her at the soiree, and the improvement in Harriet's hair and dress should be enough to insure that she would have adequate dances and flirtatious conversations at parties. Francesca would make certain of that with a few judicious hints to some of the young men who consistently danced attendance on her. Given that neither the young lady nor her father seemed to have any real interest in Harriet landing a husband this Season, there would be little maneuvering left for Francesca to do.

It was no wonder, therefore, that she felt a trifle bored, even lonely. Nor was it remarkable that her mind kept returning to the bizarre episode that had transpired between her and Rochford.

Thinking of what he had done, she could not help but feel a little tremor of remembered sensation. She closed her eyes, letting herself drift for a moment in the memory.

Why had he done what he had? she wondered. What sort of game had he been playing? She did not for an instant believe that he had expected her to accept his premise that he was asking her for advice. If it had been any other man, she would have said that he was seducing her. But that was absurd.

Wasn't it?

Rochford was capable of flirtation, of course. He had flirted when he was courting her—in his own very dry, understated way. And there had even been a faint element of flirtatiousness in the various casual conversations between them over the years—though it had been of a kind that hovered very close to sniping at times.

But he had never tried to seduce her—or any other lady that she knew of. Oh, she was not naive enough to think that he had never had a mistress. She had been wrong about Lady Daphne, but it would be foolish beyond belief to think that a gentleman of his age and station had never kept a fair Cyprian—some opera dancer or actress or professional courtesan. With those women, he might very well have acted as he did last night.

With a woman of good birth, however, the rules were different. A gentleman courted and wed a lady. He did not seduce her late at night in her home. At least, a gentleman like the Duke of Rochford did not.

On the other hand, she had to admit with a blush, a lady would not have come down to secretly open the door to a gentleman so late at night. Nor would she have slipped him past the servants and closed herself in a room alone with him.

Not only that, she had imbibed brandy in his company—she had even been the one to suggest it. Worst of all, she had thoughtlessly run down to meet him wearing only her dressing gown, under which she had on only her undergarments. No doubt any man might be forgiven for thinking that she was not averse to seduction.

When she looked at it in that light, it was enough to make her cringe with embarrassment. Widows were often considered to be more lax about their morals than a maiden; they were, at least, far more knowledgeable. Widows were not closely chaperoned, and when a woman was childless throughout years of marriage, as she had been, then there was unlikely to be the scandal of a child born out of wedlock. And in the sophisticated world of the *ton,* once a woman had married it was not unusual for her to engage in affairs without being ostracized for it, so long as she kept the matter discreet. However, Francesca had always been extremely careful not to give anyone even the slightest reason to believe that she was loose in her behavior.

Whatever had possessed her to act as she had last night? Had Rochford assumed that, given how she was dressed, she was open to seduction, perhaps even inviting it?

How could she face him again if he had thought that about her?

Yet she could not help but wonder—if he had thought her open to seduction, then why had he stopped? She had certainly done nothing to make him think she was unwilling. And that, she realized, was the most lowering thought of all: that he had grown uninterested in her.

Perhaps he had not felt the same excitement that she had. Maybe, even at that early stage, he had sensed in her the coldness that had so frustrated and angered Andrew. Tears sprang into her eyes at the thought. She had long ago stopped crying over her husband's disappointment in her. In truth, she had been glad that it had at least caused him to seek her bed less and less often. She had hated knowing that she was inferior to other women, but it had stopped causing her sorrow that Haughston was disappointed in her.

But now, thinking that Rochford might have realized the true coldness of her nature, she wanted to cry. And as one day passed and turned into another, she could not help but think that his absence was due to the same reason that had made him cease kissing her and leave.

It should not make her feel so dejected, she knew. She would not have gone to bed with him if he had stayed—*surely* she would not have. She did not want an affair with him or any other man. Fortunately, the part of her life where she had to submit to a man's pleasure was over. So there was absolutely no reason to feel downhearted because the man she had once loved had not tried to complete the seduction he had started.

And she would not dwell on it any longer.

She forced herself to turn to her neglected correspondence, but…within five minutes, her thoughts were going over the same well-trodden path.

When she did manage to put the matter of Rochford and their kisses from her mind, it was only to replace it with worry over Perkins. She had feared that he would appear at her door again to rage about Rochford's treatment of him, but he had not. That fact should have been a relief, but it was not. Knowing that he might pop up at any moment kept her nerves on edge, and her anxiety only increased as the days crept along toward her day of reckoning with him.

Francesca had no idea what she would do, what she would say to the man when he came again to demand her payment. She racked her brain to think of some argument that would convince him not to go through with his plan, some way to disprove what he said, some schedule by which she could pay off the debt that he claimed she owed him. But her thoughts were scattered and disjointed, and nothing she could offer seemed adequate. He would know as well as she that she could not pay off that much money in her lifetime, and he certainly would not want to wait. Perkins was not a man to display any kindness.

Two days after the party, Francesca was in the sitting room, trying to add up all her assets in the hope of making them amount to something close to the figure Perkins was demanding, when she heard Callie's voice in the hallway.

She jumped to her feet, thinking Rochford would be there, as well.

But it turned out that Callie had come alone, and Francesca chided herself for the faint spurt of disappointment she felt. Putting that aside with a smile, she stepped forward and took her visitor's hands, squeezing them affectionately.

"Callie, I was just thinking of you. I was going to call on you this very afternoon."

"Then I am glad that I arrived before you left to see me," Callie responded with an answering smile.

Francesca rang for tea, and the two of them sat down for a good cozy chat. The night at the party, they had barely scratched the surface of conversation. Unfortunately, Francesca learned, her friend was departing the next day for her husband's estate in the country.

"No, you must not! You have just gotten home," Francesca protested.

"I know. But Brom has been away from his estate far too long already. He says he has neglected it dreadfully. He went back to it only briefly before our wedding."

Francesca grinned at her friend. "Yes, I remember. He said he was going back for the whole two months of your engagement, but he could not stay away from you longer than two weeks."

Callie laughed in a throaty, self-satisfied way. "True. Of course, at the time he claimed that there was less to do than he had thought."

"I shall miss you terribly."

"You must come visit me," Callie told her. "I shan't know a soul there. It will be terribly lonely. You should come as soon as the Season is over."

"You will have Bromwell," Francesca reminded her. "And somehow, I suspect that he will be enough. I don't want to intrude on a newly married couple."

"It will not be an intrusion. Why, I will be an old married woman by then. And Brom will be busy. It will be harvest time."

"Well, perhaps for a little while."

"At least a month," Callie insisted, and Francesca, laughing, gave in.

They went on to talk of other things, chief among them the gowns that Callie had purchased in Paris. She was wearing one of them today, a lilac silk day dress with short petal sleeves overlying puffed sleeves of lilac net. This topic occupied them quite happily until Fenton entered to inform them that Lady Mannering had come to call.

It was a disappointment to have her time alone with Callie cut into by another guest, but Francesca gestured for the butler to show their visitor in. Lady Mannering was one of the hostesses whom she was hoping would issue an invitation or two to Harriet in the future.

"Lady Haughston. And Lady Bromwell," the newest guest said happily. "What a pleasant surprise to find you here, as well."

There was polite chat about Francesca's party, as well as about the beauty of Callie's wedding. Then Lady Mannering leaned toward Callie with a knowing smile and said, "One has to wonder, Lady Bromwell, if there isn't another Lilles alliance in the offing."

"Excuse me?" Callie stared at the other woman blankly.

"Why, your brother, dear. He seems most interested in Calderwood's eldest, does he not?"

Francesca felt a sudden cold clutch in her stomach. "Lady Mary?"

"Yes, that's the girl." Lady Mannering nodded her carefully coiffed head. "I saw him talking with her the other night at your party, Lady Haughston. I remarked to Lord Mannering about it—how long they talked and how unlike the girl it was. Quite pretty, she looked, too. Once she gets past that dreadful shyness of hers and actually smiles, you can see that she is rather attractive."

"Yes," Francesca agreed. "And sweet, as well. But, surely, one conversation at a party does not make a romance."

Her guest's eyes sparkled. "Ah, but that is just the thing. Yesterday I saw her with him again. They were riding along in that phaeton of his. She was chatting away as if they were old friends. It is so unlike her. And him. One cannot help but wonder if there is a courtship afoot."

Francesca kept a polite smile on her face. "Indeed."

"I would not refine overmuch on that," Callie told the other woman. "If Rochford has any especial interest in anyone, I have not heard of it."

The look on Callie's face, Francesca thought, could almost rival the duke's when it came to damping pretension. Lady Mannering quickly abandoned the topic and instead began to talk of the dinner she was planning in a week. Did Lady Haughston think that nice Sir Alan and his daughter might like to attend?

Francesca forced herself to put any other thoughts out of her head and concentrate on helping Harriet Sherbourne. As their conversation progressed, she had the feeling that it was Lady Harriet's father and his single state that spurred Lady Mannering's interest more than anything else. However, Francesca was not above taking advantage of that interest to advance Harriet's social career. Lady Mannering was one of the city's most prolific party-givers, and her events were always well attended.

Besides, if she could stir up a romance for Harriet's father, as well as enliven Harriet's Season, surely that was to the good. So she answered Lady Mannering's questions about the Sherbournes with alacrity and even added a few tidbits of information beyond what the woman asked.

Francesca managed to keep her attention on their conversation, but later, when both Callie and Lady Mannering had departed, she told Fenton that she was not at home to any more callers and took herself off to her bedroom.

She went to the window and stood looking out at the street below, but her mind did not really register what she saw.

So it was Mary Calderwood who had taken Rochford's fancy.

Francesca supposed that she should have known that the duke would not do what she expected. Lady Mary would have been the last of the women whom she would have guessed Rochford would want. Not that there was anything wrong with her, of course. Her reputation was impeccable, and her lineage was excellent.

It was just that Francesca would not have thought that the duke would be drawn to a such a quiet, shy girl. She was, well, exactly the opposite of Francesca herself. Though there was really no reason, she supposed, to think that Rochford would want someone similar to the choice he had made fifteen years ago. Still, she had thought that he would be more drawn to beauty and vivacity than other qualities.

But then, as Lady Mannering had pointed out, Mary was pretty when her face became more animated, and clearly Rochford seemed to be able to put the reticent girl at ease. Besides, Rochford was fifteen years older now. Doubtless he had realized over the course of the years that there were more important reasons for choosing a bride than the physical attraction he had felt for Francesca when they were young.

He enjoyed reading and corresponding with learned men. It was likely that he would enjoy being married to a woman with whom he could talk about serious, important matters. Even at the time, Francesca had known that she was too light in thought and manner for the duke. He must have come to realize that himself, as well.

Of course, it was early on yet. There was nothing to say that he would marry the girl simply because he had paid attention to her a time or two. Yet, like Lady Mannering, Francesca knew how rare it was for Rochford to show any sort of particularity toward a young woman. He was the sort of man who avoided gossip like the plague, and, moreover, knowing how highly he was rated on the marriage market, he was too much a gentleman to raise hopes in any available female's breast.

For him to be seen with a marriageable girl, particularly spending an appreciable and concentrated time alone with her, such as taking a drive together, indicated a high degree of interest in her. Moreover, to do that after having a fairly long conversation with her at a party only a day or two earlier was bound to cause speculation and lead to rumors. Rochford knew these things as well as anyone in the *ton*. Yet he had done them anyway.

Those facts raised what in another man might have been only an expression of some degree of interest to a much higher level. If he were to dance with her a time or two at a ball, it would really set tongues to wagging.

Of course, Francesca had the advantage over Lady Mannering in knowing that the duke was looking for a wife. It did not strike her as odd that he had talked with or called upon or in some other manner spent time with the various young women he was considering. However, knowing that, she also was more aware than anyone else that any interest he showed was leading toward marriage. Moreover, she knew that by taking Lady Mary for a ride in his phaeton, he was paying more marked attention to her than to any of the others.

Francesca could not imagine any reason for Rochford's actions other than the one Lady Mannering had arrived at: the duke was seriously considering Lady Mary for his wife.

She should feel glad, she knew, that her efforts were already bearing fruit. This was what she had wanted: to make up for the wrong she had done him. She wanted him to find a woman to whom he could give his heart. She wanted him to find happiness.

So why, then, had this odd weight settled in her chest? Why did she find it difficult to see the street for the tears pooling in her eyes?

THE FOLLOWING AFTERNOON, Francesca was at her desk, opening her most recent invitations, when Fenton appeared in the doorway.

"His Grace, the Duke of Rochford, is here."

Francesca jumped to her feet, knocking her knee painfully against her desk in the process. It had been almost four days since her party, and after her visit with Callie and Lady Mannering the day before, she had convinced herself that she was unlikely to see Rochford again except in the old sporadic way she had for the last few years.

Yet here he was.

Heat spread into her face, and she felt faintly embarrassed, wondering if her old servant had noticed her response.

"Please show him in," she said, schooling her expression into one of polite welcome.

Rochford strode in a moment later, and the moment

he stepped into the room, it seemed suddenly smaller. Francesca had thought she was prepared; she had spent much time advising herself on how she should react upon seeing him, given what had happened between them last time—and given his apparent interest in Lady Mary Calderwood.

But now, faced with him in the flesh, she found it harder than she had imagined. She could not keep the memories of his kisses from flooding her mind. She felt herself flushing, and she quickly dropped her eyes. *What was he thinking? What did he feel upon seeing her?*

She forced herself to look up at him again and go toward him, holding out her hand in greeting. "Rochford, what a pleasant surprise. I confess, I had not expected to see you again."

"Indeed?" He came forward, his eyes on her face, his own gaze annoying unreadable. "And here I thought I had become such a frequent guest that my presence would occasion no more than an 'oh, is it you again?'"

"I am sure that your presence never occasions that sort of remark," Francesca retorted.

His hand closed around hers, and he bowed over it. She was very aware of the feel of his skin on hers—the warmth, the slightly rougher texture. *Why was it that his touch evoked a feeling in her that no one else's ever had?* She found herself wishing that he had kissed her hand rather than simply bowing over it.

She pressed her lips together and turned away, gesturing toward the chairs grouped together in the small, casually intimate arrangement. "Pray, sit down. Would you care for refreshment?"

He shook his head, and they spent a few minutes in the usual polite exchange, commenting on the weather and asking after one another's health, as well as agreeing how pleasant it had been to see Callie again, and how sorry they were that she was so soon traveling to her new home.

Finally Francesca felt enough time had passed to broach the subject that was uppermost in her mind. "I am glad to hear that you have been paying court to Lady Mary."

His brows lifted a little, and he smiled faintly. "Indeed? Is that what people are saying?"

"I understand that you took her for a drive in your phaeton."

"Yes, I did." He continued to look at her, the same slightly quizzical smile hovering on his lips. "It hardly seems an event worth noting."

"My dear duke, any sign of favor from you is sure to garner attention."

He made a small, noncommittal noise.

"You feel a preference, then, for Lady Mary?" she went on after a moment. It was not her custom to press for information, but she could not seem to stop herself.

Still, his face gave nothing away. "She is a pleasant young woman."

Francesca reflected that Rochford could be irritating in the extreme. She would not let herself be one of those horrid women who chased down gossip, but it was more difficult than she would have thought to turn away from the subject. Why would he not just admit whether he had developed a *tendre* for the girl?

"Yes, she is," Francesca agreed. "Quite intelligent."

"So it would seem."

"Still, I presume that you are continuing to consider all the options we discussed."

"Of course." Again the corners of his lips twitched into a smile. "That is the reason for my visit today."

"Really? You wish to discuss the young women in question? Or perhaps you would like to consider some other choices. These do not suit?" Francesca felt a distinct lifting of her spirits. "I am sure that I can think of a few others."

"No. I believe these are entirely adequate," he told her. "What I had in mind was creating another opportunity in which to woo my future wife. I have decided that I should host a ball."

"Of course. That would be an excellent idea."

"I want you to help me make the arrangements."

Francesca felt a rush of pleasure. "Indeed? I am most flattered." Reluctantly, she added, "However, it is scarcely my place to do so."

"Who better?" he challenged. "There are none who can surpass your talents as a hostess."

"That is most gratifying to hear, of course, but there is no reason…I mean, it would be considered odd, surely. I have no connection to you."

"Do you not?" he asked, and for a moment his gaze, undeniably warm, rested on her face. Then he moved, and the look in his eyes was gone. "In the past my grandmother arranged such things, and in recent years, of course, Callie has acted as my hostess. But neither of them is here now. I can hardly ask my grandmother, at her age, to come rushing to London to put on a ball for me."

"No, of course not. But I am sure that your butler would be more than capable of arranging it."

"Cranston *is* quite capable, of course," Rochford agreed amiably. "But he is a man accustomed to implementing plans, not making them. Nor does he have the skill that you do. The task requires a lady of taste, such as yourself."

"You think flattery will bring me around?" Francesca asked, doing her best to look severe.

"I certainly hope so."

She could not help but laugh. "You are shameless."

"So I have been told."

"You know it would not be seemly. People would gossip."

"There is no reason for them to know." He shrugged. "I will not ask you to receive guests with me." His dark gaze was penetrating as he asked, "Would you be willing, then…if we hid it from the world?"

Francesca's heart picked up its beat, and she wondered suddenly, crazily, if his words somehow meant more than the obvious.

"Perhaps," she replied quietly. "Though it would seem to me that there must be someone else who would better serve."

"No." He continued to look steadily into her face. "It must be you."

CHAPTER ELEVEN

Francesca stared at him, his words reverberating through her, and for a moment the very air seemed to shimmer between them. She abruptly broke their gaze, fearing suddenly that he must see how her breath had quickened, that the pulse roaring in her ears might become as audible to him.

"Very well," she told him quietly, "if that is what you wish."

"It is." There was the faintest undertone of triumph in his voice as he stood up and came over to her. He reached down to her, and automatically, Francesca took his hand and rose to her feet. He smiled. "What should we do? I suppose Lilles House would be the place to start, would it not?"

"You intend a large ball?" she asked.

"I think so. Something that will give your skills adequate range."

Francesca cast him a mischievous look. "You might regret doing that."

He grinned. "Never—although I have no doubt you will do your utmost to put that resolve to the test.

However, you have carte blanche to do whatever you wish—and I mean that in the most respectable way, of course."

His last words highlighted the double entendre of the phrase, a term often used to describe the relationship a man made with his mistress, and Francesca felt her cheeks grow warm. Whatever was the matter with her? she wondered. You would think she was a naive girl instead of a sophisticated woman a decade and a half removed from her come-out.

"Ah, I see I have made you blush. Pardon me." Rochford's voice sounded more pleased than sorry, despite his words.

Francesca glanced up at him and found his dark eyes twinkling.

"You are not sorry in the slightest, you detestable man. But I can assure you that 'tis the heat of the summer, not your words. No doubt I look like a kitchen maid." She touched her cheek self-consciously.

"Whatever the cause, you look lovely." For a moment his face turned serious, but then he smiled and went on lightly, "As you very well know." He took a step back. "Come. Ring for the servants to fetch your hat. We shall go to Lilles House."

"Now?"

"Yes, why not? No reason not to get started, is there? Bring your maid, if you are worried about propriety. You must look the place over, see the ballroom. How else are you to plan?"

"How, indeed?" He was right about that, Francesca knew. Still, there was something illicit-seeming in going to a gentleman's house with him when there was no female relative residing there.

Maisie rode in the carriage with them. Though a widow enjoyed far more independence than a woman who had never married, Francesca knew that she could not be seen going into a bachelor's house alone. However, when they reached the imposing white-stone Lilles House, Maisie made her way with the footman to the servants' quarters, leaving Francesca in the foyer with the duke.

"I am surprised you do not insist that your maid accompany us through the house," Rochford teased. "Am I so fearsome a creature?"

Francesca rolled her eyes. "Really, Sinclair, you know I could not come here without her. *You* were the one who suggested it, after all. It is as much for your sake as mine. I can imagine the look on Cranston's face if you had walked in here with an unaccompanied woman." She paused, glancing at him. "That is to say, with me. I suppose that you have brought women of a certain sort here before."

The duke gave her a long, level look.

"Come, Rochford, I am not naive," she told him. "You are a man in your thirties, after all. I realize that you must have had women."

"Not here," he replied simply.

Strangely, she felt warmed by his answer. Rochford

was not the sort of man who would dishonor his house, his family or his wife in any way. He would not conduct casual affairs in the home that had been his parents', and that would someday be his wife's and children's. Had she married him, she would always have had his honor, she knew, and for a moment regret swelled in her throat. How different her life would have been if she had married Sinclair.

Francesca turned her head away from him, afraid that her feelings showed too readily on her face. Rochford had always been able to see what she thought.

Sternly, she reminded herself that however little Sinclair was like Andrew, he was, after all, a man. He would have given her his respect, treated her with honor, but she had no reason to think that he would have been any happier in her bed. He would have done it more discreetly, of course, but he, too, would have sought other women when he found her cold and passionless. And, really, it was nothing but a pipe dream to think that, had she married Sinclair, her basic nature would have changed, that she would have blossomed with desire.

Pushing aside her foolish, useless thoughts, Francesca looked around her. The entry hall of Lilles House was vast, stretching up two stories, with a sweeping double staircase as its centerpiece. Behind the staircase, a hallway stretched back to the conservatory and garden entrance, while to the left lay the hallway to the kitchen and servants' area.

To the right, however, the room opened up to the gallery, a stately hallway floored in Carrara marble, and lined with large portraits of former dukes and duchesses, as well as their children and pets. Elegant wall sconces provided light in the evening, but by day the tall, paned windows along the outside wall flooded the corridor with a golden light. Long velvet curtains, the color of dried moss, hung beside the windows, looped in artful swags over round metal holdbacks.

"I've always loved Lilles House," Francesca said.

He glanced over at her, and she wondered if he, too, was thinking that the house would once have been hers. The idea flustered her, and she glanced quickly away, heat rising in her cheeks. *What if he thought she regretted losing the magnificence of the house?*

"I am fond of it, as well," he replied, and to her relief she could detect nothing in his voice that indicated he found her words anything but normal. "Though it is somewhat dated, I fear. No doubt my bride will wish to change things. Put her own mark upon it."

"Oh, no!" Francesca protested, a little surprised at how fiercely she disliked the idea. "I hope she will not. It is beautiful just as it is. I would not change a thing."

But she had nothing to say about the matter, of course. She colored, once again aware of how her remark might be misconstrued, and she cast a glance at her companion. Fortunately, Rochford was looking in another direction and seemed not to have noticed her misstep.

He opened a set of double doors on the left. These doors, as well as a second pair farther down the hall, opened into the large ballroom, which stretched all the way to the rear of the house. Three huge chandeliers hung from the ceiling, and the floor was of the same pinkish-veined marble that lay in the gallery. Along the side wall was a row of tall windows, shaded in heavy brocade draperies of a deep maroon shade, and across the rear wall stood three sets of double French doors opening out onto a terrace.

"If you hold it in this room, it will have to be a grand ball," she warned. "Else it would not suit. It will take time to prepare for it."

"An end of the Season party, then. Mayhap one to announce an engagement."

Francesca felt the now-familiar clutch of nerves in her stomach. Was he so sure, then, of his choice? It must be Lady Mary. Given what he had said, she was certain that he was not considering Caroline Wyatt any more than he was Althea Robart. Damaris seemed a better choice, and Lady de Morgan was more lovely. But it was Mary Calderwood to whom he had talked for so long, whom he had taken riding in his phaeton.

Of course, he had taken Francesca herself for a ride in his phaeton, but that was an entirely different matter.

"You will have enough time to prepare, will you not?" the duke went on.

Her heart dropped. Would she even be in London in a few more weeks? If Perkins made good on his threats, she would be out of her house. How could she possibly still manage Rochford's party?

She forced a smile on her face, however, and told him, "Yes, of course. One does not need to add much decoration here."

They strolled through the grand ballroom to the sets of doors at the other end. Francesca stood, gazing out onto the terrace and the garden beyond. It was a very large yard for a house in the city, with an expansive garden.

"Would you like to extend the party into the garden?" she asked, turning toward him. "We could string up lights between the trees."

"Like Vauxhall Gardens?" he asked.

"Well…yes, I suppose so. But less ostentatious, perhaps—and hopefully without some of the behavior that takes place there. But perhaps we could set up a few tables and chairs on the terrace." She pointed. "There, where it is more secluded. We could have lights on the steps, and we could add decorations to the benches surrounding the fountain."

"It sounds very pleasant," Rochford agreed, reaching out to open one of the doors. "Let us go look at the garden more closely."

He offered her his arm, and they strolled across the terrace and down into the garden, moving at a leisurely pace and looking all around them. Francesca pointed out where stands of candelabra could be placed, and how wide ribbons twined through the railings would add a festive touch to the terrace and stairs. It would be a delight to plan for this party, she thought—if it were not for the knowledge, sitting in her chest like a lump of lead, that she was planning the joyous occasion for another woman.

"We would not have to use the whole garden," she went on as they circled the fountain and moved deeper into the garden. "We could mark off the paths at certain points to restrict them."

He shrugged. "No doubt the head gardener will disapprove, but I think 'twould be pleasanter to have it all open."

A tall, green hedge divided the garden, with an arch cut into it, leading into the back reaches. Beyond the great hedge, roses grew by the hundreds, filling the air with their heady scent. Here the garden grew less formal, the flower beds no longer contained in neat symmetrical shapes, but sprawling in gloriously bright abandon.

"It's beautiful," Francesca breathed. Though she had been to several parties over the years at Lilles House, and had called on the dowager duchess and Callie many times, she had never gone deeper into the garden than the section in front of the dividing hedge.

"My mother loved the garden," Rochford said quietly. "She clashed with my grandmother over it— the only times I ever heard her dare to disagree with the duchess. She encouraged the gardener to keep the rear garden wilder."

"I did not know your mother well," Francesca said. "But I am sure I would have liked her if this garden is any example."

"She did not visit Dancy Park much after my father's death. You were still a child when he died—twelve or thirteen, I suppose. My mother was…she was a sweet woman, a romantic one. Theirs was a love match. Her family was quite good, but not as lofty as the Lilles. My grandparents thought my father could have made a better match, and no doubt Mother felt it. She was intimidated, I am sure, when she married my father. Well, you can imagine coming into a family with in-laws like my grandmother and Great-Aunt Odelia."

"Sweet heaven!" Francesca said, much struck by the idea. "Either one of those women is enough to strike fear into anyone's heart. Your poor mother."

He smiled. "I do not think she minded as much as some women would have. She was glad enough at times, I think, for Grandmother's counsel and advice. She was not always comfortable in the role of duchess. However, as a wife she was perfect for my father. They were very much in love. She was a good, kind mother, as well, one who did not leave her children entirely to the nurse and governess."

"Well, those are the important roles she played. Being a duchess would not count as strongly."

He glanced at her. "That is what I thought. And my father. With Grandmother, of course, duty is paramount. The family. The name."

Francesca shrugged. "We have to face our responsibilities, of course. But surely happiness and love are more important."

"Do you think so? I would not have said so, from your admonitions to me about marrying."

Francesca stopped and turned to face him. "Are you again comparing me to the dowager duchess? Really, Rochford…you can be most maddening. I did not say you should marry for your family. What is important is that you be happy."

He studied her for a moment, a smile playing at the corners of his lips. "I am glad to hear you say it."

Francesca felt an odd quiver run through her. She did not care to think about it, so she turned and started forward again, saying, "Why did your mother dislike Dancy Park?"

"She did not dislike it so much as she found it hard to leave Marcastle. After Father died, she retreated from the world. She rarely came to London for the Season. She had lost her enjoyment of it. Indeed, she had lost most of her joy in life. She traveled less and less, preferring to stay where she and Father had spent most of their lives together. She felt closest to him at Marcastle."

"How sad. I mean, 'tis very sweet, as well, but it seems a sad life to live."

"It was. I felt sorry for her. And yet…"

"And yet what?" Francesca asked when he did not continue, unconsciously tucking her hand into his arm again.

He shook his head slightly. "You will find me very selfish, I fear. I wished she had not been so wrapped up in her grief. It was almost as if both our parents had died. Callie was just a child. She soon could not even remember our father. But for her our mother was…a wraith. A pale imitation of the woman she had been. Callie cannot remember the vibrant woman who was once our mother. She grew up with a quiet, sad person, one who was always a bit removed from everyone else's life."

"You must have missed her, as well," Francesca offered.

He glanced at her. "I did. There were times when I badly wished for her counsel. I was but eighteen and often overwhelmed by the title. There was my grandmother to advise me, of course."

"The upholder of Duty and Responsibility," Francesca murmured.

Rochford smiled faintly. "Yes. At least with Grandmother, one did not have to fear a lack of opinion. She was always certain of the correct thing to do."

"But not the most loving of women, I warrant."

"No. Not that. She did not approve of you, you know."

Francesca turned her face up to him, startled. "She knew? That you and I—"

"I did not tell her," he assured her. "But she could see the attention that I paid to you that last year. She knew the inordinate amount of time I spent at Dancy

Park instead of at the family seat, and she was able to guess the reason. Grandmother has always been astute."

"Oh, dear." Francesca winced. "She must have been furious with me, then, when I—"

"No. As I remember, she told me it was exactly what I should have expected. And she assured me that it was the best thing that could have happened to me, that it would allow me to ask for Carborough's younger sister."

"Lady Alspaugh?" Francesca asked in astonishment.

"Well, she was not married to Lord Alspaugh at the time, but yes, Lady Katherine."

Francesca continued to stare at him, slack-jawed, until he burst into laughter. "Oh!" she exclaimed then, playfully slapping his arm. "You are telling me a Banbury tale."

"No, indeed, I am not. She was my grandmother's choice. It had to do with her lineage and her dowry, primarily. A sizeable portion of land, which she was to inherit on her grandmother's death, also played into it. The land in question abutted my acres in Cornwall and would have made it a very nice estate."

"But she is buck-toothed and hasn't a humorous bone in her body," Francesca protested. "And she is several years older than you."

"Four," he admitted. "Still, duty called."

Francesca let out an inelegant snort. "Not a clarion call, I presume."

"No. It was a very soft whisper, indeed, as far as I

was concerned. Grandmother took it hard, but she rebounded with another choice in a few months—and after that, another. The past few years, however, she has grown rather silent on the matter, except for the occasional sigh and significant look, especially when she reads the news of some heir or other being born."

"I suppose I am to blame for it all." Francesca let out a martyred sigh.

"No, not at all," Rochford answered. "She is quite happy to lay the entire blame in my lap. Indeed, in recent years, she likes to remind me that I was quite foolish to let you go."

"Sinclair, I'm so sorry...."

"No, do not be." He covered her hand on his arm with his other hand. "I made my own mistakes. I let my damnable pride stand in my way. I should have—" He broke off, shrugging. "It does not matter now. But I do not want you to feel responsible. We were both young, and it was a long time ago. It is long past time to forget."

His hand was warm on hers, and Francesca was aware of a strong urge to lean her head against his arm. She could imagine him sliding his arm around her shoulders, pulling her close, and she would lay her head upon his chest, hearing the steady thump of his heart beneath her ear. Something flickered deep in his dark eyes, and Francesca suddenly feared that he had guessed her thoughts.

She turned away quickly, dropping her hand from his arm and starting forward again. Rochford moved along with her, and after a moment, he asked, "Would you like to see Mother's garden?"

Francesca turned back to him. "I thought this was her garden."

"It is, but not her own private one. It's a secret garden."

Francesca glanced around the yard curiously, intrigued. Rochford smiled and took her hand in his.

"Come. I'll show you."

He led her toward the rear of the garden, where a row of beeches lined the aged brick wall. At the end of them, the wall jutted forward, then continued east for a time before meeting the side wall of the estate. Both the side wall and the short wall beyond the beech trees were covered with ivy, green and vibrant. A slight breeze rustled the leaves, creating a soft whispering.

Rochford walked around the corner, and there, between the wall and the last beech tree, was a narrow, low wooden door with a metal ring set into it. Rochford tugged on the ring, and the door opened with a reluctant creak. He stepped aside, motioning for Francesca to enter, then followed her in, closing the door behind them.

"Oh!" She let out a happy cry.

The small garden was centered by a calm pond upon which water lilies floated. In the far corner, a stone face spilled water from his mouth into a basin below, from whence it trickled down onto artistically placed rocks. The soothing sound permeated the garden, joined now and then by the stir of leaves from the trees and ivy beyond the wall. A willow tree graced another corner of the garden, and an ornate wrought-iron bench was set near the pond.

Everywhere else, flowers bloomed in a riot of colors and scents. In some places they grew up the walls along carefully delineated paths, and in other areas, they spilled downward like a box of jewels overturned. They stretched upward on tall stalks, their heads bobbing heavily, or spread like a carpet across the ground, or mounded up in bright clumps.

It was clear, Francesca thought, that the garden was carefully tended. No weed dared show its head. Yet there were seemingly no constraints upon the flowers, which spread and bloomed and mingled with each other in glorious abandon.

"It's beautiful…." she breathed, turning around to take it all in. "And so wonderfully…"

"Excessive?" Rochford guessed.

"No, not at all," she protested. "*Sumptuous* is the word I would use. I love it."

"So did my mother." He followed her as she trailed through the flowers, stopping to admire first one plant and then another. "My father had this part of the garden walled and filled with plants just for her. It was a gift to her on their second anniversary. She always missed the gardens at Marcastle when they came to London for the Season, so he had all her favorites planted here. She could come here and lock herself away whenever she wanted."

"It locks? I did not see a key."

"It locks only from the inside." He gestured back toward the door, where, indeed, a metal bar could be pulled across to secure the door. "No children, no servants, no mother-in-law, could bother her here. Not even a husband, if she so wished. She liked to paint or read or simply sit and be…not a duchess."

"And you kept it as it was." Francesca turned to look up at him.

"Yes. It's been many years since she was here. She came to London only a time or two after Father died. But I could not change it."

"Of course not. It is lovely." She glanced around again. "Do you visit it often?"

"Sometimes. But…it is the duchess's garden."

She looked up to find him watching her. A stray bit of breeze lifted a curl of her hair and brushed it against her cheek. Rochford reached out and smoothed the curl back from her face with his knuckles.

Would this garden be Mary Calderwood's, then? Francesca wondered, and her heart tightened in her chest at the thought. She wanted this place to be hers, but she knew that the stab of possessiveness she felt went much further than that—she wanted this *man* to be hers.

She ached for what she had lost. For him. For a life that she would never know. For children and hopes and laughter.

But she knew that her wishes were futile. The time

when she could have had those things, when she could have embraced love and lived a different life, was long gone. However much she ached for it, she could not have it back.

Was she really so selfish? she wondered. How could she begrudge Rochford his chance at happiness? If Lady Mary was the woman he wanted for his duchess, then she should do everything she could to help him win her.

And however sweet it might be to feel the stroke of his hand across her cheek, it would be folly to indulge in any nostalgic attempt to recapture the romance that she and Sinclair had once shared. Though he looked at her now in a way that made her want to melt into his arms, though her mouth yearned to press against his and try to recapture the sweet fire that it had felt the other night when he kissed her, she knew that to do so would be nothing but folly.

Sinclair might want her, might want the *memory* of her, at least. And she knew that at this moment she wanted him. If she leaned toward him, if she put her hand upon his chest and gazed up into his eyes, she was certain that he would bend to kiss her. And she was filled with a tingling anticipation, a burgeoning hope that if they kissed again, she would once more know the new and wondrous sensations that had flooded her the other night. For a few minutes she might feel gloriously alive.

But that was a fleeting thing.

What Sinclair needed was a woman he could marry, a woman who could bear his children and share a life with him, who could return his passion and fill his life with love. He did not need a woman who was, at the deepest center of her, barren and cold. And she knew, after her years of childless marriage with Andrew, that she could not give Sinclair either the passion or the children he deserved.

She turned away, saying in a low voice, "It is growing late. I should return home."

"Francesca…" He reached out, grabbing her wrist. "Wait."

"No." She looked back at him, her eyes wide and dark with the turmoil of emotions inside her. "No. We must go."

She jerked her arm from his grasp and hurried out of the garden.

CHAPTER TWELVE

FRANCESCA DID HER best not to think about what had happened with her and Rochford in his mother's garden. Anything between them was out of the question. The love she had felt for Sinclair had died long ago, and she was not certain that he had ever really loved her. All they felt now was desire, fueled no doubt by the knowledge that their romance had died an abrupt and bitter death.

The last thing either of them needed at the moment was an affair. Rochford was ready for marriage. And she should be concentrating on doing whatever she could to avoid losing her home to Mr. Perkins. Besides, it was bound to end badly. The flickerings of desire in her would wither and die once they reached the bedchamber, and she would be left shamed before Sinclair. She could not, would not, allow that to happen.

She spent the next morning tallying up the things Maisie and Fenton had managed to sell. Fenton had gotten rid of a number of objects, though he had held stubbornly to the silver flatware and a few large serving dishes, as well as the crystal goblets and china. She had not pressed the issue. The pearls, too, were gone, which cost her a bit of a pang, as well as all the candelabras in the house except those used in the drawing room and formal dining room. Even so, the amount of money they had amassed fell woefully short.

But she had known that would be the case. Perhaps it would be enough money for her to hire a solicitor. The thought of going to court turned her stomach to ice.

The afternoon she spent making plans for Rochford's party, an occupation that greatly brightened her mood. It was wonderful having a huge room and an unquestioning source of money with which to work, and she let her imagination roam free.

However, she could not help but remember Sinclair's offhand remark that it would perhaps be an engagement ball, and that thought deflated all her happiness.

The Haversley soiree was to take place the following evening. Francesca had not planned to attend, but she knew that the Calderwoods were certain to be there, as Lady Calderwood and Mrs. Haversley were cousins and friends. If Lady Mary was there, wasn't it likely that Rochford would attend, as well? If the rumors she had heard were accurate, he certainly would.

She wanted to see them together. She was not sure why, but the idea was persistent. If she watched them, she was certain she could gauge the extent of Rochford's interest in Mary. The more she thought about it, the more she wanted to see that for herself.

Besides, she reasoned, it would be another way to

help Harriet if she asked Harriet and her father to accompany her. By the time she went up to dress for supper, she had convinced herself to attend the party, and she sat down and dashed off a note to Sir Alan, asking them to go with her to the soiree the following evening.

As it turned out, she was correct in her supposition that the Calderwoods would be at the party. Francesca felt an unbidden sense of relief when she saw that the duke was not there, but he arrived a few minutes later. Well, at least he had not come with them, she thought.

She managed to keep her eyes on Rochford and Lady Mary throughout most of the evening. She saw them together once in earnest conversation, and later he brought the young girl a cup of punch. Of course, she also saw him talking at one point to Lady de Morgan, and later to Damaris Burke and her father. Indeed, if anything, he talked to Damaris the longest, but Francesca found it difficult to judge the depth of his interest in the girl, since most of the conversation appeared to be between the two men.

She tried not to be obvious about the direction of her attention, but at one point Sir Lucien, standing beside her, commented dryly, "Spying on the duke, are we?"

"What?" Startled, Francesca turned at him. "No, of course not. Don't be silly."

However, she feared that her words of innocence were spoiled by the blush she felt creeping up her face. Confirming her fears, Sir Lucien cast her a knowing look.

"Mmm-hmm. Then I am sure that you are not interested in hearing the word going around the clubs."

"Word? What word? About Rochford?"

"The very same."

"People love to talk," Francesca said casually, looking off across the room as if she had no interest in the matter. However, when Lucien did not continue, she finally had to prompt him, "What do they say?"

A little smile touched his lips, but he said only, "Oh, that the duke seems to be in the market for a bride."

"Really?" She turned to him, abandoning all pretense of disinterest. "Has he said something?"

"I doubt it. He's a closemouthed one. But it has been noticed that he has been far more social than in other years. Attending parties and plays. Making social calls. Taking rides in the park in the company of ladies. And at those parties, he rarely leaves soon after his arrival, as he has been known to do in the past. He is often seen conversing, not only with friends and family, but with a number of young women—few of whom he even seemed to notice in years past."

"I see." Francesca paused. She knew all this, of course. Indeed, she was the one who had urged him to do these things. But somehow this information, coming as it did from general Society gossip, made it seem terribly real—and final. "And do they link him with any name in particular?"

"One I have heard more than once is Lord Calderwood's youngest."

"Mary."

"Yes. She is a shy sort, yet she has been observed in animated conversation with the duke. Moreover, he has called on her and taken her for a ride in his phaeton. All unusual signs of interest."

Francesca shrugged. "I suppose so. Still, it seems little enough to make people speak of marriage. Rochford is a notorious bachelor."

"Which is precisely why such small signs are pored over and declared proof of wife-shopping. He is so disinclined to have his name linked with any lady that even the smallest indication is magnified. In one man, being in the market for a wife might involve showering a young girl with attention—flowers, walks, calls, rides, poetry. In Rochford, however, a few visits might suffice."

"Still, I think people are being a bit premature. It could be only that he is making a bit more effort now that Callie is no longer living at Lilles House. He might want company."

"Perhaps. But usually that entails spending more time at White's, not taking up with marriageable young women."

Francesca nodded a bit absently, turning to glance around. She could not find Rochford now. But she spotted Mary Calderwood sitting against the wall with one of her sisters.

Beside her, Lucien followed her gaze. "Of course, he would have to put up with Calderwood as a father-in-law. That should be sufficient deterrent."

Francesca smiled. "That hardly seems reason not to choose a girl."

"I don't know. One would have to talk to him if he was one's father-in-law, and the chap is a dead bore."

"True. Perhaps you ought to point it out to Rochford."

He let out a little snort of derision. "You won't find me attempting to give the duke advice on his love life. Some may find my life of little worth, but it's quite valuable to me."

Francesca tilted her head, considering Lady Mary and her sister. "She seems a bit…bland for Rochford, don't you think?"

Sir Lucien cut his eyes toward her speculatively. "I don't know. She is shy. Perhaps when one gets to know her, she sparkles with wit."

"I cannot imagine her being able to meet the duke's social obligations. She blushes and drops her gaze whenever she is introduced to someone."

"Becoming modesty, some would say," Lucien suggested.

"Nor are her looks exactly what one would expect Rochford to be drawn to."

"Do I detect a note of jealousy?" Sir Lucien drawled.

Francesca turned to find her friend smirking at her. "Nonsense. Why would I be jealous?"

He did not reply, only studied her for a moment, then commented, "There is another name bandied about as the woman who has drawn the duke's interest."

"Who?" Francesca asked, surprised.

"Lady Haughston."

For a moment she simply stared at him, his words having effectively rendered her speechless. Finally, she squeaked out, "Me? How absurd." She rolled her eyes. "Why, Rochford and I have known each other forever."

"Knowing one a long time does not necessarily preclude marriage."

"We are friends, that is all."

"Neither does being friends rule out marriage. Though one would have to assume that it would not continue after the ceremony." He paused, then added, "You cannot deny that you and the duke have been a good deal friendlier in recent weeks."

"Whatever do you mean?" Francesca opened her fan and began to waft it gently. The ballroom had become much warmer, it seemed.

"You have gone for rides in the park, just as Rochford and Lady Mary have."

"One ride," Francesca corrected swiftly.

"As Rochford and Lady Mary have," he repeated. "You have stood up to dance with him several times."

"It is not unusual for Rochford to ask me for a dance."

"Three times in two weeks?"

"Have you been keeping count?" Francesca gazed at him in astonishment. "No doubt it is that many only because the duke has been attending so many more balls."

"And he has called on you a number of times."

"We are friends. You know that."

"How often did the duke pay social calls on you in the past several years?"

Francesca searched her mind frantically. "I cannot remember," she said at last. "But I am certain that he has. Why, in January, he called on me a time or two, I am certain."

"Sometime other than when his sister was staying with you."

"Really, Lucien, how can I be expected to remember every little detail?" She gave him an exasperated look. "I do hope you are not fueling such idiotic rumors."

"Of course not. I would never gossip about you." Sir Lucien looked wounded. "However, one cannot help but notice things. And one would think that one's friends might inform one if—"

"Pray do not get on your high ropes, Lucien. I did not tell you because there is nothing to tell. Rochford is not interested in me, and I am not jealous."

He looked at her for a moment, then gave in. "Very well. I shall just continue to look mysterious and say nothing when people ask me."

"Lucien! You must disabuse people of the notion!"

"Are you mad? One can scarcely dine out on denials."

Francesca had to chuckle. Lucien began to talk of the gossip swirling around the Countess of Oxmoor, which centered on her relationship with an artist her husband had hired to paint her portrait. Francesca only half listened to him, once more scanning the room.

She saw that Mary Calderwood was now seated by herself against the wall. It was, Francesca thought, the perfect opportunity to start up a conversation with the girl.

"Pardon me," she inserted quickly into the first pause in Lucien's chatter. "I need to speak to someone."

She left almost as soon as she spoke and did not see the speculative glance her friend cast at her as she wound her way through the throng to the chairs where Mary sat.

She paused a time or two to say hello to someone or compliment a gown or hairdo, not wanting it to seem as though she had made a straight line to the girl. When she felt she was close enough, she turned and let her gaze fall upon Mary as if she had just seen her sitting there.

"Lady Mary," she said, smiling and going over to her. "How nice to see you again."

The girl jumped up and bobbed a quick curtsey toward her, saying, "Lady Haughston. Hello. Um, it's very nice to see you, as well."

Pink crept along the girl's cheeks, and she looked down at her shoes.

Francesca pretended not to notice Mary's awkwardness. *How in the world did the girl manage to converse so easily with Rochford, who regularly intimidated people far braver than she?* Francesca sat down in the chair next to Mary's. Mary looked faintly alarmed, but took her seat again. Francesca noticed that the girl sat at the front edge of the chair, as if she might bolt at any second.

"I am so glad you were able to come to my little soiree last week," Francesca began.

Mary's blush deepened. "Oh, yes. I beg your pardon—I should have said— That is, I am, um, very glad that you invited me. Us, I mean."

"I hope that you enjoyed it," Francesca went on, ignoring Mary's blushes and stammering about.

"Yes, it was most beautiful." Mary smiled, looking as though it was rather painful to her, and quickly glanced away.

"I hope your parents are well," Francesca said, working her way through the customary polite chat.

Mary was of little help, answering in brief phrases and making no attempt to open up any topics of her own. Francesca felt as if she was being cruel to continue talking to the girl when she was so plainly uncomfortable, so she gave up the social niceties and simply jumped into the topic that had brought her over, trusting that Mary would scarcely notice the awkwardness of the transition.

"You seemed to enjoy a nice chat with the Duke of Rochford at my party," she began.

Mary's demeanor changed instantly. She lifted her head, her face suddenly glowing, as if lit from within. The lights glinted off the glass of her round spectacles as she said, "Yes. He is the most wonderful man, is he not?"

"Very admirable," Francesca agreed, suppressing a sigh. Clearly the young lady was topsy-turvy over Rochford. It was no wonder, of course; any girl would be, even a bookish sort. Sinclair was handsome, witty and strong, everything a woman could want in a man.

Mary nodded enthusiastically. "He is ever so kind. Usually—well, I am sure you noticed—I do not talk easily to anyone. But the duke is so pleasant and attentive. Indeed, I scarcely realized that I was conversing until I heard myself babbling away."

Francesca nodded agreeably, although she could not help but be amazed. She wondered if Caroline Wyatt would agree that the duke was so easy to talk with. But then, she supposed, it made all the difference in the duke's demeanor if the girl who was talking was one who had caught his fancy.

"You must think me very silly," Lady Mary went on, smiling in a self-deprecating way. "You have been friends with the duke so long."

"Yes, indeed, I have." Francesca forced herself to smile, to ignore the hard knot that had taken hold in her chest. "He is a wonderful gentleman."

Mary beamed back at her. "I know. I am so lucky."

Francesca fought to keep the pleasant smile on her face. *Already the girl counted herself lucky? Was she that sure of herself and her hold on the duke?* In another woman, Francesca might have termed the statement foolish arrogance, but Mary Calderwood was not the arrogant sort. No, she was simply too inexperienced to know that she should not speak with such certainty until the duke had actually asked for her hand.

But then, perhaps he had already asked and just had not told her. The thought cut Francesca like a knife.

Suddenly she could not bear to sit there anymore, listening to the happiness bubbling in the young woman's voice, seeing her eyes shine. She smiled and uttered a few pleasantries that she could not remember afterward, then took her leave.

Francesca walked away from the rest of the crowd, ducking into a hallway. She found an alcove that was blessedly secluded, and she sat down, drawing a deep breath.

Could it be that Lucien was right, and she was jealous? She wanted to laugh and say that it was absurd, as she had told him, but she could not do it. All the time that she had been planning the party for Sinclair, the thought that it would be an engagement ball had preyed on her mind. It was wicked of her, she told herself, not to want Rochford to find love with Mary. There was naught wrong with the girl; she seemed sweet, and the love had been clear to see on her face. That was what Sinclair deserved, a girl who loved him, who would make him a good wife. That was what she wanted for him. Wasn't it?

Yet neither could she deny the ache in her chest when she thought of the two of them together. She burned with resentment to think of him in love.

She knew it was wrong…and wicked. And she was determined not to feel this way. She would fight the nasty burning inside her. She would not allow herself to be the sort of woman who wished a man to be unhappy simply because she could not have him.

It could be done, surely. Perhaps she was not a deep person, but she was sure that she was not a bad person, either. She had started this whole thing because she wanted Sinclair to be happy, and she still wanted that. If Mary Calderwood was the woman who would make him happy, she would somehow bring herself to be glad.

The only problem was figuring out how to do so.

THE DEADLINE Mr. Perkins had set loomed before Francesca, but she refused to think about it. Barring a miracle, she could not possibly have the money for him, leaving her with nothing but the decision of whether to refuse to leave or to go meekly. And though she quailed inside at the thought, she was rather certain what she would do when it came down to it. Whatever else the FitzAlans may have been, her family had always been warriors.

Instead, she kept herself busy with the plans for Rochford's party. She soon realized that she needed to discuss her plans with Cranston, Rochford's efficient butler. She could have sent a note to him, requesting him to call on her. She knew that would be the most correct thing to do. Instead, she decided that she would go to Lilles House to consult with him. She would take Maisie with her, so it would be quite proper. And it would be easier to show the man what she wanted if they could actually go into the ballroom.

She might run into the duke, but she had taken herself firmly in hand after the Haversley soiree. She was sure that she had exorcised the demon of jealousy from herself. It had been just a momentary emotion, after all, and reason would overcome it. Besides, it was quite likely that Rochford would not even be at home.

He was not, as it turned out, and she told herself that things had worked out perfectly. Cranston looked rather surprised to see her, though he hid it well, only his light blue eyes revealing a hint of curiosity at finding Francesca and her maid standing in the entryway of Lilles House. When she explained that she was there to consult with him on the duke's upcoming ball, his carefully polite expression vanished, and he beamed, the first time Francesca could ever remember seeing him do so.

"My lady, of course. I would be more than happy to assist you. I have seating charts, as well as plans for the ballroom."

"Excellent," Francesca said, her eyes lighting up. Such efficiency would make Fenton jealous, she thought. "If there is a table where we could sit…?"

"Naturally. If her ladyship would not mind, there is the table in the servants' hall, where I do most of my planning. Or, um, the library might be more suitable."

"The table in the servants' hall sounds just the thing."

So while Maisie went off for a bit of tea and gossip with the Lilles House housekeeper, having earned that woman's friendship the last time they were there by praising Callie, Francesca settled down at the table in the servants' dining hall, one of Cranston's drawings of the large ballroom spread out on the table before her.

The dining area was a cozy place, separated by a short hall from the kitchen, and while there was the clanging of pots and pans and the usual bustle of a working kitchen, the sound was muffled enough that it provided only a low background noise. Cranston solicitously brought her a cup of tea and a pot for refills, as well as a small plate of biscuits, then stood a little behind her and to the side.

"Do sit down, Cranston," she told him, indicating the chair beside her.

"Very kind of you, my lady, but…"

She knew that he was a stickler for correct procedure in every detail, but she was also aware that the older man had grown increasingly stiff in his knees over the past few years. She was well-versed in dealing with aging servants.

"Please do," she insisted. "It will be much easier for us to talk. I shan't have to crane my head around to see you that way."

"Of course, my lady, if you wish it."

The butler sat down beside Francesca, though he remained poised on the edge of the seat, as though ready to spring up at any moment, and he kept his chair slightly behind hers.

"Here is the preliminary list of guests," she told him, laying a sheet of paper on the table. "I thought you might look over it and see if I have by chance missed someone who ought to be on it or put someone there who would be quite wrong."

"I am sure your opinions are absolutely correct," Cranston assured her, though he set the list aside for later viewing.

Francesca took up a pencil and began to describe her ideas for the decorations, marking them on his map of the ballroom. Cranston nodded approvingly, jotting down notes on a piece of paper as he went.

They moved on to the refreshments, which meant that the cook had to be brought in on the discussion, as well. The cook, obviously another Lilles retainer who had been there for many years, was a rotund woman with iron-gray hair and the beefy arms of one who had spent her life kneading bread and stirring soups. As possessive of her territory as most cooks Francesca knew, she came into the room with a slightly wary expression on her face. It did not take long, however, for Francesca's charm to work its usual magic, and soon she, too, was nodding and agreeing to all Francesca's suggestions.

"Well, well," came a cultured male voice from the doorway. "Are you poaching my servants, Lady Haughston? Should I take umbrage?"

All three of the occupants of the room swiveled around to the door, where the duke was leaning against the frame, a smile starting on his lips.

"I should love to, I can assure you, but then I would have to face the wrath of my own staff," Francesca replied, smiling back at him.

It occurred to her, as it had the other day when she was here, that had she married him years ago, this scene would have been a common occurrence. How many times would she have looked up to see him standing in a doorway, watching her?

"Then I can only assume that you are here laying plans for the ball," Rochford went on.

"Yes. Would you like to hear where I intend to put the decorations?"

"Come show me instead," he suggested. "Then perhaps we could have tea, if you would like."

"That would be lovely," Francesca answered honestly.

"Excellent. Cranston, tea in the morning room, I think. Twenty minutes?"

Cranston nodded, and he and the cook quickly disappeared into the kitchen. Rochford turned to Francesca, offering her his arm, and they walked back through the long hallway to the foyer, then along the even longer gallery to the large ballroom.

"I thought it would make sense to show Cranston where the decorations should go," Francesca said, thinking that Rochford might wonder why she had come to his house to talk to Cranston instead of the other way around. "But he had plans of the ballroom, with everything marked, so I was able to jot it all down for him there."

"He is a wonder of organization. I have little doubt that he has the layout of every room in this house, with each stick of furniture marked in its place. Nothing escapes Cranston's attention. No doubt he was ecstatic at having someone who takes an interest in decoration and menus. I fear that he finds me hopelessly lacking when it comes to such things. I am sure he feels the loss of Callie deeply."

Francesca smiled and squeezed his arm a little. "As do you, I imagine."

He glanced at her and allowed a small smile. "You are right, of course. I had thought that I had become accustomed to her absence when she was staying with you, but I discovered that it is quite a different feeling when one knows that she is not returning after a month or two. I have to be glad for her, for I know she is happy with Bromwell, but I cannot help but wish that his estates were not so far as Yorkshire."

"At least Marcastle is much nearer there," Francesca put in consolingly.

"Yes. No doubt we shall visit more when I am back home."

Francesca could not keep from feeling a pang of loneliness, thinking that then she would be here quite alone. It took her a moment to realize that she was being nonsensical—she was rarely alone in London, even when the Season was over. Besides, given the threat that loomed before her with Mr. Perkins, it was all too likely that she would not be in London at all, but immured at Redfields.

Determinedly, she steered the conversation in a new direction as they entered the ballroom. "I thought that you might have a Midsummer's Night Eve party—what do you think? We could have it on that date and make the place appear a fairyland. Cranston thought that it could be done in time. We can have lots of greenery and, amidst all that, white flowers of every sort."

She went on happily describing the wonders that could be done with net and tulle sprinkled with silver sequins and draped in swags across the ceiling to catch the lights. After a few minutes, she stopped and arched an eyebrow at him.

"I am boring you to tears, am I not?" she asked with a sigh.

"Not at all. I could not be more transported," he assured her, one side of his mouth quirking up in a grin.

"Liar," she told him without heat.

He chuckled. "I am sure it will be delightful. Everyone will be dazzled. They will dance away the night and go home declaring that no one can entertain like Lady Haughston."

"But it will be *your* party, not mine," she pointed out.

"I think all and sundry will be aware that mine was not the genius behind it. Such elegance and whimsy could only be yours. Will you come as Titania—a vision in white and silver?"

Francesca's eyes sparkled. "There's an idea. Perhaps we should make it a fancy-dress ball."

He let out a groan. "No, please, not that. Aunt

Odelia's fancy-dress ball was more than enough for one year."

"You did not even come in costume!" she protested. "It could not have been so hard."

"No, but I was plagued to death to do so, which is perhaps worse."

Francesca shook her head at him, smiling. They had been strolling around the large room as they talked, but he stopped now and turned to look at her. She raised her eyes questioningly, not sure what he was doing.

"You must save the first dance for me," he told her.

Under his gaze, she felt suddenly, strangely shy. She shook her head. "But I must oversee the arrangements— make sure everything runs smoothly. I won't have time for dancing."

"Nonsense. That is what Cranston will be doing. You will open the dancing with me."

She looked up into his face. There was something in his dark eyes that made her breathless. "But surely… one of the young ladies—Lady Mary, for instance— should have the honor."

"No," he replied. "Only you."

He surprised her by taking her hand and sweeping her out onto the floor, humming a waltz. Francesca laughed and fell into the easy rhythm of the dance, and they whirled around the room. It might have been daylight, and the grand room utterly empty of any decoration, but it felt for a few moments quite magical to her.

She was very aware of the hard muscle of his arm beneath her hand, of his long, supple fingers at her waist, guiding her subtly. Finally he stopped, and for a long moment they simply stood there gazing at each other, her hand still in his, his hand still at her waist. Though they had not danced long, his breathing was visibly harder, his chest rising and falling. His eyes glowed with a dark light. Francesca could feel the sudden surge of heat in his hands, and his mouth softened. He leaned closer.

She knew that he was about to kiss her, knew that she should move away. Instead, she closed her eyes.

CHAPTER THIRTEEN

THEN HIS LIPS were on hers, soft and seeking. His hands did not move from the position they had been in as they danced. He did not pull her against him or touch her anywhere else. Only his lips spoke for him, sweetly, yearningly kissing hers—entreating, teasing, tempting her.

Francesca trembled. She wanted to go up on tiptoe and throw her arms around his neck. She ached to hold on to him and kiss him, to press her body into his. She wanted to throw everything else aside—all caution, all sense—and indulge herself. To forget that he was on the verge of making an offer for another woman. To ignore her past and not think about where this kiss could lead.

But if she could not bring herself to pull away, neither could she allow herself to move forward. She simply lived in the moment, fragile and sweetly aching, drinking in the pleasure of his mouth.

At last he broke the kiss and raised his head. Neither of them spoke.

There was the sound of footsteps in the long gallery outside, and Rochford moved away. A footman appeared in the doorway to announce that tea was served. Rochford turned to Francesca and offered her his arm, as apparently cool and reserved as ever.

She took his arm, hoping that she seemed equally unfazed, and they strolled out of the room. However, instead of following the footman, Rochford led her out the French doors and onto the terrace, cutting across it to another door.

"This is the morning room," he said as they stepped inside. "It is my favorite, although I actually prefer it late in the afternoon, like this."

Francesca could understand his pleasure in the room. Spacious and comfortably furnished, it was graced by a wall of tall, wide windows facing the terrace and the extensive gardens beyond. Protected as it was from the west sun, it was delightfully cool and shaded, yet open to the lovely view.

"It's beautiful," she murmured, moving across the room to the chairs and low table where the butler had set out their tea tray.

She poured for them, and was struck once again by the thought that this might have been her life. It seemed so natural and right. His face across from her was as familiar as her own. Yet she knew, too, that it would never have grown commonplace to her, even if they had been married for years. Now, as whenever she saw him, her pulse leapt a little.

They chatted as they sipped their tea, and ate the square cakes and slivers of sandwiches. They talked of the ball and of Francesca's letter from home that morning. Dominic was pleased with what they had accomplished on the estate this spring planting, and Constance, it seemed, was contentedly growing larger as she moved into her seventh month.

"Will you travel to Dancy Park to be with her?" he asked.

Francesca nodded. "I shall stay here another month or six weeks and then go. She has no family, you know, besides us—except for that excessively annoying aunt and uncle of hers, and I cannot imagine she would want that woman there at such a time. Nor is my mother a woman one would choose at such a time. Not, of course, that I am any hand with babies, but the nurse can provide that. I, at least, can keep Constance entertained."

"I am sure you will be a great comfort to her. Perhaps I shall see you there. I intend to visit Dancy Park again before autumn."

Francesca glanced at him, a little surprised. "I would have thought that you would remain here after—" She stopped abruptly.

His brows pulled together in a frown. "After what?"

"Nothing. It is none of my business, really. I only thought that, well, you would be making wedding plans."

He looked at her steadily for a moment. "Did you?"

"Yes. After all, you seem to be moving in that direction. You as much as said you would be announcing your engagement at the ball, and you have shown a marked interest in Lady Mary. I must say, she seems an excellent choice. Only the other night, at the Haversley soiree, she was expressing her fondness for you."

"Was she?" His black brows rose. "How interesting."

"Oh, yes." Francesca felt the now-familiar crawl of jealousy through her stomach, but she was determined not to give in to it. It did not matter what had happened minutes earlier in the ballroom; it did not matter how she felt.

She started to go on, but at that moment there was the sound of raised voices in the hall, something so uncommon in the quiet and aristocratic atmosphere of Lilles House that both Francesca and Rochford stopped their conversation and glanced toward the door.

"—must see him!" came a male voice, raised in agitation. "I don't care what he's doing!"

His words were followed by the deeper, calmer tone of Rochford's butler, but it was clear that his attempt at reason had little effect.

Rochford rose to his feet and started toward the door at the clear sound of scuffling. "Cranston? What is going on here!"

"I must see you!" Though Francesca could not see the clearly agitated young man in the hallway, she could hear him well enough. "I am Kit Browning. Christopher Browning. I think you will know why I am here."

Rochford scowled. "You were supposed to call on me tomorrow morning." He sighed, then motioned for the visitor to come in. "Very well. It is all right, Cranston. I shall see him."

He turned back toward Francesca. "I am sorry. This should take but a moment."

Christopher Browning burst into the room. Francesca saw, with some surprise, that he wore the black suit and clerical collar of an Anglican priest. His thin, blond hair stood out all over his head, as though he had been worrying at it with his fingers, and his lean, ascetic face was pale and taut. He appeared at once frightened and angry, and he faced the larger duke with an air of defiance.

"I will not allow you to do this!" he announced to Rochford.

"Indeed?" Rochford studied him somewhat curiously. "And what exactly is it that you will not allow?"

"I will not let you have her! You may have dazzled her with your grand airs and your huge house and all the gold you no doubt have. But I know that those things will not make her happy. She is a quiet, studious girl. She loves nothing so much as a good book by the fire or a quiet ramble down the lane. She cannot be happy as a duchess."

"I daresay," Rochford replied quietly, and the corner of his mouth twitched in the way that told Francesca he was suppressing his amusement. "Am I to take it that you are speaking of Lady Mary Calderwood?"

"Of course! Who else would I be talking about? Do you have some other poor young woman dangling on a string?"

Francesca's interest rose even higher at the mention of Lady Mary, and she inspected the young man more carefully.

"I was not aware that I had Lady Mary 'dangling,' let alone any other. Perhaps you would be so kind as to tell me what you are talking about."

"I'm talking about your pursuit of her. Oh, do not think that I have not heard about it. Rumors reach even into the sacred halls of the church."

"Yes. No doubt. So these rumors that have reached you in the church…"

"Do not sneer at me!" Browning flared, color flaming in his cheeks. "Just because you are wealthy and powerful does not make you a better man. It does not give you the right to push me aside with a laugh."

"No, you are quite correct," Rochford replied. "Indeed, I was not sneering at you. I am, I admit, somewhat taken aback, however, by your, um, ferocity."

"No doubt you thought you would have a clear path to the lady. But I, sir, stand in your way."

"So I see." Rochford put his hand to his lips, and Francesca suspected that he was firmly suppressing a smile at the young man's florid manner of speech.

"Lady Mary loves me! She and I are to be wed. We have promised each other. I know it was not before the church, and that her father disapproves. But in her heart, I know that she considers it as sacred a vow as I do. This is her father's doing, I know. He is pushing her to marry you."

Then Rochford had *already asked Lady Mary to wed!* Francesca felt as if a great hand had reached into her chest and squeezed her heart.

"My dear Mr. Browning," Rochford said, "as enlightening as all this is, I fear that I must move the conversation along. You have caught me in the middle of tea, you see."

"Oh, yes, I see!" the young man retorted, and he turned a flashing gaze on Francesca. "Consorting with your lightskirts while my sweet Mary—"

Francesca's eyes widened at the man's description of her, and she started to protest, but Rochford had taken a step forward and fixed Browning with a hard look that shut up even that wordy young man.

"I will make allowances for your poor manners because it is clear that you have been driven to some disorder of the mind by your affection for Lady Mary. However, I assure you that you will not malign this lady, either in my presence or elsewhere. Is that clear?"

"Y-yes." Browning swallowed and took a step back. His gaze flickered over to Francesca, and he murmured, "My apologies, ma'am."

Francesca inclined her head regally. She was too interested in the conversation to spend any time discussing this side issue.

"Now, as to your…problem with me," Rochford continued. "Are you aware that I invited you to visit me tomorrow morning?"

"I knew it. I presume that it is your intention to

inform me of your engagement to Lady Mary. But what kind of man do you take me for, to think that I would stand idly by and let you take her from me?"

"I took you for a man of better judgment than was warranted, apparently," Rochford snapped. "Have you not spoken to Lady Mary? Did she not tell you why I wished to see you?"

"No," Browning replied somewhat stiffly. "I have not yet seen her. She sent me a note to meet her in the park this afternoon, but I did not go. I—I had to confront you first. I could not let her tell me she was marrying you without putting up a fight for her." He straightened his shoulders and lifted his chin, staring Rochford in the eye.

"Well, if you *had* gone to see her," the duke said, "I feel sure that she would have told you that I have a living available. I am considering giving it to you. St. Swithin in the village of Overby, near my manor house at Dancy Park."

The clergyman looked first stunned, then eager. Then, as if remembering what he was about, he pulled his face into sober lines and grew even stiffer, if that was possible. "It is, of course, a position that anyone would love to have. However, I cannot accept a bribe to look the other way while you marry the woman I love."

"Good Gad!" Rochford exclaimed. "If I have to suffer much more of this inanity, I can guarantee you that I will *not* make the offer. I am not trying to bribe you, you young fool! I have no interest in marrying Lady Mary Calderwood."

Mr. Browning gaped at Rochford. Francesca stared at him in almost equal astonishment.

"But everyone says you—you have been dancing attendance on her," the young man sputtered.

"I have spent a great deal of time with her, listening to her sing your praises," Rochford responded. "I can only assume from her vision of you that you must display better sense when you are around her."

Browning had the grace to blush at those words, and Francesca had to press her lips together to keep a gurgle of laughter from spilling out. She felt suddenly a great deal more cheerful, almost buoyant.

"Lady Mary has told me the entire story of your blighted hopes," Rochford went on. "And she related her father's not unreasonable demand that she shall not marry a man who cannot provide for her. A living would give you the ability to provide for a wife and family, and would, presumably, encourage the lady's father to approve of your suit. She asked me for my help, and I agreed to speak to you about the living at St. Swithin's, which opened up quite recently."

Mr. Browning simply stood, staring at the duke, as his face slowly registered a realization of the opportunity that had opened for him and of exactly what his actions might have cost him.

"Oh," he said at last, weakly. Finally, squaring his shoulders again, he went on in a subdued voice, "I beg your pardon, sir. I—I shall not bother you further." He bowed toward Rochford and then toward Francesca. "Ma'am."

He turned to leave, and Rochford said, "Tomorrow morning at ten o'clock."

Browning swiveled back around to face him. "Then you—you'll still interview me?"

"Yes. Love makes fools of us all, I fear. I would like to speak to you under…better circumstances."

"Thank you, Your Grace." The young man's face underwent a lightning change, eager hope spreading over his features. "I am so… Thank you."

He seemed to think better of any lengthier speech, and simply gave another bow and strode out of the room.

"Well," Francesca said lightly. "So now you are finding husbands for your prospective wives."

He turned back to her, giving her a half smile. "I did not find him. He was presented to me."

"But you are going to make it possible for her to marry him."

He shrugged and returned to his seat opposite her. "I find I have little interest in wooing a woman who is in love with another man."

"Were you interested in wooing her?"

"I tried to be."

"So all these things—the ride in the park, calling on her—they were—"

"Conversations about her desire to marry Mr. Browning and how that could be achieved."

No wonder Mary Calderwood had sung the duke's praises the other night! Now her conversation with the girl appeared in an entirely different light. Mary had thought herself lucky not because the duke wanted her, but because he was helping her to obtain the husband *she* desired.

Francesca chuckled. "I should be cross with you. You led me to believe that you were interested in her!"

"I did not say any such thing."

Had he not? She could not remember exactly what had been said. But he certainly had not told her the complete truth regarding the girl; he had never mentioned a word about this scheme to find employment for the man she loved.

It was probably something she should be miffed about, she thought, but she could not bring herself to care.

"Do you still intend to give the man the living at St. Swithin's?" Francesca asked.

"Probably." He shrugged. "It would be a welcome change, I imagine, to the people of St. Swithin's, to have a vicar who cared passionately about anything. The last one could barely keep his eyes open during his own sermons."

"You do not think he is a trifle…impulsive?"

A grin touched Rochford's lips. "He is that. One hopes today may have taught him a lesson. If he seems seriously unstable tomorrow, I shall not offer it to him, of course. But he is young and in love, and one does foolish things at such times."

"Yes, one does," Francesca agreed quietly. That was one thing she knew far too well.

She finished her tea in the best of spirits and was, frankly, tempted to linger. However, as she had plans to attend the opera that evening with Sir Alan and his daughter, she had to take her leave.

Rochford, unsurprisingly, insisted that she and her maid be driven home in his carriage rather than walking the few blocks to her house. Francesca, leaning back against the luxurious leather seats, contemplated the meaning of her discovery. Rochford had already ruled out Althea Robart and Caroline Wyatt, and now it was clear that he had no interest in Mary Calderwood, either.

Was he not serious about pursuing a wife? In that case, what was she to make of his comment regarding an engagement announcement at the ball?

It could be that one of the two choices remaining would catch his interest—or had already done so. After all, Damaris seemed the most prepared to take on the duties of a duchess, and Lady de Morgan was the most attractive of all the prospects. However, Francesca had seen little about the duke that bespoke a man in love with either prospect. He had not mentioned either of the women even once. And according to the gossip, only Lady Mary had appeared to be the object of his pursuit.

But if he was not serious about marriage, then why had he come to her and asked for her help with the ball?

And in light of the ball and its intent, why had he kissed her?

LOST IN SUCH MUSINGS, Francesca went straight to her room when she returned home. It was already time to start preparing for her evening out with the Sherbournes. She bathed and ate a quick supper, which was brought to her on a tray in her room. It was often what she did when she dined at home alone in the evenings, especially when she had to dress for an evening out. It was easier on the servants, and, besides, she invariably felt a trifle foolish dining alone at the long table.

She hummed to herself as she sat down before her mirror and Maisie began the lengthy process of putting up her hair. Maisie was an artist at arranging hair, and she would not be rushed. Francesca opened her jewelry box and glanced over the earrings within. She picked up a pair of jet bobs, then set them down, and opened the small, secret drawer in the bottom. She took out the sapphire earrings Rochford had given her fifteen years ago and laid them in her palm.

She studied the rich, dark blue stones, their depth brightened by the tiny diamonds surrounding them. She had never worn them. At first she had not done so because their engagement was secret, and after that, the thought of wearing them had been too painful. Even when the years had worn away most of the pain, she had been reluctant to put them on. It had seemed somehow wrong.

However, it struck her now that it was quite foolish to hide away such lovely jewelry. Especially tonight, when she was going to wear an evening gown of deep blue. She put the earrings in her earlobes and turned her head from side to side, studying the effect as the diamonds caught and reflected the light.

"Oh, my lady!" Maisie sucked in her breath in appreciation. "Those are beautiful, those are. And won't they look a treat with your dress?"

"I was just thinking the same thing." Francesca smiled at her maid in the mirror.

"Are you going to wear the bracelet, as well?"

"I don't know." Francesca pulled out the circlet of diamonds and sapphires.

It was not a heavy bracelet, but the work was exquisite, and the jewels were of the highest quality, exactly the epitome of taste and elegance that one would expect Rochford to choose. She slipped it on her wrist and admired it.

"You know…I believe I will."

Maisie helped her into the blue ball gown, a gossamer voile dress of deep blue laid over a lighter blue underskirt, the contrast of colors repeated in the sleeves. Francesca had just stepped into her slippers when there was the sound of a thunderous knock downstairs.

Maid and mistress looked at each other in surprise. It was too early for Sir Alan's arrival, and in any case, he would not have pounded so rudely upon the door. Curious, Francesca went to the door of her bedchamber and opened it as Maisie went on about her business, pulling out Francesca's light evening cloak, fan and gloves, and laying them out on the bed.

A man's voice reverberated downstairs, strident and aggressive. Francesca stiffened. She did not recognize the voice so much as the manner. What was Mr. Perkins doing here? He had promised to wait until Saturday.

Her hand tightened on the doorknob, her insides clenching. She should have known that he would not keep to his promise. She hesitated. She did not want to go down and face him, and for a short moment she was tempted to stay there and let Fenton deal with the man.

It was only a fleeting thought, however, for she knew there was no way Fenton could make Perkins leave, and Perkins was exactly the boorish sort who would refuse to go. Indeed, it would not surprise her at all if the man decided to bully his way up the stairs to find her. She had to get rid of him before Sir Alan arrived.

So, with a sigh, she started downstairs. The voices were rising in volume and heat as she approached, and as she rounded the corner of the stairway, she saw Perkins reach out and grab her butler by his shirtfront, bunching the material in his fist and giving the man a shake.

"By God, she will see me, or I'll know why!"

Fenton's face turned dangerously purple with rage, and Francesca ran quickly down the last few steps.

"I am here, Mr. Perkins, so you can stop your bellowing."

He let go of Fenton and swung around. Only a few

feet from him now, Francesca could see that his eyes were bloodshot and his face puffier than the last time she had seen him. The distinct smell of alcohol hung on the air around him.

"You," he said heavily.

"Yes. I."

"My lady," Fenton began, almost quivering with rage.

"Yes, Fenton, I know. You did all you could to stop him. But I think it is best that I speak to Mr. Perkins. If you will come with me…?" She gestured toward the drawing room, then strode off in that direction, and Perkins followed her.

When they reached the drawing room, she turned around to face him. "Now. What are you doing here? I have plans for this evening. I did not expect you until Saturday."

"Maybe I don't want to wait until Saturday," he retorted. "After the way you tossed me out of your party last week, I decided I needn't stand on formalities."

With an insolent grin, he plopped down in a chair without waiting for her to sit first.

Firmly suppressing her distaste, Francesca took a seat on the couch across from him, saying evenly, "I had nothing to do with that. However, when one arrives at a party uninvited, I imagine one might expect a bit of rudeness."

"I expect nothing else from the high and mighty duke," he sneered. "He's always held himself better than the rest of us. Haughston'd be spinning in his grave if he knew Rochford was sniffing around you." Perkins cast a baleful glance at her. "No doubt he's hoping to set you up as his next mistress."

Francesca drew in her breath sharply, startled by his words. Anger followed an instant later, and she jumped to her feet. "How dare you speak such lies? Rochford would never do such a thing."

Perkins let out a short laugh. "Any man would."

"That's absurd," Francesca told him stiffly. "Rochford is an honorable man."

"Honor's got nothing to do with it. 'Tis lust that pulls that cart."

"You could not possibly understand a man like Rochford."

He quirked an eyebrow at her. "A man's a man, for all the fine airs he puts on, I can tell you that." An ill-humored grin split his face. "Don't tell me you're thinking you can bring the man to marry you?"

"Of course not!" Francesca turned and walked away from him.

"Best not be," he continued. "That one'll marry for duty and naught else."

She stopped and turned back, facing him with all the hauteur of which she was capable. "I am well aware of that. I can assure you that I have no intention of trying to 'bring' him to marry me. Nor do I have any intention of discussing my personal life with you."

"All right, then. Let's talk business. Do you have my money?" He crossed his arms and waited, looking at her.

Francesca, gazing back at him, felt her momentary anger drain out of her, leaving only the apprehension than had been haunting her for the past two and a half weeks. She took a step forward even though it felt more comfortable to be standing several feet away from the man. She suspected that it was important, as it was with an animal, not to let Perkins see that she was afraid.

"I—" Her voice was shaky, and she stopped, beginning again, injecting some iron into her words. The moment was upon her, and she had to try to save her house.

She started again. "I have a proposition for you."

CHAPTER FOURTEEN

"Do you?" He leered. "And what might that be?"

"I am prepared to pay you a sum of money today—two hundred pounds, say." Now that she had started, Francesca felt calmer. She had thought about it a great deal, and this, she had decided, was her best hope. "The money will be above and beyond the debt you claim my late husband owed you. In return, you will give me a reasonable time in which to raise the whole amount."

"Will I? And just what is 'a reasonable time'?"

"Six months."

"Six months? You ask me to wait for six months to take possession of a house that is rightfully mine? My lady, I think you overestimate your powers of persuasion." He rose to his feet.

"You cannot lose," Francesca assured him quickly. "If I am unable to raise the money, you will keep the two hundred pounds." Of course, she did not tell him that she had not raised the whole £200 yet. If he agreed, she would have to sell her team and carriage to reach that amount.

"And if I am able to pay you the five thousand

pounds in six months, you will get two hundred more than you asked for," she went on. "If you will but think about it, I believe you will see the advantages for you."

"So you are saying that I should let you live in the house free for six months." Perkins sauntered toward her.

Francesca faced him, refusing to retreat. "Hardly free. It seems to me that two hundred pounds is a very sizable rent for that period of time. And you would not have to face the trouble and expense of taking me to court. You must be aware that it will not be as easy as you said to take my home from me in court."

"Just how do you intend to raise the money in six months if you cannot raise it now?" he asked. "What do you think you will do—sell the house? I can sell it as soon as I take possession—and get the entire price, not just the debt your husband acquired. Why should I let you do it?"

"Because what you are doing is reprehensible!" Francesca shot back. "To take my home because of some foolish bet my husband made years ago!"

"Reprehensible, am I?" His mouth curved up again in his cocky sneer. "Seems you've always thought poorly of me. You never liked me dirtying your house, did you? You looked down on me from the moment I walked in the door. I wasn't good enough for your husband."

He was close enough now that she could again smell the alcohol on his breath, but Francesca continued to stand her ground, carefully schooling her face.

"You encouraged Andrew in his follies," she told him. "I never said that he was superior to you."

"You didn't have to say it. I could see it in your face. His, too. He was a Haughston, family came over with the Conqueror, but I was just some squire's youngest son. Well, my birth was as good as any."

"It was not your birth that I objected to. It was what you chose to do with your life."

"I was no worse than your esteemed husband."

"Small compliment there!"

"Yet he was good enough for you to marry, whereas I wasn't even worth a smile." He closed the distance between them, and there was a dark look in his eyes that made Francesca back up a step. "If I came near you, you moved away. Just like now. If I paid you a compliment, you sneered at me. If I touched you, you shoved my hand aside."

"What did you expect?" she retorted. "I was a married woman. I was not about to dally with you or any man. My husband was your friend. Only the basest sort would have made advances to his wife."

"The basest sort, eh?" He took another step, and Francesca backed up again. The wall was behind her. She knew that if she retreated any more, she would come up against it, so she turned to move away.

But Perkins' arm shot forward, his hand slapping into the wall, barring her passage. "Not so fast, my lady. *I* have a proposition for *you*."

Francesca faced him. Her heart was pounding wildly

in her chest, and her stomach was suddenly icy, but she would not let him see that he frightened her. She was sure that was precisely the reaction he was hoping for.

"And what might that be?" She was pleased at how coolly her voice came out.

"You can continue to live here. No rent. No two hundred pounds. I'll even forgive the debt…after a while." He smiled coldly, and there was a look in his eyes that made Francesca's stomach turn. He raised his other hand and stroked his forefinger down her cheek. "All you have to do is…be *mistress* of the house."

Francesca stared at him, too stunned to speak.

"Don't look so shocked. It's what women like you do every day, except you like to wrap it up in fancy words and ceremonies. You sell yourselves to live like this. You did it with Haughston. You'd do it with Rochford. If you want to stay here, you will do it with me."

Francesca finally broke free of her paralysis, and she jerked away. "You must be joking!"

"No, that I'm not." His voice was laced with amusement as he added mockingly, "If you will but think about it, I am sure that you will see the advantages for you."

"I would never be your mistress," Francesca spat back, the revulsion she felt written so clearly on her face that even in his inebriated state, he could see it. "I would rather starve than sleep with you!"

"Is that right?" His face went cold and hard, all the amusement leaving it, as his hand lashed out and grabbed her arm. "Why don't we just see about that?"

He jerked her toward him so suddenly and roughly that Francesca stumbled and fell forward, coming up heavily against his chest. He let go of her, but only to wrap his arm around her and crush her to him. His other hand clamped down on her face, turning it up toward him.

Terror rushed through her, and she stamped down as hard as she could on his instep, grateful that she had worn slippers with a bit of a heel. His arm loosened automatically as he let out a small cry of pain, and she wrenched away from him.

She ran to the fireplace and grabbed the poker, swinging around to face him, her improvised weapon brandished in the air. "Get out of here or I'll have you thrown out!"

"Really?" he sneered, starting toward her. "You think that old fool can throw me out? I'd like to see him try."

"Stop! If you touch me, I shall have you thrown in gaol. Do you want to run for the Continent again?"

"You won't be talking much once I'm done with you," he told her, and the smile that spread across his face was cold with menace. He took another step toward her. "I'm going to enjoy taking you down a peg."

He rushed at her then, and Francesca shrieked, swinging at him with all her strength. To her surprise, she managed to land a blow on his upper arm hard enough to make a satisfying *thwack*. But as she pulled back to strike again, he wrapped his fist around the poker and jerked it out of her grasp, tossing it behind him, where it crashed into a small table.

She screamed again and turned to run, and he lunged after her. However, the five glasses of blue ruin he had consumed before he came to see her impaired his judgment of distance, and he hooked a foot in the leg of a chair and stumbled, falling heavily to his knees. He struggled to his feet, but stopped short at the distinctive sound of a pistol cocking.

"Do not take another step unless you want a hole through you," came Fenton's voice, rather less calm than normal.

Both Francesca and her attacker swung around to face the speaker. Had she been less afraid, Francesca might have laughed at the sight of her aged butler standing there, crisp as ever, not a hair out of place, holding one of Andrew's dueling pistols. Beside him, the cook wielded an iron skillet.

As they stood there, locked in a silent tableau, there came the sound of running footsteps on the stairs. A moment later, Maisie and the parlor-maid burst into the room. Maisie carried a pair of scissors, and the parlor-maid held a broom at ready. And last, there was the pot boy running in, gripping the cook's cleaver in both hands.

Francesca's eyes filled with tears at the sight of her loyal servants. "Thank you, Fenton. Everyone. I think Mr. Perkins is leaving now."

Perkins shot her a look filled with hatred. "You think you've won? You think I'm going to quietly fade away?

You made your choice, and now you have to live with it. I withdraw my offer. You'll have to beg me to service you now."

"That will never happen!"

"You think not?" His face contorted with rage. "We'll see how fine a tune you're talking after I've tossed you out into the street. Humiliated in front of all your fine friends. Penniless, homeless, facing debtors' prison…or worse." He let out a bitter laugh. "I can see you now, trying to scrape by, living in a garret, freezing, hungry. What do you think you'll do? Become a seamstress, squinting your eyes out over your stitches, hands so cold you'll get chilblains, because you can't afford to heat your bare room? Or maybe you think you'll turn to selling hats to the women who were once your friends.

"They won't hire you, you know. Even for such lowly tasks. You can swallow your pride, mayhap, and go looking for work, but no one will take you. You aren't smart enough to be a governess, and no sane wife would hire you anyway. You can't sew well enough to do that, either. Scrub floors? Cook? Wash dishes?" He sneered. "You haven't got any skills, my lady. The only way you could make a living is on your back."

"Shut up!" Francesca cried, trembling with fury. "Just stop it. Get out of my house and never come here again. Do you understand me?"

"Oh, aye, I understand you well enough," he replied. "Now you understand me. If you aren't out of this house by tomorrow evening, I am taking it from you. And none of your…defenders—" he cast a contemptuous look at the servants clustered in the doorway "—will be able to stop me."

With that, he turned and strode off. The cluster of people in the doorway moved back quickly to let him pass, Fenton carefully staying beyond the other man's reach and keeping the pistol trained steadily on him.

Francesca sank into a chair, her legs suddenly too weak to stand. The servants trailed after Perkins, except for Maisie, who scurried over to Francesca and knelt beside her chair, gazing worriedly into her face.

"Are you all right, ma'am?"

Francesca nodded. She was still trembling, and her thoughts were scattered. She wanted to burst into tears, and only the sense of decorum ingrained in her since childhood kept her functioning.

"Yes, of course," she managed to say, though she had to swallow back the tears before she could continue. "I—I think that I shall go up to my room."

She rose to her feet, hoping they would support her as far as her bedchamber, and Maisie popped up with her. "Shall I help you?"

Francesca shook her head and summoned up a faint smile. "No. I am fine. I just…need some time alone to think."

She walked out of the room, Maisie trailing uncertainly behind her. The other servants were clustered in the entryway, speaking in hushed urgency, but they broke off immediately when she emerged from the drawing room. Fenton stepped forward, and the others remained behind him, all gazing at Francesca with mingled anxiety and sympathy.

"My lady, if there is any way in which I can be of service to you…" Fenton began in his measured tones, his face tight with concern.

"Thank you, Fenton. If you would inform Sir Alan when he arrives that I am indisposed…"

"Of course, my lady." Fenton bowed gravely.

Francesca nodded and started upstairs. She climbed on shaky legs, hand on the banister to help pull herself up. Emotions were boiling and bubbling in her chest, threatening to burst out of her in shrieks or tears—she was not sure which, perhaps both. She could feel all the servants' concerned gazes on her back as she climbed, and it was all she could do to hold back her tears.

She barely made it to her room and closed the door before she burst into sobs. She collapsed on the floor, laying her head on her arms on the seat of a chair, and cried. Fury and fear and shame swirled within her, tangling and warring and blending into a cataclysmic outpouring.

What was she to do? How would she live? Perkins' words battered at her, ripping through the barricades she had constructed over the past few weeks. She knew that her brother would take her in; she would not have to live on the streets as Perkins had pictured. But she burned with the humiliation, the utter defeat, of spending the rest of her life as a dependent relative.

She would have no home of her own, nothing that belonged to her, other than the clothes on her back. She would be living always on another's kindness, hovering at the edges of Dominic and Constance's life—observing their children, their marriage, their happiness. She would have to give up the life she had struggled so hard to keep since Andrew's death. All her cleverness, all her scrambling to find enough money to keep herself and her little family of servants afloat, would now be for naught.

Not only would she be displaced, but Fenton and the others would be turned out, as well. She could hardly expect her brother to absorb the cost of several more servants, even if any of them wished to uproot their lives and remove to the country to live. She had failed them, and she knew that mixed in with their concern for her was a very real fear for themselves. Cook would have little problem, of course, but what about Fenton? He was growing rather old now to find a new position.

Almost worse than anything else, though, was the knowledge that everyone in the *ton* would know of her plight. She would be an object of pity to some and a subject of scorn to others. Whatever any of them felt for her, there would be a certain condescension laced through it. Everyone would know that she had failed. Everyone would know what sort of husband Haughston had been, how little he had cared for her, how foolishly he had thrown away both their lives. No matter how little love she held for Andrew, it shamed her unbearably to have others know what a pitiful wreck her marriage had been. Even if she were to survive a battle in court with Perkins, her life would have been splashed all over the gossip circuit for everyone to pick over.

Her skin crawled at the thought. She felt almost physically ill at the idea of Perkins living in her house—walking through her rooms, owning her beloved little sitting room or sleeping here in her bedchamber.

Desperately, she tried to think of some way to save herself, but her brain skittered about wildly, unable to focus on anything.

Downstairs she heard the sound of a man's voice, and she knew that Sir Alan must have arrived. He was a good, kind man, and he was a little entranced, even dazzled, by her. If she gave him any encouragement, he would fall in love with her. She could marry him and escape the bleak life before her. She was sure that most women would offer him that encouragement.

But she could not. She could not bring herself to marry a man she did not love simply to make the rest of her life secure.

But what other path was open to her? She had been trying to find a way to escape this mess for over two weeks, and still she had discovered no way out.

She jumped to her feet and began to pace the room, wiping at the tears that streaked her face. Her nerves vibrated wildly, and she could not keep still. In fits and starts, tears continued to come, and now and then she could not hold back a little hiccuping sob.

In her despair, she could think of nothing. Only one thought penetrated the fog; only one word sent any ease through her: *Sinclair.*

She turned and grabbed up the light evening cloak that Maisie had laid out for her. Flinging it around her shoulders, she went out her door and lightly down the stairs. Peering carefully around the corner of the staircase, she was relieved to see that the servants had apparently retreated to the kitchen to discuss the evening's events.

On tiptoe, she slipped down the last few steps and out the front door, closing it softly behind her. Pulling up the hood of her cloak to hide her face, she hurried off down the street.

A FOOTMAN IN ELEGANT blue-and-white livery opened the door. He frowned at the sight of a woman on his doorstep.

"Go on, get away from here! What do you think you're doing?" he told her bluntly, starting to close the door.

"No!" Francesca cried, holding out a hand to stop him.

She knew that the fellow must take her for a prostitute or some other low creature, and she understood why. No respectable woman would show up on a gentleman's doorstep like this, certainly not unaccompanied. But she could not let him keep her out.

"Fetch Cranston," she told him, and the combination of her cultured voice and the use of the butler's name must have given the man pause, for he hesitated.

"Wait here," he said finally, closing the door, and a few minutes later the door opened to reveal Rochford's starched, efficient butler.

Cranston peered out the door at her, his expression full of disdain until she reached up and pushed back her hood far enough that he could see her face. His eyes widened. "My lady!"

"Please, I must see him," she said in a low voice.

"Of course, of course, please come in. I am so sorry."

Francesca pulled her hood forward again, not eager to let any of the other servants glimpse her face, and Cranston led her quickly down the hall to Rochford's study. The room was empty, but the butler ushered her inside and took her cloak.

"I will inform His Grace immediately that you are here," he assured her, no trace of the curiosity he must feel registering on his carefully blank face.

"Thank you, Cranston."

He left, closing the door behind him. Francesca turned away. The frantic despair that had sent her flying to Rochford was ebbing now, giving way to doubt. *What would he think of her, coming to him this way?*

There was the sound of hurrying footsteps in the hall outside, and the duke rushed in, frowning. His eyes went to her, taking in at once her tear-streaked face and tense posture.

"Francesca! My God. What happened?" He swung the door shut behind him and came to her, hands outstretched. "Are you ill? Is it Dom? Selbrooke?"

She shook her head. "No, no, it is none of that."

He took her hands in his, and they felt so warm and strong that tears sprang into her eyes and she let out a single shuddering sob. "I'm sorry! I should not have come here, but I didn't know what to do!"

"Of course you should come to me," he told her, leading her over to the small sofa and pulling her down onto it with him. "Where else should you go? Just tell me what is wrong."

"And you will take care of it for me?" she asked, trying to smile, but she could feel it wobble.

"I will strive my utmost to do so," he assured her.

Suddenly she was crying. She tried to hold it back; she would have said that she had no tears left to cry. But the kindness in his smile, the concern in his eyes, pierced her, and the tears came flooding out.

"Oh, Sinclair, I'm sorry, I shouldn't—I'm so scared—"

"Francesca, dearest…" He pulled her over and into his lap, cradling her in his arms.

The endearment, the comfort of his embrace, somehow broke her heart, and she sobbed, burying her face in his chest, her hand digging into his lapels. She cried, unable to speak or even think coherently.

He stroked her back and head, his hands knocking loose some of the curls that Maisie had so carefully arranged. He murmured soft, soothing sounds as his hands moved gently over her. Francesca's sobs gradually began to wind down. Her breathing slowed, and the tears stopped. She leaned against his chest, comforted by his strong arms around her, the steady thump of his heart beneath her ear.

The movement of his hands was incredibly comforting. She felt, at least for the moment, safe and secure, warmed by his heat. She could believe that nothing bad could ever happen to her here.

Yet, she realized, at the same time his touch stirred something inside her. She closed her eyes, amazed that she could feel such a thing, especially at a time as this. Something brushed against her hair, and she realized, wonderingly, that he must have kissed her.

His hand drifted down her arm. She could feel the brush of his breath against her neck, and then his lips pressed lightly against her skin. Francesca drew a shaky breath, her body flaming to life. Her nipples prickled, hardening and pressing against her dress.

She bent her head down, exposing her neck further to him, and she felt him stiffen, his skin suddenly searing. He pressed his mouth upon the back of her neck, velvety soft upon her skin. His breath rasped harshly in his throat, tickling her flesh, raising goose bumps along her arms, and she shivered.

She wanted to melt into him, to open herself to him. She had never felt this way before—so vulnerable, yet at the same time reveling in that vulnerability. A pulsing heat began low in her abdomen, and she was aware of an ache deep inside her. She yearned, she realized, for him to lay claim to her, to sink deep inside her. The depth of her desire was so new and different that it startled her into stillness.

He tensed. "Oh, God, I'm sorry, Francesca. You came to me for help, and I've—"

Rochford gently lifted her and set her from him. She felt bereft and wished that he would take her back into his arms. But she was at least fully enough in possession of her senses to realize that she could not ask that.

He handed her a snowy white handkerchief, and she took it, not looking at him, and stood up, walking away as she dried the tears from her face. Rochford let out a small sigh and rose, too, watching her.

She turned back and found him studying her. A blush started up her throat. "I am sorry."

"Stop saying that." His voice was harsh, and he seemed to realize it. He closed his eyes and visibly relaxed. "Francesca…tell me what is troubling you. You said that you were scared. Who has frightened you? What happened?"

She drew a breath, gathering courage. Suddenly the thought that had seized her back home in the midst of her despair no longer seemed so feasible. "I—I came to ask you for a loan."

He stared at her, dumbstruck.

She hurried on. "I know it is terribly improper, and

I had sworn that I would not ask you, but I can think of no other way, and I cannot bear to think of that man in my house. I must do something!"

"Man! What man? Are you telling me that a man broke in to your home?"

"No, no. He did not break in. It is Perkins."

"Galen Perkins?" Rochford's dark eyes were suddenly a little frightening. "Perkins is in your house?"

He started toward the door, and Francesca hurried to grab his hand. "No! No, he isn't there now. I am telling this all wrong. Please, come back and sit down. Let me begin at the beginning."

"All right." He allowed her to lead him back to the small sofa and sat down with her. Her hand was still in his, and he curled his fingers around hers. "Tell me."

"Lord Haughston—"

"It starts that far back?"

"Yes, it does. Andrew was…imprudent."

He let out a short, harsh laugh that held no humor. "Lord Haughston was a fool."

Francesca started to protest, then shrugged. "Yes, he was. You were right about him." She turned her face away from him, unable to look into his eyes as she went on. "I was an idiot to marry him. You tried to tell me, and I would not listen. I'm sorry."

She looked at him then and was surprised to see the pain that flashed in his eyes. "It is I who am sorry. I knew it was useless to tell you, with you in the throes of new love, but I had to try. I made a mess of it."

"I was certain that you warned me against him only because you were…bitter."

Rochford had come back from his estate after her engagement was announced and had told her in a cold, hard voice that she was making a mistake to marry such a fool as Andrew Haughston. She remembered the pain that had sprung up in her afresh when she saw him, and she knew that it was that pain, more than any love for Andrew, that had made her storm out of the room, refusing to listen to him.

"I *was* bitter," he admitted with a grimace. "But it did not mean I was not telling you the truth. I handled it poorly. I would have been better served writing you a letter instead of appearing on your doorstep. I could have presented my case more clearly. I fear that I have never been very clearheaded around you. I should have proved to you what sort of man Haughston was— stayed there until you listened to me and believed. But I let my deuced pride rule me."

Francesca smiled and squeezed his hand. "Oh, Sinclair. Pray do not blame yourself. It was my fault and no one else's that I married the man. I should have been more careful. Should not have rushed into marriage. It was just— I wanted to love him. I wanted to believe that he was the perfect man for me. I was hurt and lonely, and angry at you."

She looked into his eyes. "You called Andrew a fool, but I was ten times that, hastening to marry because I wanted to prove to you that my heart was not broken."

He went still, his fingers tightening on hers. Realizing how much she had just revealed, Francesca jumped to her feet and walked away.

"But that is not the point of my story. What is pertinent is that Lord Haughston left me almost nothing when he died. Indeed, he left me with a number of debts to pay. Since he died, I have been barely scraping by."

"I know," he told her quietly.

Francesca stared. "You know?" Heat rushed into her cheeks. "Is it common knowledge? Does everyone in the *ton* know?"

"No, no," he hastened to assure her, rising and crossing to her. "It is only I. I had my suspicions how he might have left you, knowing the way he was. I…made a few discreet inquiries."

Her embarrassment deepened. All these years, the man from whom she had most wanted to hide her financial problems had known about them. "You must have thought me a terrible fool."

"No, of course not."

She sighed. "I suppose it should not matter. You have always known the worst of me."

A faint smile touched his face and was gone. "True. As you have seen the worst of me."

His remark brought a smile to her face. "Have I? Then your worst must be a trifling thing."

"As is yours."

Her heart warmed within her, and she had to swallow

hard to suppress her emotion. She turned away, clearing her throat and saying, "Well, I learned to economize— you would be most surprised to see me shop." Looking away from him as she was, she did not see the pain and regret that colored his features. "I have managed to get by. But now Perkins—"

"What the devil does Perkins have to do with anything?"

"He won my house from Andrew in a card game!" Francesca whirled back around, rage rising up in her all anew. "That...*bastard* threw away my home on a hand of cards!"

A red light flared in Rochford's eyes, and he let out a string of curses. Francesca was not certain whether they were directed at Perkins or her late husband. She knew only that they made her feel strangely better.

"Perkins told me that if I repaid the money Andrew owed him, he would tear up the paper Andrew signed giving him ownership of the house. I have sold what I can, but it is completely beyond my means. But if—"

She swallowed, not daring to look him in the face. What she was asking was completely improper. A woman could not take such a large amount of money from a man without compromising her virtue, and she feared that he would think terribly of her for doing so. For a moment, she thought she could not go on.

Then, in a rush, she said, "If you would but loan it to me, I could give him the money. I would pay it back,

I promise. I will sell the house and that will give me enough money to—"

"You will not sell your house," Rochford told her flatly.

"It is either that or lease it during the Season, but it would take me years to repay the loan then, and, truly, if I sold it, I could repay you and purchase a smaller house."

"You are not leasing it. You are not selling it. And there will be no loan."

Francesca turned to stare at him, her stomach clenching in despair.

The duke's face was so stony, his eyes so flat and cold, that any words she might have spoken died. "I'll be damned if I'll let that bloody ivory-turner have your house. Cranston will call the carriage and send you home." He started toward the door.

"Rochford! What are you doing?" Anxiously, Francesca started after him.

He turned and said shortly, "I am going to see Perkins."

CHAPTER FIFTEEN

"SINCLAIR! NO!" Francesca ran after him, grabbing his arm and tugging him to a stop. "What are you going to do? I won't let you simply pay off my debt for me."

"Do not worry yourself about that. 'Tis highly unlikely that there will be any exchange of money involved. It is my opinion that Perkins will find he needs to return to the Continent forthwith."

"Sinclair!" Francesca's eyes widened in alarm. "You mean to go over there to fight him? No, you must not. Truly, it is not worth it. You will get hurt."

The duke cocked an eyebrow at her. "Are you suggesting that I cannot take care of a weasel like Perkins?"

"He killed a man!"

"I am considered something of a shot, as well—in my own humble way."

"I know that." Francesca grimaced. "But you are a gentleman, with a code of honor, whereas Perkins is not bound by any such rules."

"Quite frankly, where Perkins is concerned, I don't feel particularly bound by the rules, either."

"No, please…you must not get involved in a duel. I

would never forgive myself if something happened to you."

"Your faith in me is a trifle underwhelming, my dear." As she started to protest again, he shook his head and placed his forefinger against her lips. "There will not be a duel. I can promise you that. I can deal adequately with Perkins without that."

Francesca released his arm, though she still frowned. "He will not fight fair. You cannot trust him."

"Believe me, I do not intend to."

He stepped away and walked to the door, then turned to look back at her. She was standing in the middle of the room, watching him forlornly. Her dark blue eyes were huge in her pale face.

Rochford muttered an oath beneath his breath and strode back to her, sweeping her up in his arms and kissing her. Startled, she did not move for an instant, but then she wrapped her arms around his neck and pressed her body up into his. He kissed her thoroughly, taking his time, and when at last he set her down, she was breathless, her heart beating like a wild thing.

Then he was gone, striding out into the hall, calling for Cranston. Francesca sank down into a chair, dazed. She heard Rochford and his butler talking in low voices in the hallway, but she could not understand what they were saying. A short while later, Cranston appeared in the doorway and bowed.

"My lady, the carriage is at the door to take you home."

"Thank you, Cranston." She summoned up a smile, though she suspected that it was not a very successful effort.

He held out her cloak, and she slipped into it, tying it in the front. Pulling the hood up to conceal her, she followed the butler to the front door. As promised, Rochford's carriage waited outside, and Cranston handed her up into it. She wondered what he must think about these peculiar goings-on, but his face, of course, revealed none of his thoughts.

She had hoped to see the duke again before she left, but she thought that he must have gone straight out after giving his butler instructions. Nerves jittered in her stomach, and she drew a deep breath, trying to calm them.

Sinclair would be perfectly all right, she told herself. She had heard Dominic say that Rochford "showed to advantage" and was one he would want to have on his side in a "mill," both of which statements Francesca took to be compliments to Sinclair's fighting skill.

But she could not help but worry. Perkins would not hesitate to shoot an unarmed man. If Sinclair were killed trying to help her, she would never forgive herself. She wished that she had never taken it into her head to go to Lilles House. Better by far to lose her house than to bring about injury or even death to Rochford.

And yet, beneath the guilt and the worry, there was another feeling, a giddy uprush of emotion—gratitude, yes, but more than that. Certainly there was elation at the thought that she might not have to leave her home, but it was greater than *that,* as well. It was a deep, sweet warmth, an inner satisfaction at the realization that Sinclair still cared what happened to her.

THE DUKE OF ROCHFORD wasted little time finding Galen Perkins. He went first to a gambling hall on Pall Mall that he had known Lord Haughston to frequent years ago. It was still in business, but there was no sign of Perkins. A quick inquiry to the proprietor brought the news that Perkins was no longer welcome at his club, having left the country owing a substantial sum of money. He usually could be found, however, a few doors down on Pall Mall or at a club on Bennett.

Perkins was, in fact, at the second place, so happily engaged in a game of Hazard that he did not even glance up when Rochford entered the room. The duke quietly left and, giving the doorman a gold coin to bring Perkins to him, took up a post outside.

It was ten minutes later that the burly doorman opened the door and ushered Perkins out. Perkins glanced around, saying plaintively, "What the devil are you talking about? I don't see anyone."

The man shrugged. "I don't know. He just said he had a debt to pay you."

Rochford stepped out of the shadows. "It is I."

Perkins' eyes widened, and he started to turn to go

back inside, but Rochford clamped his hand around the man's upper arm and steered him firmly into the street.

"You and I are going to have a talk."

Perkins tried to pull away. "The devil we are. I am not going with you."

"You think not?"

Rochford released Perkins' arm and planted his fist in the other man's stomach instead. Perkins doubled over as the air went out of him in a whoosh, and Rochford finished him off with an uppercut to the chin that left his lip bleeding. Perkins staggered and landed hard on the sidewalk.

The doorman had been watching them with great interest, and the duke gestured to him now. "Help me get this fellow up and into a cab. I believe it's time for him to go home."

The corner of the doorman's mouth quirked up for an instant, and he came forward, reaching down to grab Perkins' arm and haul him to his feet. Rochford signaled a hackney, and the two men bundled the pale and wheezing Perkins into it.

Rochford settled down in the seat across from Perkins. "Where are you rooming?"

Perkins regarded him in baleful silence.

Rochford sighed. "Do you really wish to have another go? I have no problem continuing, of course, but I fear you might tire of it before long."

This time Perkins muttered an address. Rochford relayed it to the driver and sat back in his seat, arms crossed, regarding the other man steadily. Perkins, his arm still wrapped protectively across his stomach, leaned in the corner of the coach, avoiding the duke's gaze.

When the hack pulled to a stop in front of a narrow, brown brick building, Rochford leaned across and took Perkins' arm, jerking him out of the coach. He released the other man for a moment to pay for the ride, and Perkins took the opportunity to bolt.

Almost casually, Rochford stretched out his foot, catching Perkins at the ankles, and he went sprawling. Rochford handed the driver his money and bent down to pull Perkins to his feet. Now bleeding from a fresh cut to his cheek, as well as the old one to his lip, Perkins offered no more resistance as Rochford steered him up the stairs and into the building.

There was another flight of stairs to climb once they were inside, and Perkins spent a few moments fumbling through his pockets for his key, but finally they were inside the room. With a contemptuous shove, the duke sent the other man sprawling onto his bed.

"Bloody hell!" Perkins burst out. "What the devil do you think you're doing?" He struggled to an upright position.

"I am sending you back to the Continent."

"What? I'm not going anywhere."

"Oh, but I think you are. First, you are going to give me the note that Lord Haughston supposedly wrote turning over his house to you. Then you are going to leave this country and never return."

"The hell I will!" Perkins' defiant cry would have been more effective if he had not staggered when he jumped to his feet and had to grab the bedstead to stay upright. "You can't make me go anywhere."

Rochford cocked one eyebrow expressively. Perkins regarded him stubbornly for a moment, then turned away.

"All right, all right," he whined, making his way to the wardrobe and pulling a handled cloth bag from the bottom of it.

Opening the bag, he set it down on the bed, then turned to the small table beside it. His back turned to Rochford, he reached inside. As he pulled his hand out of the drawer, he whirled and charged Rochford, a blade glinting in his grasp.

Rochford sidestepped neatly and sent a sharp jab into his kidney as he passed. Perkins stumbled forward under the force of the blow, and Rochford followed, grabbing the arm that held the knife and twisting it behind his back. His hand was like iron around the other man's wrist, and he jerked Perkins' arm up painfully, pulling the knife from his fingers.

"Now," he said, dropping the knife into the pocket of his jacket. "I hope we can proceed to your packing. Another stunt like that one, and you will be departing without any of your things."

"You nearly wrenched my arm out of the socket," Perkins whined, rubbing his shoulder. "Have you gone mad?"

"I am quite sane, I assure you."

"I never did anything to you. You've no right to be pushing me about."

"You have offended a lady of my acquaintance. That gives me every right. Now, hand over the note."

Perkins' mouth twisted bitterly. "That doxy! So that's her price for becoming your plaything, eh?"

Rochford's fist shot out, slamming into Perkins' cheek and knocking the man flat on the floor. Before Perkins could move, Rochford strode forward and set his boot across the other man's throat.

"I could do whatever I wished to you," he pointed out conversationally. "I hope you are intelligent enough to understand that. If I wanted, I could crush your throat right now." He pressed harder against Perkins' windpipe. "I could kill you in an instant and then have my servants toss your body in the Thames. And no one would either know or care that you are gone." He paused, then went on. "Now...I will tell you one last time. Give me the note."

Perkins had turned as white as chalk during the duke's speech, and now he dug frantically in his inner pocket and pulled out a sheet of paper. He held it upward, waving it.

Rochford relaxed his pressure somewhat and reached down to pluck the note from the other man's fingers. He unfolded and perused it, his mouth tightening as he read; then he folded up the paper and stuck it in his pocket.

"Tell me," he said conversationally. "Just as a point

of curiosity…was Haughston really so great a gudgeon as to write that note?"

Perkins set his jaw stubbornly, and Rochford pressed his foot down harder.

"No!" Perkins gasped. "I wrote it. I could always do his hand. The bird-witted clunch! I don't know how many times I wrote his vowels. He was always too disguised to remember."

With a noise of disgust, Rochford removed his foot from the other man's throat, and Perkins rose gingerly to his feet.

"You will leave England tomorrow," Rochford told him in icy tones. "And if you ever come back, I can promise you that I will put the full weight of my name and my fortune to seeing that you are prosecuted for murdering Avery Bagshaw. Do I make myself clear?"

Hatred shot from Perkins' eyes, but he nodded, reaching up to wipe the fresh blood from his mouth.

"Good." Rochford nodded. "It is my sincere hope never to see you again. Make sure I am not disappointed."

He turned and strode out the door. Behind him, Perkins glared at the door for a moment, then turned and walked stiff-legged over to the bag on the bed. He picked it up and flung it against the wall.

"We'll see about that," he muttered sullenly. "We'll bloody see about that."

FRANCESCA SAT IN the drawing room, not bothering to go upstairs and change. She was certain that Rochford would come to her when he was finished with Perkins, and if he did not, she feared that it would mean the worst. She could not possibly go up to bed with that hanging over her head.

So she kicked off her shoes and curled up in the most comfortable chair in the room, angling it so that she could keep watch out the front bow window. Time moved by at an agonizing pace.

She told herself that she did not need to worry. Rochford would take care of Perkins without coming to any harm. She had never known him to be unprepared or caught off guard. He was intelligent, as well as strong, and he would not let Perkins get the better of him, no matter how underhandedly Perkins went about it.

But no matter how much she reassured herself, Francesca could not vanquish her fear. If anything happened to Sinclair because of her, she did not know what she would do. The thought was crushing.

She closed her eyes, clasping her hands together tightly in her lap. She should not have gone to Rochford. It had been foolish. Selfish.

Yet she knew that she could not have done anything else. And if she were somehow given the chance to do it all again, she would undoubtedly do the same thing. The fact was, in all the world, out of all her family and friends, it was Rochford to whom she would always turn when she was in trouble.

And that, she realized, was the central truth of her

life. Rochford knew her better than anyone. He was the rock at the center of her world, the one person on whom she could rely.

She had ignored that fact for years, denied it, done her best to pretend that it was otherwise. She had lived as another man's wife, faithful to him in every way except the one that mattered most. Her heart belonged to Sinclair, and it always had.

It always would.

She did not fool herself that there could be any future for them. It was clear that Rochford felt some degree of passion for her—given his kisses and caresses, it would be hard to deny that fact. But she was wise enough to know that passion did not mean love, and it most certainly did not mean marriage.

Francesca had lost any hope of those things when she broke off their engagement. The duke was too proud a man to propose a second time to a woman who had jilted him. Even if, by some wild stretch of the imagination, she could believe that he would want to marry her, it would be a dereliction of his duty to his name and family for him to marry a barren widow.

No, Rochford knew where his responsibility lay, and he would marry the sort of woman he had to. Why else had he committed himself to finding a bride?

She would have no satisfaction from her love. But still, there was something deep inside her that could not help but warm to the knowledge. Her heart had been a cold thing in her chest for so many years that it was a heady experience to have it swell again with sweet emotion.

She leaned forward, spotting a man walking toward her house. She waited tensely as he came closer.

"Sinclair!" Tears sprang to her eyes as the tall figure resolved into that of the duke.

Jumping to her feet, she picked up her candle and hurried to the door. She set the candle down on the entry table and shot back the bolt, then carefully pulled the door open. Rochford was turning off the street onto her walkway.

"Sinclair!"

He looked up at her and smiled. Francesca flew down the steps and launched herself at him. He wrapped his arms around her, lifting her up and into him, and his mouth came down to meet hers.

They stood that way for a long moment, their lips sealed together and the rest of the world lost to them. But finally Francesca recalled where they were and what she was doing, and she released him and stepped back, letting out a shaky little laugh.

"I was so worried. Come in, come in…." She took his hand and led him inside, casting a glance around the darkened street.

As they had the other time he had visited her late at night, they slipped quietly down the hallway to the cozy sitting room and closed the door behind them.

"What happened?" she asked, turning to face him. "Did you see Perkins?"

"I did." He reached inside his jacket and pulled out a piece of paper. Unfolding it, he handed it to her. "Here is the note. I suggest that you burn it."

Almost unbelieving, Francesca reached her hand and took the piece of paper. She noticed that it trembled in her fingers. "You did not—you did not pay him, did you?"

"No. I swear it."

"Or kill him?"

A faint smile lifted one corner of his mouth. "Nor kill him. I persuaded the fellow to leave England. I do not think you will see him again."

"Oh, Sinclair!" Francesca raised a hand to her eyes, pressing it against them to stem the tears that threatened her. "I suppose it is very wrong—legally the house may be his—but I cannot feel anything but glad that you sent him away."

"The house is not his. Perkins admitted that the note was a forgery, just as I thought. Haughston was, God knows, mutton-headed enough to do it. But if Perkins had had this paper in his hands for the last seven years, he would have done something about it before now, even if he was in exile. Nor would he have been willing to accept money from you in lieu of taking the house. He would have gone straight to court with it when he returned home."

"Oh." Francesca thought about it. "No doubt you are right. I could have fought him in court. I should have, instead of bothering you with it."

"You did exactly as you should have. If you had

challenged him, he would have made you miserable with lies and gossip. The man is a snake. It was no bother to me. I am sorry only that you waited so long to tell me what was wrong. I would have liked to save you the weeks of worry."

His words, the gentle expression in his dark eyes, finally broke through her control. She began to cry.

"Francesca…sweetheart, no…" He went to her, pulling her gently into his arms. "Do not cry." He kissed the top of her head. "I meant to make you happy."

"I am!" Francesca let out a watery little laugh. "I am happier than I have been in—in so long."

He chuckled, his arms tightening around her, and he rubbed his cheek against her hair. "So happy that you cry."

"Exactly."

She pulled back a little and looked up into his face, wiping the tears from her cheeks. Her blue eyes shone as she gazed at him, full of tenderness and joy.

He sucked in his breath sharply. "Francesca…"

"You have been so kind, so good. I am more grateful to you than you can know."

"I do not want your gratitude," he answered, his voice rough with emotion.

"You have it anyway—and more. Much more."

Boldly she went up on tiptoe and pressed her lips to his cheek. Her hands came up to cup his face, and for a long moment they gazed into each other's eyes. Then she rose again, her mouth moving to his.

They kissed, lips hot and hungry, tongues tangling in a primal dance of desire. Heat surged between them.

His hands went to her hips, moving restlessly over her, and he pulled her more tightly against him. Francesca wrapped her arms around his neck, pressing up into him, delighting in the hard feel of his body against her softness. A deep, formless yearning grew inside her, deepening with every brush of his fingers, every movement of his mouth. Her senses sprang to life as they had done only with him. Her skin was supremely sensitive, aware of the merest touch of air upon it. Sight, sound, smell—all were magnified until she felt almost overwhelmed with the rush of sensations.

She slipped a hand up his neck, feeling the prickle of the short hairs at the back of his head, then the silken slide of the longer hair above that, thick and soft. She dug her fingers into his hair, letting the locks trail across her skin, pressing the pads of her fingers against the solidity of his skull.

He moaned as she twined her fingers through his hair, and the sound sent desire leaping through her. Her heart slammed inside her chest, her pulse racing madly. His arms went tightly around her, almost bruising in their strength, as though he could meld their bodies together.

It was, she realized, what she wanted—to feel him inside her, part of her, to be so entwined with him that there was no separation between them. She trembled, almost frightened by the intensity of her eagerness.

"No." He pulled away, gasping for air. "I don't want you this way—you must not feel that you owe me anything." He ran a hand back through his hair, taking a deep breath and visibly struggling to bring calm to his words. "I will not take advantage of you."

He looked at her, his black eyes so heated, so intense, that his very gaze sent desire lancing through her. "You do not need to repay me for what I did. That isn't why—"

"Hush." She reached up and laid a finger against his lips. "I know that is not why you helped me."

She gazed at him, drinking in his beloved face, her senses stirred by the lines of desire etched on his features. "It is my own free choice. I want to."

She realized as she spoke how very true her words were. Despite the fear that lurked inside her, despite the dread of finding that this heat and hunger would once again disappear into cold ashes, despite all the reasons why they should not continue what they were doing, she wanted to. She wanted to more than she had ever wanted anything in her life. Indeed, all she wanted in this world was him.

With a smile, she stepped forward into his arms, her face turning up to meet his.

CHAPTER SIXTEEN

"FRANCESCA…" Her name shimmered with hunger and hope on his tongue, and he wrapped his arms around her, lifting her up.

He kissed her hungrily, desperately, and Francesca clung to him with equal fervor, returning kiss for kiss, her hands digging into his jacket. He was her anchor in a maelstrom of emotions and sensations. The creator of her hunger and, at the same time, the only one who could ease it.

Untutored and clumsy with need, she moved her hands over his shoulders and up into his hair, desire increasing with every touch, driven by the awareness that it was not enough. She knew that it was his flesh she wanted to explore, his bare skin that her fingers trembled to touch. With a brazenness heretofore unknown to her, she slipped her hand beneath the edge of his jacket. The silk of his waistcoat was slick and cool beneath her fingers, and the texture of it sent tendrils of desire twisting down through her, but that was not enough, either.

She wanted to touch *him,* feel *him.* Most of all, she wanted to have *his* hands on *her.*

Sinclair set her down and reached back to pull off his jacket, flinging it carelessly to the floor. Francesca undid the buttons of his waistcoat, fumbling a little in her haste and hunger. He ripped at his carefully arranged neckcloth and tossed it in the general direction of his jacket, following it an instant afterward with his waistcoat.

He pulled her to him then as if he could wait no longer and pressed his mouth into hers. Francesca, no longer restricted by his outer garments, ran her hands over his back and chest. She could feel the heat of his skin through the thin lawn of his shirt, but still she wanted more. Bunching his shirt up in her hands, she tugged until it came free of his breeches, and she slid her hands up under the cloth onto his bare skin.

She felt his flesh twitch beneath her touch, felt the heat that flooded through him. She rubbed her hands over his back, then trailed them across it lightly, her fingernails barely scraping over his skin, testing and exploring, now digging in, now tracing the faintest of swirling patterns upon it.

His breath hissed in sharply, and Francesca felt a tremor run through him. He dug his hands into her hair, sending pins popping loose and curls tumbling, and he kissed his way down her throat, lingering on the tender white flesh. His fingers went to the back of her dress, and he let out a low curse as the row of tiny pearl-like buttons impeded him.

Francesca could not hold back a chuckle, and he

raised his head, eyes glinting with a mixture of amusement, frustration and hunger.

"You find that funny, eh?" he mock-growled.

"I find it very familiar," she returned, and then reached out to unfasten the ties of his shirt. "Much better to have these, I think."

His only reply was a murmur as he returned to kissing her neck, moving up this time to lay kisses in a line along her jaw up to her ear. His lips grazed her earring as they moved along the curve of her ear.

He paused, then once again lifted his head, narrowing his eyes as he looked at the earring. He traced his thumb across the jewel. "You are wearing the earrings I gave you."

Francesca blushed, feeling suddenly embarrassed. "Yes."

Rochford looked into her eyes, his gaze searching. She could not read his expression, and a prickle of unease crept up her back. What if the earrings reminded him of the rift between them, the anger and resentment he must have felt when she broke off their engagement? What if he thought she was presuming too much?

But he only smiled and said, "They are lovely on you."

He turned his head to look at her wrist, where the bracelet lay, then lifted her arm and placed a soft kiss upon her skin just above the jewels. Francesca felt her pulse jump beneath his mouth, betraying her.

Rochford traced his finger across the bottom of her

throat. "You need something there to match them, don't you think?"

Before she could protest, he bent and kissed the vulnerable hollow of her throat. Francesca's eyes fluttered closed, and she hoped her knees would not give way. Funny, how one tender little gesture like that could turn her insides to wax.

"Sinclair…" She smoothed her hand over his hair. "Oh, Sin."

His mouth left a hot trail up the side of her neck, and he nuzzled her ear, sending shivers through her. He murmured her name, his voice husky with desire.

He had never been like this with her before, she thought—never so bold, so tempting…so *hungry*. Desire fountained in her in response, hot and swift. She slipped her hands beneath the edges of his open shirt and slid them outwards, exploring the ridged muscles and the smooth skin with its roughening of hair. Her fingertips found the small, hard masculine nipples and circled them.

He made a noise low in his throat, and his mouth came back to claim hers. His fingers worked at the fastenings of her dress, making short work of the rest of her buttons—Francesca was rather sure that she heard a snap as a button or two popped off, as well as a rip here and there, but she did not care. All that mattered was that now his hands were on her skin, gliding across her back, bringing every inch of her flesh tinglingly alive.

Sinclair pulled her dress down over her arms, and it fell to her feet. He bent to kiss her shoulder, then moved along the hard line of her collarbone, and finally down to the softly swelling mounds of her breasts. Francesca's breath caught in her throat. Gently he edged down the lace of her chemise, and the movement of the fabric across her delicate skin was a caress. The top ruffle skimmed over her nipple, making it tighten.

His eyes, heavy and dark with desire, were fixed on her breast, watching his fingers follow the path of the cloth. Francesca trembled at the touch of his skin on her nipple, and the bud hardened even more. He traced his fingertip around the rosy button, teasing it, and moisture pooled between her legs in response. The blossoming warmth there startled her, but then he bent and took the fleshy bud into his mouth, and all thought was lost to her.

Francesca moaned, catching her lower lip between her teeth, and the noise seemed to excite him further. He wrapped his arms around her, lifting her up, as he pulled her nipple deeper into his mouth. He sucked at it gently, his tongue circling and caressing, driving the hunger in her ever higher. With each movement of his mouth, the heat deep in her abdomen grew, moist and pulsing, aching for fulfillment. She wanted to wrap her legs around him, to move against him in a way that would have made her blush if she had thought of it at any other time.

Roughly, he dragged down the other side of her

chemise and turned his attention to that breast. Francesca had to suppress a whimper, and her fingers dug into his arms.

Finally he let her slide back down his body to the floor, and his hands swept over her buttocks in a parting caress, his fingers digging into the fleshy mounds and pressing her flush against the hard ridge of his desire. With a wantonness that would have shocked her a few weeks ago, Francesca moved her hips, rubbing herself against him, and she smiled with satisfaction at the swift and unmistakable response of his body.

He tugged at the ribbon that fastened her chemise. Stretched as it had been, the bow had tightened, turning into a knot, but after a few seconds struggle, the narrow ribbon ripped, releasing her. Impatiently, he shoved the garment back from her shoulders and down. Stepping out of her slippers, Francesca reached back to untie the ribbons of her petticoat and pantaloons, circumventing the destruction of any further ties at his hand.

Her underclothes slid down to pool at her feet. Sinclair's eyes moved slowly downward, taking in every inch of her body. Francesca remembered her embarrassment the first time her husband had looked upon her naked body in bed, the urge she had felt to cover herself before him and the impatience with which he had shoved her hands away.

It made the heat rise in her face to stand like this beneath Sinclair's gaze, but she knew that only a small part of it came from any embarrassment, for her body flamed with desire at the touch of his eyes as surely as if his hands had swept over her.

He shrugged off his opened shirt, and Francesca found herself exploring the naked expanse of his chest with her eyes just as eagerly as he had looked at her. She wanted, she realized with a twinge of surprise, to see even more of him. More than that, she was filled with a yearning to touch him, to kiss and caress him. Something deep within her longed to know him in every possible way, to possess and be possessed by him, to become a part of him.

She watched as he quickly divested himself of his boots, then the rest of his clothes, the throb of her pulse quickening with every garment that slid down his skin. He came to her then, taking her by the hands, and knelt on the floor, pulling her with him. Francesca lay back upon the tangle of her petticoats, her hair spreading out around her like a shimmering golden fan.

She tightened a little, thinking, *Now is when it will come—the cold, the indifference, even disgust.* This would be the moment when she learned that nothing had changed inside, nothing was different with Sinclair. She would grow stiff, and the warm pleasure in her loins would melt away, and she would know that she had been mad to think that it could end any other way.

Rochford lay on his side next to her, propped up on his forearm, and he gazed down at her, his eyes searching her face. "I always dreamed of making love to you in my bed, of seeing your hair spread out over my pillows."

He ran his hand across her hair, then brought it back to caress her cheek and throat, saying, "But I want you too much to wait."

Lowering his head, he kissed her slowly and tenderly, his mouth moving with a gentle lack of haste that was at odds with the words he had spoken. But Francesca sensed the barely leashed passion that lay beneath his actions. It was there in his thrumming pulse, the quick intake of his breath, the searing heat of his skin. She knew that he was restraining himself by force of will, like a dam holding back the floodwaters, tamping down his desire in order to savor the pleasure of each moment.

And all she felt was that same delight. Her body warmed, and the tightness relaxed. There was no trepidation, no anxiety. She was floating on pleasure, reveling in emotions she had never expected to feel.

Francesca trailed her hand up his arm, learning the texture of his skin—the tender skin on the inner side of his elbow, the firmness of muscle beneath his upper arm, the faint coarseness of hair. Her fingertips tingled from touching him, sending tendrils of desire wriggling down through her abdomen. She let her hand stray up onto his shoulder and over his back as far as she could reach.

How could she ever have feared that this would not be wonderful? Yet even as she thought it, she reminded herself that things might change at any moment, that Sinclair would leave off kissing and stroking her and would shove himself between her legs, eager for his fulfillment.

When he lifted his head, she thought it would change then, but he left her mouth only to explore her neck and chest, his lips and tongue tasting and teasing her skin, arousing her more with each kiss. As his mouth moved over her, his hand slid down her body, caressing her in slow, lingering strokes.

Her legs moved restlessly at the touch of his hand, and the ache between her legs grew and pulsed, flooding with passion. His mouth crept over her breast, moving slowly, inexorably toward the nipple, and anticipation grew in her. She waited for him to take the hard bud into his mouth once more, and with each touch of his tongue, his lips, his teeth, the eagerness heightened and swelled until she was taut as a bowstring, her skin damp and her breath rasping in her throat. She dug her fingertips into his shoulders, aware of a primitive urge to rake her fingernails down his back and sink them into the soft flesh of his buttocks.

Then, at last, his mouth closed around her nipple, velvety soft and damp, and he began to suckle, pulling at the sensitive button of flesh with long, hot strokes. Francesca could not hold back a moan of satisfaction, so intense it was almost painful, and her hips moved on the bed of her petticoats.

Answering her unspoken urging, Sinclair's hand slid up her thigh and over onto the flat plain of her abdomen, circling and inching closer to the thatch of hair between her legs. His fingertips edged into the silky triangle, tangling in the hair, and gliding to the center and down into the slick, heated folds of flesh. Francesca jerked and tried to move away, embarrassed that he should feel the unusual flood of moisture there.

But his searching fingers followed her, gliding insistently over her, pressing into her in a way that made her gasp and dig her heels into the floor. Then his clever fingers were parting and exploring her in the most intimate way, stroking over the supremely sensitive nub of flesh until she was almost wild with hunger, her hips circling and pressing up against his hand. Soft whimpers of passion escaped her lips, and she turned her head to muffle the sounds against his arm.

Something was building inside her, a hard, aching knot of yearning, until she felt, desperately, as if she were going to scream. Then it burst within her, and she did cry out, sinking her teeth in his arm. A tidal wave of pleasure washed through her, and she trembled under the force of it, lost in the pure physical sensation.

She heard him groan, and he rested his head against her chest for a moment, as though fighting for control. And when, at last, she lay limp and languid beneath him, rendered utterly nerveless, he moved over her, parting her legs. She opened her legs to him eagerly, for despite the mind-numbing satisfaction of what she had just experienced, there was still an ache, a hunger that would not be filled until she took him inside her.

But he did not move into her just yet. Instead,

propping himself on his elbows, he began a leisurely pleasuring of her other breast, kissing and teasing it, taking the nipple into his mouth and repeating the slow, hard suction. To her amazement, the tension began to rise in her again—if anything, she was more eager this time, knowing what waited at the end.

He pulled back, blowing a soft breath of air upon the damp berry-colored nipple and causing it to prickle and lengthen, and he teased the other nipple between his forefinger and thumb, rolling and gently tugging. The hunger built in her until she was almost sobbing with need.

She moaned his name, and her hands drifted down his back to his buttocks, caressing the fleshy mounds. "Please," she murmured. "Please…"

He moved into her then, lifting her hips and pressing slowly, steadily into her. She gasped at the sensation as he filled her, shocked by the sense of completion, the wonderful rightness of the joining. Sinclair began to stroke within her, pulling almost out, then thrusting back in, creating an intense, delightful friction that pushed the tension inside her ever higher. Then, once more, she convulsed, and this time she did indulge her primitive desire, raking his back with her nails and digging her fingers into his buttocks.

Sinclair let out a hoarse cry, jerking against her, and they met in a cataclysm of passion. Francesca wrapped her arms and legs around him, clinging to him as the storm engulfed them.

HE WAS A HEAVY WEIGHT upon her, his face pressed into the crook of her shoulder, but Francesca did not mind the pressure. She was so buoyant with joy that she was not sure she would not simply float away otherwise. She held on to him tightly, reveling in the feel of his body upon hers, his skin hot and damp, his breath tickling her neck.

Tears gathered in her eyes and spilled over, trickling down her face, and she reached up to wipe them away.

"Francesca?" He rolled away from her then, gazing down into her face, a frown forming on his brow. "What is it? Are you crying?"

She nodded, embarrassed, and gulped back her tears. "I'm sorry."

"Are you all right? Did I hurt you?"

"No! Oh, no," she hastened to assure him. "I don't know why I'm crying—it was just so beautiful." She began to tear up again, and she dashed the moisture away impatiently with her hand. "Oh, bother…"

He chuckled, his voice rich with satisfaction, and gathered her up in his arms, pulling her back against his chest so that they lay curled together like spoons in a drawer. He nuzzled into her hair and pressed a brief kiss on the back of her neck. "It *was* beautiful."

"I have never felt anything like that before. I thought—" She stopped, suddenly realizing that perhaps she was giving away too much.

"Never?" There was astonishment in his voice. "You

mean…" He paused, then went on thoughtfully, "You mean you never felt— Oh, blast, I cannot think of any genteel way to put it—you never reached satisfaction before?"

She shook her head. Her voice was small as she replied, "No. I know you must find me very odd. And, really, there is no point in talking about it."

Why had she ever brought this subject up? she wondered, cursing her own thoughtlessness. There was no reason for Sinclair to know about her former coldness. It was bound to make him wonder about her.

"I don't find you odd at all," he replied, kissing her hair again. "I find you—" he trailed his hand down her side, following the curves of her waist and hips "—delectable." He laid another kiss on the point of her shoulder. "What I don't understand is your late husband."

"It was so different with him. I—I hated it!" Her vehemence shocked her a little. "I am sorry—I know you must think I'm terrible." She pressed her lips together, trying to stem the flow of words.

"Of course I don't think that." He pulled her even closer into his body, surrounding her with his warmth and strength. "I think Lord Haughston must have been an even greater ass than I realized."

The words poured out of her now, and she seemed helpless to stop them. "Andrew said that I was cold, an ice princess. I tried not to be, but I could not help it. It was…it wasn't at all like tonight. I hated for him to touch me. I know I was a terrible wife. I should not have married him. I did not love him. I tried to make myself think I did, but as soon as we were wed, I knew what a dreadful mistake I had made. It was so awkward and—and painful. I cried half my wedding night." She swallowed, then added lightly, "'Tis no wonder, I suppose, that he found me unappealing. Or that he turned to other women. I made a horrible mess of it all."

"Stop it," Sinclair told her crisply. He went up on his elbow, pulling her over onto her back, so that he could look down into her face. "Listen to me. You are a lovely, extremely passionate woman. I detected not the slightest sign of coldness in you. You are utterly desirable, and whatever that fool Haughston told you, there was no fault in you." He bent and kissed her, hard and fast. "Understand?"

She nodded, a blush creeping along her cheekbones.

He stroked his knuckles along her cheek, his face softening. "I am sorry for your unhappiness. For the pleasure you didn't know. But I am a base enough fellow that I cannot help but be glad that he never...*had* this with you." He smiled, his dark eyes lighting wickedly. "And I am...well, I am quite detestably smug and self-satisfied to know that you found satisfaction with me and not him."

Sinclair bent to kiss her again. "Furthermore," he went on, punctuating his words with kisses across her face and down her neck, "I intend to devote a good deal of my time to showing you exactly how lacking you are in coldness."

A little gurgle of laughter escaped her. "Do you now?"

"Indeed. I shall make it my solemn mission. We shall discover exactly all the things that excite you." He trailed a finger down her body, skimming over her breasts, smiling a little at the tightening response of her nipples. "It will take some time and effort, I fear, but I think it is my duty to discover each one."

He bent and brushed a kiss on each hardened point.

"You are a very dedicated man," Francesca told him.

"I am," he agreed, his hand drifting lower.

She drew her breath in a little gasp, arching up at the sudden sizzle through her body. Her eyes clouded over in desire as she murmured, "Already?"

"Mmm. I believe so." His voice turned husky. "I think it is imperative that I begin my research immediately. I would not have it said that I shirked my duty."

"No…" She sighed on a new wave of pleasure as his fingers sought out the very center of her passion. "We cannot have that."

He kissed her, and everything else faded from her mind.

CHAPTER SEVENTEEN

FRANCESCA AWOKE LATE the next morning. She was lying in her bed, the sun streaming into the room past the draperies. She blinked, confused for a moment. Then memories of the night before came rushing back into her mind. A blush stained her cheeks, but she smiled, snuggling deeper into her covers. She stretched out a hand to the pillow where Sinclair's head had lain last night.

He was gone, of course. After they had made love again downstairs, he had whisked her up here to her bed, and they had lain together for a while, holding each other in a quiet glow of contentment. She had fallen asleep finally, and he must have slipped out after that. She had known he would. Rochford would do his utmost to protect her reputation, even from her own servants.

On that thought, her eyes flew open and she sat up quickly, glancing around the room. When her eyes fell on the pile of her clothes in the chair by the bed, she let out a sigh of relief and sank back onto her pillow. Thank goodness he had thought to bring up her things and not leave them in a telling heap on the floor of her sitting room.

She stretched, enjoying the feel of the sheets sliding over her naked body. Perhaps she would eschew nightgowns altogether now, she thought, and giggled to herself. Somehow Sinclair had turned her into a wanton overnight. She had barely awakened, and already she was thinking of what this night would hold and whether Rochford would come to her again.

But that was perfectly acceptable, she told herself. After all, she had a number of years to make up for.

Francesca rose and wrapped herself in her dressing gown. Her maid had apparently decided not to awaken her and had left her morning tray on the low table beside her chair. Both the tea and the toast had grown cold, but Francesca gulped them down anyway. She was suddenly ravenous.

She rang for her maid and ordered a bath. She could feel Maisie's curiosity fairly radiating from her. She knew that her maid and all the servants were dying to know what was going on after the scene they had witnessed last night with Perkins. She would have to tell them that the problem had been taken care of so that they could stop worrying about their futures, but for now she kept silent. All she wanted was to soak in a hot bath and daydream about Sinclair.

There could be no long future for them, of course. Francesca was realistic enough to know that despite the blissful night they had spent together, it could lead only to an affair. Yes, she loved Rochford, but while he had certainly enjoyed their lovemaking, he had not given any indication that he *loved* her. Passion did not mean the same thing for men that it did for women. Sinclair's desire was not charged with love, as hers was. And even if he did love her, it would not make any difference.

The Duke of Rochford had to marry to produce heirs, no matter what Sinclair Lilles might want. And Sinclair was responsible. He followed his duty, not his desires. He could not marry a barren woman. He would have to choose a younger bride and have children with her.

But surely he would not have to do that just yet. He was clearly not interested in any of the women she had picked out as possibilities for him. Indeed, he positively disliked two of them, and he had helped a third become engaged to another man. Nor had he ever raised the hopes of any of them; he had been his usual circumspect self. He could wait for a few more months, even a year…or two. A man could produce offspring, after all, at a far greater age than his.

Until he had to marry, they could be together—or at least until he grew tired of her. They could have an affair, and no one in the *ton* would care, as long as they were discreet. After all, she was a widow, and he was single. No one would be hurt by what they did. It was often the case, even among the married nobility, to conduct affairs, though usually after the question of heirs had been settled.

There would be whispered rumors, perhaps, but as long as they were careful—and given Rochford's reputation as a crack shot—it would not be blown up into a scandal. Even if it was, well—that was something she was willing to risk. It would be her reputation that would suffer the damage, after all, not his.

It would be hard, she knew, to give him up eventually, but she was willing to risk that, as well. She was determined to seize this moment of happiness. Afterwards, of course, she would do the right thing; she would not damage Rochford's life. But for now, she intended to enjoy her bit of pleasure.

She sailed through the day on a cloud of happiness. Once she was dressed, she went downstairs and called the servants together in the kitchen. She thanked them for their efforts on her behalf the evening before and assured them that the problem with Mr. Perkins had been taken care of. He would not, she told them with a smile, be coming around again.

Their relief was obvious, though she could also see that a good deal of curiosity remained. However, she was not about to explain about running to Rochford or what he had done to get rid of Perkins. She might tell Maisie some of it later. A woman's personal maid was, after all, the person from whom it was most difficult to keep secrets. But for now she wanted to hug to herself everything regarding the duke. She suspected that any talk of him would bring a glow to her face that would reveal the truth.

She tried to go about her daily tasks, but she found it hard to concentrate. She sat down at her desk to update her correspondence, which had been dreadfully tardy of late. She should have written to Constance days ago. However, as soon as she pulled out paper and started to write, she found her thoughts drifting away to Sinclair and the way he smiled, his eyes crinkling up at the corners, or to things they had done the evening before. And *those* sorts of thoughts soon had her pulse racing and warmth blossoming deep within her.

She pulled her wayward thoughts back and started to write again, but after a while she gave it up and decided to take on a task that required less concentration. She turned instead to her mending, but it soon became apparent that darning stockings and sewing on ruffles kept her no more occupied than letter-writing.

Afternoon callers would, she reasoned, make the time pass more quickly, but she soon found that having visitors was the worst way of passing the time, for she had to struggle to appear to be listening and interested. At least no one had seen when she dropped her mending in her lap and started gazing sightlessly at the wall, a dreamy smile playing on her lips as she recalled Sinclair's kisses.

She lost the thread of the conversation so many times that one of her callers asked her if she was feeling unwell, and a later one gave her an icy look when she left. Then the Duke of Rochford came to call.

Fenton announced him as she was sitting in her

drawing room with Lady Feringham and her daughter. Francesca's heart leaped into her throat, and she jumped to her feet before she realized what she had done. Gravely, trying to look as if she rose for every visitor, she bowed her head to the butler, saying, "Please, show him in."

She dared not glance at Lady Feringham or her daughter as she braced herself to see Sinclair again. She must not let anything of what had happened between the two of them show in her face. Discretion, after all, must be her watchword.

Rochford walked into the room after the butler, and Francesca saw the flicker of dismay on his face when he noticed her other visitors. He checked at the doorway before continuing into the room and bowing to her.

"Lady Haughston."

"Rochford. How very pleasant to see you," she greeted him, her voice carefully even. Her cheeks were a little warm, and she hoped that she was not blushing—at least not deeply enough that the others would notice.

She extended her hand to him. She wanted desperately to feel his touch, yet she knew that she must not allow any of that to be seen on her face. His fingers closed around hers, and she felt him squeeze briefly before he released her hand. She allowed herself one glance up into his eyes; it was all she could do to tear her own eyes away.

She gave a bright, general smile and gestured vaguely toward one of the chairs. "Do sit down. You know Lady Feringham and her daughter, Lady Cottwell, I believe."

"Yes, of course." Rochford bowed to the other women and greeted them politely while Francesca sat down and sought to gather her composure around her.

It was absurd, she told herself, that all she could think about right now was the way Rochford had looked looming above her, his skin slick with sweat, his breath ragged, his eyes black as the pit, as he plunged into her.

She slipped out her handkerchief and dabbed surreptitiously at her face. *Was anyone else looking heated, or was it just her?* She wondered if it would appear odd if she called for Fenton to open another of the windows.

The room was silent, and Francesca glanced around, realizing that something was amiss. From the expectant looks on the others' faces, she knew that they were waiting for some response from her.

"I—I beg your pardon. I fear my mind, um, wandered for a bit. I was thinking that it seemed a bit warm. Shall I have a window opened?"

"Oh, no, it's quite pleasant," the younger visitor assured her. "I had just asked you whether you enjoyed Lady Smythe-Fulton's rout last week. I found it such a crush, I confess."

"Indeed. But is that not the goal of a rout?" Francesca asked with a smile, doing her best to recall anything about the party. *That was not where she had*

*watched Rochford talk to Mary Calderwood, was it?
No, surely that had been the Haversley soiree.* She
could remember almost nothing of that evening except
with whom the duke had chatted and the praise Lady
Mary had heaped upon him.

She sneaked another glance at Rochford. He was
watching her, and there was something in his gaze that
made her skin flare with heat. She tried to give him an
admonitory glare, but she feared that it did not come
out looking that way at all. *When were these women
going to leave? Had they not been here long past the
polite limit for an afternoon call?*

But still Lady Feringham prattled on. She had gone
on to a discussion of Lord Chesterfield's new
phaeton, which his youngest son had apparently
wrecked only this morning in an absurd race with Mr.
William Arbuthnot. Francesca did her best to gasp
and sigh and smile in all the right places, but she
could not keep her eyes from straying back time and
again to the duke.

She was swept with relief when at last Lady Feringham announced that they must take their leave. She
could only hope that they did not see the joy flare in her
eyes as she rose to bid goodbye to them.

When they were gone, Francesca whirled back to
Rochford, who came to her in two quick strides and
grasped both her hands in his, bringing them up to his
lips and planting a hard, brief kiss on the knuckles of
each one.

"I was beginning to think that they had taken root here," he told her between kisses.

Francesca let out a giddy little laugh. "As did I. Oh, Sinclair…"

She let out his name on a sigh, gazing up into his face, her own features glowing as if lit from within.

He let out an oath under his breath and drew her into his arms, bending to kiss her fiercely. When they at last emerged from the embrace sometime later, Francesca's face was rosy and her eyes shining, her lips soft and almost bruised-looking.

"When you look at me like that, I forget all else," he told her hoarsely. "We must talk."

"Must we?" she retorted lightly, grinning in a deliberately provocative way. "I can think of a number of things I would rather do."

"Vixen." He raised her hand again and turned it over to press a kiss into her palm. "You know that I would, as well. But I have to tell you—"

There was the sound of a discreet cough in the hallway, and they sprang apart, Rochford swinging away to inspect the mantel as though it held some deep fascination for him. Francesca grimaced, but composed her expression and turned to face her butler.

"Yes, Fenton?"

"Mrs. Frederick Wilberforce to see you, madam."

She would dearly have liked to instruct him to tell the woman that she was not at home, but she knew that Mrs. Wilberforce must have seen the other callers leaving, and if she was then turned away, her feelings would be hurt. Mrs. Wilberforce, having "married up," was especially sensitive to any sort of slight.

Suppressing a sigh, Francesca instructed Fenton to send the woman in. She turned back to Sinclair, saying in a low tone, "I am so sorry."

He shook his head, giving her a crooked little smile, and said, "I will wait."

Francesca turned back to smile at the woman entering the room. She hoped that there was nothing in her face to reveal what she had been doing before Mrs. Wilberforce arrived. Certainly, her pulse was still thundering, and she dared not look over at the duke.

Fortunately, Rochford knew Mrs. Wilberforce's husband, who hailed from a town near the duke's property in Cornwall, and he was able to engage her for a few minutes in a conversation about the man. After that, it was slow going. For once Francesca was unable to summon up the usual social chatter to aid her. All she could think of was her desire for the woman to leave and allow her to be alone with Sinclair.

When she left, Francesca thought, she would tell Fenton that she was no longer receiving visitors. However, she was not sure what excuse she could make for Sinclair's continued presence. By the rules of polite behavior, of course, he should leave before Mrs. Wilberforce. He had already been here longer than was customary for an afternoon call. She wondered if Mrs. Wilberforce would notice or would be too overawed by talking to a duke to even be aware that he had made a social misstep.

Finally, surprising her, Sinclair rose, saying that he must take his leave of them. It was all Francesca could do not to utter a protest. She managed a brittle smile, however, and gave him her hand.

"It was so good of you to come," she told him stiffly.

He smiled. "I hope to return soon."

Her eyes flew up to his at his words, and she saw a smile lurking in their dark depths. "Oh. Well, yes, please do. I should like very much to show you my garden."

He grinned. "I am sure it is beautiful. Good day, Lady Haughston."

"Duke."

She waited out the rest of Mrs. Wilberforce's visit with a barely concealed frustration. The woman chattered on at length about the duke's graciousness and pleasant manner, his lack of arrogance, his handsome looks, until Francesca was ready to scream. Instead she smiled and nodded like an automaton, but offered few words of her own; the last thing she wanted was to lengthen the conversation.

As soon as Mrs. Wilberforce departed, Francesca slipped down the hallway and out the back door to the small garden behind her house. It was enclosed by walls, but beside her house, leading to the servants' entrance, was a narrow walkway that ended at the gate into the garden. She made her way to the gate now, hoping that she and Sinclair had understood one another in their leave-taking conversation.

Though it offered no handle on the outside, the garden gate could be opened from within. Francesca lifted the bar now and swung it open. The duke stood just outside, leaning negligently against the wall of the house.

She let out a laugh of sheer delight as he ducked inside, closing the gate behind him, and swept her up into his arms. They kissed, moving in a slow, shuffling circle, and Francesca clung to him, lost in a haze of passion.

Several long minutes passed before Rochford set her back down on her feet, and for a goodly time after that, she was still too dazed to speak. He took her hand and led her deeper into the garden, stopping finally at a bench. It was a lovely spot, sheltered by the garden wall and perfumed by the roses growing in profusion beside it, and Francesca sank down onto it happily, planning to snuggle against his side, his arm curled around her shoulders.

When Sinclair did not sit down beside her, she glanced up at him, puzzled. "Come, sit down with me." She smiled invitingly, holding out a hand to him.

He shook his head, his face settling into serious lines. "I came here to talk to you, and I find that if I am close to you, I forget all my intentions."

Francesca's smile deepened, her long dimple popping into her cheek. "I don't mind."

He could not keep from smiling back, but he said, "No. Not this time. I intend to get out what I have to say before someone else interrupts us."

Francesca sighed. "Very well. Go on."

He looked at her, started to speak, then stopped, and began again. "I have no facility with this." He drew a breath. "Lady Haughston…"

"Lady Haughston!" Francesca repeated, starting to laugh. "How did we come to *that?*" She went cold as she took in the grave look on his face. "Sinclair, what is it? What are you trying to say?"

She was suddenly certain that he was here to tell her that he regretted what had happened the night before, that he could not let her distract him from his purpose of finding a duchess. Her fingers knotted in her lap, and she looked down at them, trying to school herself not to cry.

"Francesca," he corrected himself. "You must know of my regard for you—of my hope that— Oh, the devil take it! I am asking you to marry me!"

Francesca stared at him, struck silent. Of all the horrid certainties that had flooded in upon her at his serious tone, this had not even occurred to her.

He glanced at her, then let out a low growl. "Bloody hell! I've made a complete botch of it." He dropped down on one knee in front of her. "I am sorry. Francesca, please…" He reached in his pocket and took out a small box, extending it toward her. "Would you do me the honor of agreeing to be my wife?"

She found her tongue at last. "No!" She jumped to

her feet, staring at him in horror. "Sinclair, no! I cannot marry you!"

His face closed, and he rose to his feet. "Again? You are refusing me again?"

"No! Sinclair, no. Pray do not be angry—"

"What the bloody hell do you expect me to be?" he lashed out. "What was last night about? Your gratitude? Thank you, but I did not need a payment!"

Francesca's head snapped back as though he had hit her, and her cheeks flared with color. "I did not pay you! I gave myself to you because—" She stopped, unable to expose her love to him when he was staring at her so stonily.

His eyebrows shot up. "Yes? Because?" He grimaced and swung away. "My God, what an idiot I've been." He took a few steps from her, then whirled back to pierce her with his black gaze. "What did you intend? One night? Two?"

"No. I— Just not marriage."

"An affair?" He appeared, if possible, even more thunderstruck. "Are you telling me that you thought we would skulk about, hiding our relationship from everyone? What was I to do? Marry another and all the while carry on an affair behind my wife's back? Is that what you think of me? Is that the sort of man I seem to you?"

Tears choked Francesca. "No! No, please, Sinclair…"

"Sweet Jesu! I thought you cared for me. I thought that, after all these years, you had realized—that you wanted—" He let out an oath, followed by a bitter laugh. "How many times can a man play the fool for you?" He shook his head. "Well, this is the last, I assure you. Goodbye, my lady, I will not bother you any further."

Francesca stood frozen in horror for a moment, then started after him. "Sinclair, wait! No!"

He whipped back around and tossed the box in his hand onto the ground in front of her. "Here. Add this to your collection."

He strode off to the gate, flung it open and was gone. The gate crashed shut behind him, leaving the garden in a ringing silence.

Francesca could not think, could not move. She began to shake, and tears rushed from her eyes. *This could not be happening! He could not have walked out of her life like this!*

She dropped to her knees, suddenly too weak to remain standing. Despite the warmth of the summer afternoon, she was chilled to the bone, and an uncontrollable trembling shook her body. She reached out, picked up the small box he had dropped and opened it. A ring lay inside, simple and elegant, a large pear-shaped yellow diamond. The Lilles diamond, the wedding ring of the Duchesses of Rochford.

Her fingers curled around it, and she sagged to the ground, clutching the ring to her chest.

"MY LADY? MY LADY?" Maisie's voice sounded close to Francesca's ear. "What is amiss? Are you ill?"

Francesca opened her eyes and looked up to see her maid kneeling over her, peering down into her face with worried eyes. Francesca blinked. She could not have said how long she had lain there, spent and despairing.

She sat up dazedly, realizing that she still held the small jewelry box clutched tightly in her fist, and that her fist was still pressed to her heart. "I am fine, Maisie. Do not worry."

"My lady, what happened? Bess saw you lying out here, and she screeched fit to wake the dead. She thought you'd been struck down."

Francesca swallowed. "I have been. But not in the way you think." She rose to her knees, and Maisie took her arm to help her up.

"Fenton thought His Grace was out here with you earlier. He never… He didn't do this to you, did he?"

"No! No, he would never hit me. No. I did this to myself, I fear." Francesca tried to smile at her maid, but she knew that her effort was not successful. "I believe that I will go up to my room now. Really, I am all right. Tell the others not to worry. I am merely… tired."

"It's not that blackguard back again, is it?" Maisie persisted as they walked to the back door.

"Perkins?" Francesca shook her head. "No. He is gone for good. I have just…mishandled something very badly. I think—" Tears welled in her eyes. "I think the duke will not be here again."

"What?" Her maid's eyes grew large and round. "But, my lady—"

"Please. I cannot talk about it now. I must go to my room and rest."

They went inside and up the back stairs. In her room, Maisie helped her mistress out of her dress and wrapped her dressing gown around her. Despite its warmth, Francesca still shivered, and Maisie lit a fire in the fireplace to warm her.

Later, she brought up tea and supper on a tray. Francesca could not bring herself to eat, but she drank the hot tea gratefully. For a long time she sat staring numbly into the fire, her thoughts running on a long, futile track.

Her instinct was to run to Rochford, to throw herself at him and beg him to hear her out—to make him listen to her somehow. She would explain it all, she thought, and he would understand why she had turned him down. He would realize that she was right. They could not marry; he would know that, if he only considered it a little.

She would tell him how she felt, convince him that it was not lack of feeling that had made her refuse him—how could he think that, after what had happened between them!

But, of course, she knew she could not run to him. He would not even see her. He had been so angry, so cold. Just remembering the icy disdain with which he flung the ring at her made tears spring to her eyes.

She decided to write him a letter, and she went downstairs to her desk, creeping like a mouse to avoid the notice of any of the servants. She wasted page after page, starting one explanation after another. Nothing that she wrote was adequate; nothing could express the horror and regret she had felt at the expression on Sinclair's face. Nothing, she thought, would make him take her back.

He hated her. Her clumsy rejection had cut him deeply. He would never forgive her.

Francesca cursed her own stupidity. She should have been better prepared. She should have known that Sinclair, with his engrained code of honor, would have felt duty-bound to offer marriage to her after he had slept with her. No matter what was reasonable or sound, he would give her the chance to retain her honor.

If she had given it any thought, instead of going blithely through her day, brimming with happiness, she would have realized that she needed to be prepared to deal with a marriage proposal. She could have marshalled her reasons and laid them out carefully. With a little forethought, she could have avoided the anger and the hurt.

But perhaps she was being foolish. Perhaps nothing could have avoided what had happened. The fact was, she had been headstrong and impulsive. She had wanted him, had wanted to experience that intimate, vital pleasure with him, and she had been certain that she could make everything work out. She had let her desire rule her, and look at the result: She had lost Rochford—not only as a lover, but as a friend.

It was the bleakest fate she could think of. How was she to live without ever having his smile warm her again? Without him turning to her and raising an eyebrow in that maddening way? Never watching him take a fence as if he were all of a piece with his horse?

With a shaky sigh, Francesca closed her eyes and leaned back in her chair. Perhaps after a few days… when his fury had had time to cool, when he was more likely to be reasonable, she could send him a letter and explain it all.

But no, it was probably better this way. She should let him go without trying to justify her actions. Put an end to it so that he could get back to his life. She should wrap up the Lilles wedding ring tomorrow and return it to him without any explanation.

But the thought pierced her like a knife. She was not sure that she had the strength to be so noble.

Tiredness overcame her finally, and she went to bed. But then, perversely, sleep would not come. She lay awake for long hours, simply staring into the dark and regretting her actions. When she did fall asleep, it seemed as though she jerked awake immediately.

Her eyes flew open, and she lay tensely, wondering what had awakened her. The house was in deep silence all around her, and after a long moment she closed her eyes again, telling herself that it was simply her own distress that had pulled her out of sleep.

A floorboard creaked then, and she rolled over. A dark male form loomed at the end of her bed. For an instant hope leaped into her heart. Sinclair!

But then the figure was rushing around the side of the bed, something dark in his arms, and she realized with horror that it was not Sinclair, coming to take her in his arms again, but Perkins.

She opened her mouth to scream, but something heavy and dark dropped around her, silencing her.

CHAPTER EIGHTEEN

FRANCESCA SCREAMED, but she knew it was so muffled that no one would hear, and began to struggle wildly, trapped in the dark cloth, but her assailant hit her with his fist, dazing her enough that she went limp. He seized the momentary advantage and picked her up, flinging her over his shoulder, and ran from the room. Francesca, hanging sickeningly upside down, the breath jouncing from her with every step he took, could bring forth only a muffled cry. She tried to struggle again, but with the blanket wrapped around her and secured by his arm tight around her legs, she could do little more than wriggle about as he thundered down the stairs.

As he flung open the front door, she thought she heard a cry from the back of the house, but with the crashing of the door, she could not be sure. The next thing she knew, she was unceremoniously dumped onto a hard floor, knocking the wind from her. She heard Perkins jump in after her and slam the door, and suddenly the floor beneath them was moving. She realized that he must have had a carriage waiting for them, and that they were now driving away at a fast pace.

Before she could recover her breath enough to tear away the blanket, Perkins himself jerked it from her. Roughly he pulled her up onto the seat and wrapped a sash around her wrists, tying them together in front of her. Francesca kicked at him and tried to pull away, but he was stronger, and though he cursed when her kicks connected, he did not pause in binding her hands.

She screamed, her wind having returned, but he ignored that, as well. She suspected that her cries would do little good; no doubt the rumbling of the carriage would cover most of the noise she made, and as for the rest of it—well, this was London, and who was going to give chase after a carriage simply because a few screams were heard from within?

When he had finished with her wrists, he reached into a pocket to pull out a handkerchief and stuffed it into her mouth, saying fiercely, "Shut up, damn you. Shut up! God, what a racket."

He began to unfasten his cravat, and Francesca seized the opportunity to throw herself across the carriage away from him. She spat the handkerchief out of her mouth and released another shriek. He cursed and leaned down to pick up the handkerchief just as the carriage went around a corner. Perkins went sprawling on the floor.

Francesca aimed a swift kick at him. She intended to hit his head, but he was quick enough to twist away, and her blow landed on his shoulder instead. She did not waste time trying to disable him further. Instead she leaped for the door and turned the handle.

The carriage had lost speed as it rounded the corner, and now it slowed still more. As the door swung open, Francesca saw that they had entered the market area. In the predawn dark, merchants were setting up their goods in stalls all along the street, so the carriage could not continue at its previous fast clip.

She was still holding the door handle, intending to swing out of the carriage and jump, but at the last second she hesitated, afraid that the vehicle was still moving too quickly. Perkins, however, was scrambling up off the floor, and he lunged for her, so she leaped, whispering a frantic prayer that she would not roll back under the wheels.

She fell, not hitting the ground as she had feared, but crashing on her side into one of the stalls and landing on a bed of fruit. The stall keeper, who was unloading boxes of plums and berries, let out a cry of rage and dropped his crate.

He swung around and grabbed her arm, yanking her up from the ruins of his display. "Bloody 'ell, woman! Wot the divil do you think yer doin'?"

Francesca pulled with all her might. Behind her, she could hear Perkins yelling at the driver to stop. With a last burst of energy, fueled by fear, she tore her bound arms away from the fruit seller's grasp and started to run.

The cobblestones were uneven and painful to her bare feet, and she realized that it was astonishingly difficult to run with her hands tied together. But she tore down the street as fast as she could. Behind her came a swell of shouts and catcalls, and one vendor let out a whistle and clapped his hands in encouragement as she ran past, as if he were watching a race.

But no one intervened to stop Perkins, and his footsteps grew louder and louder behind her. He threw himself at her, sending them both tumbling to the ground. Francesca bore the worst of their fall, with him on top of her, and once again the breath was knocked out of her. The impact jarred her whole body, bruising her side, and her head rang as her teeth clicked together sharply.

Perkins rolled to his feet and picked her up, carrying her back to the carriage. Francesca, struggling for breath, could not even protest, and her struggles were feeble.

"Hush, dear," he told her in an infuriatingly calm voice. "I know you're upset, but it will be all right." He turned toward the bystanders, saying, "I beg your pardon for my wife. She is not herself lately. Lost our child, you see—I fear it has made her a little mad."

"No!" Francesca managed to gasp out.

"There, there. Don't fret. We'll get you back home, and the doctor will make it all better."

"'Ere now!" The burly fruit vendor rushed up to them, gesturing at his stall. "'Oo's goin' to pay for all this? Quality! Tearin' 'round and breakin' everfin' up."

Perkins dug in his pocket and pulled out a few coins, tossing them to the fruit vendor, which seemed to mollify the man. Then he swung Francesca up into the carriage.

"There, now, darling, calm down," he told her loudly as he climbed into the carriage and slammed the door shut after them.

She came up clawing, but he managed to dodge her hands and wrap his arms around her, bearing her back down on the floor. The vehicle rolled off down the street as the two of them wrestled inside. Since Perkins was stronger than she and her hands were tied, it proved to be little contest. Though Francesca fought as hard as she could, he soon had wrapped his ascot around the lower half of her face, effectively silencing her cries, and he went on to grab her ankles and hold them together, tying a length of rope around them.

"Well!" He leaned back against the edge of the seat, looking down at her. "Aren't you the feisty one? I'd never have figured you for it." A slow, evil grin spread across his face. "Maybe tonight will turn out more interesting that I'd thought. Never did like a woman who lay there like a stick. Mayhap you'll give me a good ride, eh?"

He slid his hand casually down her body, and Francesca's gorge rose in disgust.

"There's more curves to you than I thought, too," he went on and laughed as she glared at him. "Ah, yes, it's much better when you can't say anything."

He shoved himself up and onto the seat, not bothering to help her up from the floor. Francesca managed to sit up, then crouch and lever herself up onto the seat opposite, positioning herself as far from him as she possibly could. Her feet hurt from running on the cobblestones, and the rope was so tight that she knew they would soon be numb. Her hands, too, were bound too tightly, and her hair had been caught in the gag wrapped around her head, so that it pulled painfully against her scalp. She was sore and bruised in numerous places all over her body, but she almost welcomed the pain. It kept her from falling into a daze of despair.

Where were they going? Why had he taken her? She feared that she had all too accurate an idea of what he planned to do with her whenever they eventually reached their destination. She swallowed hard, an icy cold filling her at the thought of what lay before her.

She tried to turn her thoughts to something else. She wondered if any of the servants had seen Perkins carrying her from the house. Certainly he had not been quiet when he had run down the stairs with her. He was bound to have awakened some of them. But even if one of them had come running and recognized Perkins, what could her servants do?

They would have no idea where he had taken her. And where would they go for help? Fenton might think of Rochford, but if he went to the duke, would Sinclair even care what had happened to her? Her heart squeezed inside her chest as she thought of him turning away, still cold with anger.

Maisie might go to Irene. With Callie out of town,

Irene would be her closest friend and the one most able to help. Dominic, of course, would be more than willing to help, but he lived at Redfields, a good day's ride away. If Fenton decided to go to him, the trail would be terribly cold by the time Dominic got to London. And she—well, she had no doubt that Perkins would have taken his revenge on her by that time.

Her best hope was that they would go to Irene. She would help, and her husband was the sort of man who would have a good idea what to do. She would put her hopes on that—that one of the servants had come out in time to see Perkins carry her out the door, and that Fenton or Maisie would have the good sense to run to Irene immediately with their story.

If they did not…but no, she refused to think of that. She would plan instead what she could do to escape, how she might loosen her bonds or surprise Perkins.

She turned away from him as best she could, curling in on herself. She suspected that he would think her posture sprang from fear of him, and she hated to give him that satisfaction, but it was more important that she hide her hands from his sight. Surreptitiously, she began to work at her bonds, stretching the sash as much as she could. The cloth dug painfully into her skin, but she would not let that stop her. It was a much softer material than the rope he had used on her ankles, and while that meant that he had been able to tie it more tightly and securely, it also meant that it would stretch more easily.

Unfortunately, in an attempt to keep what she was

doing hidden from her companion, she had to make her movements small. No matter how she pulled and twisted, she could loosen the ties only a fraction, nowhere near enough to enable her to slip her hands through. Moreover, all the tugging had managed to tighten the knot into a hard, tiny ball, almost impossible to undo. She needed something sharp that would cut the bonds, but nothing like that was in evidence.

As she worked on the sash that tied her hands, she also moved her feet as much as she could without being obvious. But the ropes were even more unyielding than the cloth sash. She was, she thought with despair, utterly unable to get out of her bonds.

After a time, she could feel the carriage slowing down, and she shifted, trying to see out the window. However, the curtains covered it completely, and she could see nothing. She glanced across at Perkins, and his mouth pulled into a familiar grin, the one that made her shiver inside.

"Yes. We are here already. Surely you did not think I would take my time to get what I want. I'm not a man who likes waiting."

Francesca stiffened her spine, sending him her fiercest look. He merely laughed.

"Oh, aye, glare at me all you wish. It'll be different in a little while. You'll be begging me then." He leaned forward. "And that bastard Rochford will have to live with the fact that I got there before him. He won't like that, will he, the mighty duke? Finding out that his precious little lady is just a doxy, like any other. Knowing I've plowed that furrow long before he had a chance to."

Francesca would have dearly loved to spit back an answer at him, but of course, the gag prevented it. She waited, her body tensing. The moment when he pulled her out of the carriage would be her best chance to create a fuss, although, bound and gagged as she was, she was not sure what she could manage to do. But surely, if they had stopped at an inn, there would be people around, and the sight of him hauling out a bound-and-gagged woman would appear extremely odd. Someone might come forward and question them.

But then again, it was still night, no later than dawn. Even at an inn, there might be no one about. Far worse, they could have driven to some cottage on the outskirts of town, where there would be no one to see or wonder.

Perkins leaned across the carriage, and she squeezed back into the corner, determined to make a fight of it. But to her surprise, he did not take her arm and pull her out. Instead, he seized the dangling end of the sash he had wound around her wrists, looping it through a small bar beside the door and tying it there.

Then he took her chin between his forefinger and thumb and pinched it, giving her a wink, and left the carriage. Francesca stared after him, filled with impotent rage. She jerked hard at the tie, but it was firmly secured. Next she tried to undo it with her fingers, which had room to move a little, but the knot he had made was hard and fast, and her hands had grown so numb that her fingers were clumsy. She made little headway.

She kicked the side of the carriage in frustration. Encouraged by the sound it made, she continued kicking with both feet, making as much noise as possible. No one came to check on her.

It seemed forever that she was out there by herself, alternately kicking and working at the knots. She was beginning to wonder if Perkins intended to leave her alone for the rest of the night.

Finally, however, he opened the door and climbed back in. "You're a noisy one, aren't you? I thought you would have grown tired by now."

The stench of alcohol filled the carriage, and Francesca realized that he must have spent most of his time inside drinking.

"I've gotten my poor sick wife and me a room," he told her, reaching under the seat and pulling out a drawer. From it he extracted a large piece of fabric, which he unfolded to reveal a dark, hooded cloak.

Sitting down beside her, he arranged the cloak around her shoulders and tied it at her neck. There was little she could do to thwart him except lash out at him with her bound legs. He solved that problem by shoving her legs hard against the side of the carriage with one booted foot and holding them there. Finally, he pulled the hood forward so that it covered most of her face.

He did not try to undo the knot he had tied in the sash

but merely drew out a knife and slashed through the material close to the bar, leaving the remnant hanging there. Francesca tried to move away from him, but it was no use. He wrapped the cloak tightly around her, binding her even more, and hauled her out of the carriage.

With his arms tightly around her, carrying her as one would a child, he was able to keep the cloak tightly in place, thus hindering her movements. The cloak also hid the bindings around her ankles and wrists, and the hood, pulled far forward, effectively concealed her gagged face. She would look, she supposed, just like someone asleep or ill.

Still, she did her best to move, hoping that she might throw him off balance or arouse attention, and she screamed against the gag. But the sound was almost entirely muffled, and she doubted that anyone would notice the little wriggling movements she was able to make—if, of course, there was even anyone about to see.

They must be at an inn, given his words, but it was probably still too early in the morning for the other guests to be around. Though it was no longer the black of night, it was only pale dawn. Only the servants would be up, and they would be working in the kitchens, not waiting in the halls watching guests go up to their rooms.

She had no chance, she knew, but she struggled anyway.

It must have had some effect, for she could hear Perkins' ragged breath as he climbed the stairs, and once he grunted and nearly dropped her. He set her down to open the door, keeping one arm tightly around her. Then he jerked her inside and closed the door behind them, turning the key in the lock.

Letting loose a string of curses, he picked her up and tossed her onto the bed, then turned away and went to the small chest of drawers across the room, where a decanter of liquor and glasses stood on a tray. He poured himself a drink, quickly downed it, and poured another.

Francesca managed to wriggle to the edge of the bed. If he got drunk enough, perhaps she would be able to escape him. She knew the likely futility of trying to get away, even from a drunk, with her ankles tied. Still, she had to try. Otherwise, her only choice was to give in to defeat and despair.

He watched her as he drank the second glass. She lay still, not looking directly at him, but watching him from the corner of her eye. When he turned away to pour himself a third drink, she brought up her hands and hooked her fingers beneath the gag, tugging it down. It was tight and hard to move, but she felt it give, and she pulled harder.

Perkins let out an oath, and the glass crashed back down on the tray. He crossed the room in a few quick strides and clamped his hand down across her mouth just as Francesca drew a breath to scream. He jerked the gag back in place. She swung her legs off the bed, but he grabbed her and threw her back onto it, pushing her so far up on the mattress that the back of her head cracked against the wooden headboard.

The blow stunned her for a moment, sending pain lancing through her head. Perkins took the end of the sash dangling from her wrists and wound it around one of the bedposts, tying it firmly, then stepped back, panting, and surveyed her.

"There! You won't be getting away now, will you? Trussed like a pig for slaughter, aren't you?" He grinned, the imagery obviously pleasing to him. "I'll have you squealing like one soon enough, as well." He chuckled and returned to the decanter, pouring himself another drink.

He lifted the glass to her in a mocking toast and drank it. "How'd the duke like seeing you now, I wonder. How you think he'll like getting my leavings?" He grinned. "Won't be so full of himself then, will he?"

Pouring another drink, he sat down in the chair. His movements were growing increasingly clumsy as he drank, so that he plopped down more than sat, the whiskey splashing over the side of the glass. He leaned back, stretching his legs out in front of him. "Arrogant bastard—telling me to get out of the country. Like I'd bow down to him like everybody else." He let out a noise of disgust. "Doesn't know Galen Perkins, though, I'll tell you that. No man's my master, least of all him."

After finishing his drink, he set the glass on the chest

and stood up. He made his way over to the bed, staggering a little as he walked. When he reached her, he leaned against the bedpost, gazing down at her, his eyes glittering with malice. Then he hooked his hand in the neckline of her nightgown and jerked downward, ripping it down to her waist.

Francesca shrieked behind the gag and lashed out at him with her feet, managing to slam her shins into him. The blow unbalanced him, and he staggered to the side and went crashing into the washstand.

The malice in his eyes changed in a flash to pure hatred, and he managed to right himself and charged toward her, his hand raised to strike her.

At that moment something slammed against the door. Perkins whirled, startled, to face the door as another blow hit it and it crashed open, sending Rochford bursting into the room.

CHAPTER NINETEEN

ROCHFORD CROSSED THE room in two long strides and plowed his fist into the other man's jaw. Perkins reeled back and crashed into the wall beside the bed. As he struggled dazedly to right himself, the duke grabbed the front of his shirt and jerked him forward. He wheeled and, grasping the back of Perkins' jacket, propelled him with all his force forward, so that Perkins slammed into the wall beside the door. Perkins bounced off that wall and staggered back, falling in a heap on the floor.

Rochford turned to Francesca. "My God. Are you all right?"

Gently he pulled the sides of her nightgown together, covering her nakedness, then reached up to unfasten the gag that was wrapped around her mouth.

"Sinclair! Oh, Sinclair!" She fought back the tears of relief that threatened to flood her eyes. "Thank God you came! But…how did you get here?"

He bent to kiss her forehead, then turned to unfasten the knot that bound her to the post of the bed. Behind them, Perkins thrashed about on the floor and pulled himself up on all fours, then to his feet. Weaving drunkenly, he reached behind him, beneath his jacket, and pulled out a knife.

"No! Sinclair! Watch out!" Francesca cried.

Rochford whirled and saw the man lurching toward him, knife in hand. Dodging to the side, he grasped Perkins' arm in both hands and slammed it against the footpost of the bed. There was an audible crack, and Perkins shrieked as the knife tumbled harmlessly out of his hand. Bunching his fist into the front of Perkins' shirt to hold him in place, Rochford jabbed the other man twice in the face.

Only his hold kept the other man upright. Rochford spun him around, and, seizing his unbroken arm and twisting it behind his back, once again propelled Perkins into the wall beside the door.

Perkins let out a moan of pain, protesting, "No! No! Leave off! You've broken my arm!"

"You'll be lucky if that's the only thing I break," Rochford retorted coldly. "For daring to touch Lady Haughston, I am tempted to smash every bone in your body." For emphasis, he pulled back and shoved Perkins into the wall again. "You're a worthless piece of scum, and I wish to God I had dispatched you the other night."

"I didn't do anything! Ask her! *Ask her!* I haven't taken her. I swear it."

"Sinclair! Don't kill him," Francesca put in quickly. "It's true. He hadn't quite gotten to it yet."

Rochford's jaw clenched. After a long moment, he

growled, "Be glad for that, then, for if you had hurt her, I would make sure you died a very slow death. As it is, you are going to gaol, and I plan to devote myself to making sure that you stand trial for shooting Avery Bagshaw."

Perkins began to babble in protest, but Rochford ignored him, shoving him out into the hallway, where a small crowd had gathered and were watching the scene with avid interest.

"Here, innkeeper, take this man and tie him up." Rochford thrust Perkins into the hands of the large man who stood at the front of the crowd.

When the innkeeper began to protest, Rochford fixed him with the stare for which he was justifiably famous and told him, "Unless you plan to spend the night in gaol for aiding and abetting this criminal, I suggest that you tie him up and send for the magistrate."

His statement was followed by a goggling silence, and Rochford stepped back inside, closing the door after him. As the latch no longer worked, he shoved the chair in front of it to keep out any prying eyes and hurried back to the bed.

He snatched up Perkins' knife from where it had fallen on the mattress and cut Francesca free from the bedpost. Then he sliced the sash just below the knot at her wrists and turned to sawing through the rope that bound her ankles while she unwound the sash from her hands.

Her hands and feet began to tingle madly as the

blood rushed back into them, and she had to press her lips together at the sudden pain. Tossing the knife onto the table beside the bed, Rochford chafed her feet in an effort to return warmth to them. After a moment, he released her feet and reached up to gently brush her hair from her face.

"Are you all right? Truly? Did he hurt you in any way?"

For answer, Francesca only threw her arms around him and clung tightly. His arms went around her with equal fervor, and for a long moment they simply clung together, as if that would somehow drive the previous night from their minds.

"I was so scared," Francesca whispered. "He didn't hurt me—well, apart from some bumps and bruises. But I was so afraid. I was certain no one would come after me quickly enough."

"Thank heavens your butler and maid came running to me the instant they saw him carry you out of the house. And I went straight to his lodgings, hoping he had taken you there. His valet was there, packing up his things, and it did not take me much time to find out where Perkins was headed."

He pressed his lips to her temple and murmured, "I died a thousand deaths tonight, thinking I would not reach you in time. Afraid the valet had been more foolish than I thought and had led me astray. When I think of him hurting you—"

"I'm all right," she assured him, turning to kiss him lightly.

Then she kissed him again, her lips lingering on his this time. When she pulled away, he took her head between his hands and leaned in, his mouth seizing hers in a long, fierce kiss. All the roiling fear and rage that had eaten at him as he chased Perkins and Francesca now burst out of him in white-hot desire.

A long shudder shook Francesca, and she threw her arms around his neck. They kissed frantically, desperately, as if at any moment they might be pulled apart. They rolled across the bed, hands and mouths touching, tasting, exploring, in a maelstrom of passion.

They pulled and tugged at their clothing as they kissed, pausing only for him to wrench off his boots and throw them on the floor. Her nightgown, torn as it was, was easy to slide out of. His clothes were less so, and there was the sound of buttons popping, and even a tear as he yanked off his shirt and skinned out of his breeches.

But then, at last, they were naked and open to each other. He drove into her hard and fast, and she wrapped her arms and legs around him, clinging, almost sobbing in her need. There was no world outside of them, no thought or emotion but the desire pounding through them, so close together that they could not tell where one ended and the other began. And so they rode the storm of their passion until at last they crashed through into an explosion of pleasure that left them drained and floating blissfully.

Finally, he rolled from her and wrapped his arm

around her, reaching out with the other to pull the counterpane over them. Francesca snuggled into him, too spent and exhausted to speak, and in the delicious warmth of his arms, she drifted off to sleep.

THE NOISES OF THE INN woke her. She had slept dreamlessly, never moving from the position in which she had fallen asleep. Sinclair was still draped around her, though the cover had long since slid from their bodies. She smiled a little to think what a picture they would have presented had someone entered the room.

She must have moved, for he came awake instantly beside her. She felt the sudden tension in his arms, and he raised his head, then settled back down, relaxing.

"How do you feel?" he asked, kissing the point of her shoulder.

"Wonderful—and a trifle sore."

She felt his fingers trail down her spine, pausing at a tender spot low on her back and another on her side.

"I should have killed the filthy bastard," he growled. "Did he hit you?"

"Once, when he first captured me." She reached up to her hairline to touch a tender spot.

He gently kissed the place her fingers had found. "Perhaps I will advise the magistrate to release him after all, and then I'll make sure he's never seen again."

Francesca smiled. "Thank you for the thought, but I would not have you do that. It would cause you guilt in the end."

"I think not."

"Well, I do not wish it." She linked her fingers through his. "The rest of the bruises came from our struggling in the carriage—oh, and when I landed in the grocer's stand."

"The what?"

She giggled, finding humor in the incident in retrospect. "The grocer's stand. We drove through the market area when he first took me. There were vendors all about, beginning to set up their wares. We had slowed down, so I jumped from the carriage—that was before he had bound my legs, you see—and I landed among the fruits and vegetables. It made for a softer landing, I suppose, but it doubtless gave me bruises."

"So you led the blackguard on a chase." He let out a bark of laughter. "I should have known that you would make it hard on him."

"I fear I was reaching the end, though," she told him, then lifted his hand and kissed his palm. "Thank you for coming after me."

"Always." He kissed her neck where it joined her shoulder.

"You must get very tired of rescuing me," she went on softly.

"I would never tire of rescuing you," he assured her, going up on his elbow and turning her onto her back, so that he looked down into her face. "I hope that I am always there when you need me. But you know, it was you who rescued yourself. Had you not fought as you did—screamed and struggled and jumped into the fruits and vegetables—I could not possibly have reached you in time. *You* delayed him—your courage...your strength."

Emotion swelled Francesca's throat, and she smiled up at him. He bent to kiss her, then pulled back with a sigh.

"If I stay here much longer, I won't be able to leave at all."

"Leave?" Francesca watched as he rolled away and got out of bed. She sat up, pulling the sheet up to cover her chest, feeling suddenly modest now that he had left the bed. "Why? Where are you going?"

He pulled on his breeches and continued to dress as he explained. "To visit the magistrate about Perkins. To order you food and a bath brought up, if you'd like."

"Oh, yes!" A bath sounded heavenly, but the empty rumbling in her stomach was almost as compelling.

Rochford flashed her a quick smile and leaned over the bed, resting his fists on the mattress, to kiss her lightly on the nose. "And I thought I might find you some clothing to wear. Much as I would enjoy the trip home with you wearing only that nightrail, I imagine you would rather have a dress."

"I would indeed," she agreed. However, she could not help but feel a trifle bereft as he pulled the chair from the door and left.

It was all very well for him to tell her how brave and resourceful she had been last night in fighting off Perkins, but she knew how scared she had been the whole time—and that some of the anxiety still lingered in her now, even though she knew that Perkins was safely locked up.

Two maids brought up a long metal tub. It was a far cry from Francesca's own porcelain slipper tub at home, but the maids filled it with warm water, and it was such a wonderful feeling to sink down into the heat that she did not mind that it was a trifle cramped and anything but elegant.

Somehow the maids' chatter relaxed her and helped ease the anxiety inside her. Even their rampant curiosity and sidelong gazes were so normal that Francesca felt more herself again.

After they left, she lay back and relaxed, her lids drooping in exhaustion, but her eyes flew open when the door was shoved back. Then she saw that it was Rochford who stood framed in the doorway, and she relaxed. He stepped inside and closed the door behind him, his eyes drifting slowly down her body. A smile hovered at the edges of his lips.

"You look very inviting, I must say," he told her, tossing the bundle in his hand onto the bed.

"Perhaps you would care to join me," she suggested boldly, leaning back in the tub and making no move to cover herself.

The twitch became a grin. "I think there might not be enough room in there for both of us." He sat down on the chair and pulled off his boots. "However, I would be happy to offer my services in drying you off."

He shrugged out of his jacket and went to work on the buttons of his shirt as he walked toward her, then leaned down, bracing his hands on either side of the tub, and kissed her.

His lips moved slowly, deliciously, savoring the kiss, and by the time he pulled back, Francesca felt as warm and liquid as the water around her. She smiled up at him, the somnolent heat in her eyes beckoning him. He reached down and grasped her arms, pulling her up, and wrapped his arms around her.

She giggled. "You're getting all wet."

"I don't care," he assured her as his mouth sank into hers.

They made love unhurriedly this time, moving without haste in a counterpoint to their lovemaking of the night before. Caressing, kissing, making their way with almost agonizing slowness, they heightened their pleasure almost to the breaking point. Time and again they retreated from the intense peaks, until their bodies were slick with sweat and their breathing ragged, their flesh searing with desire. Then, at last, they came together, soaring on a wave of passion so strong that their bodies shook from it.

Afterwards, they lay curled together, lazily drifting in a state of golden, loose-limbed warmth. Sinclair brushed his hand down her arm and nuzzled into her hair.

"Francesca…"

"Mmm?"

"Whatever I missaid yesterday, I am sorry."

Francesca stiffened, suddenly wary. "Sinclair, no—"

"Please, let me finish. I want to marry you. However you say, whenever it pleases you. I want you to be my wife."

"Pray do not spoil this." She rolled away from him, but he reached out and wrapped his hand around her arm, holding her in place.

"No, I will not let you do this. You are not running away from me again."

"I am not running." She turned back. She felt suddenly naked and exposed before him, and she pulled the sheet up over her chest and sat up to face him.

"What else would you call it?" He sat up, too, releasing her arm. "I am not a fool, Francesca, no matter how much I may have acted one yesterday. That was my pride speaking, my hurt over what happened fifteen years ago. But once I let myself look at it cleanly and clearly, I knew…" He doubled his fist and tapped it against his chest. "I *know* that you love me. Do not tell me that you do not."

"Of course I love you!" Tears sprang into Francesca's eyes, and she whirled, jumping off the bed and grabbing the bundle of clothes Sinclair had tossed on the bed earlier. She could not stand naked in front of him and argue. Hastily, she began to throw on the undergarments and the simple frock.

Rochford followed her, shoving his legs into his breeches and pulling them up, buttoning them high enough to stay on his body as he strode over to Francesca. His eyes were bright with anger and frustration, and color flamed on the high ridge of his cheekbones.

"Then why, in the name of all that is holy, do you refuse to marry me?" he thundered. "Blast it, Francesca, I cannot believe that you are playing a coquette's game with me."

"Of course not!" She faced him, her jaw set stubbornly, her hands fisted on her hips. "How can you even think such a thing? If you had but listened yesterday instead of charging off like a wounded bull, I would have explained."

His brows rushed together, and a light flared in his eyes, and for an instant Francesca thought that he was about to explode into a rage. But he set his jaw and said only, "Explain, then. I will endeavor not to behave like a bull."

Francesca drew a breath. Now that she had the opportunity, she suddenly found it terribly hard to speak. Tears threatened to clog her throat and fill her eyes. She pushed them back. "I am being reasonable."

"Reasonable!"

"Yes, reasonable. I am thinking about the future, about *your* future."

"Unless you hope to see me suffer a long and lonely one, I fail to see how you are thinking of my future," he retorted.

"You are a duke. You have to marry well."

"And you are not good enough to be a duchess?" His

brows sailed upward. "I must say, my dear, I have never known you to be so modest."

"You know that I am not the sort to be a duchess," Francesca protested. "It is not my lineage at fault. It is me."

"And how, pray, are you not fit?"

"In so many ways! I am not sober or dignified. I don't think about important things or read weighty tomes or engage in learned discussions. Gossip and fashion and parties—those are what I know. I am flighty and frivolous. We are horridly unalike. You will be bound to grow tired of me and regret marrying me."

"Francesca…dearest…for someone who knows so much about love, there are times when you are remarkably obtuse. If I wanted someone exactly like me, I would be quite content living alone. I have no desire to marry a bluestocking or a bore or someone puffed up with pride of family. I promise that I will read all the weighty tomes and think all the deep thoughts that we are required to. And you…" His face softened. "You will give our parties and entrance our friends, win the love of my tenants, and make everyone wonder how I could have caught a jewel such as you. And every day you will fill my eyes with beauty."

He took her by the shoulders and kissed her softly on the mouth. "Believe me, I know a great deal about regret. I have suffered it for fifteen years. I will *not* regret marrying you. Your frivolity, your love of fun, your laughter, your smile—those are some of the things

I find most enchanting about you. I want to laugh. I even want you to stick a pinprick in my pride now and then. Sweet heavens, don't you realize—you are everything I could want in a wife."

His words made her heart swell with love. She wanted to give in, to admit that nothing would make her happier than marrying him. But she could not allow herself to do so. She had to be strong.

She pulled away, saying, "I am not young. I am a widow."

"I care not." He crossed his arms, facing her.

She stared at him, frustrated. Her throat was tight, and she felt as if it was filling with such anger, such loss, that she might explode at any moment. Finally, as if it had been torn from her, she cried, "I cannot have children!"

Sinclair stared at her. Then he stepped forward, his arms going around her gently and he pulled her to him, cradling her against his chest. "Oh, my God, Francesca...I am so sorry."

He kissed the top of her head and laid his cheek upon her hair. Francesca melted into him, unable to stand against his tenderness. She let him hold her, leaning on his strength, soaking in his warmth, taking the comfort that had never been offered her by the father of the child she had lost.

Rochford lifted her up and sat down in the chair by the window, holding her in his arms. For a long time they sat that way in silence, his head lowered to hers, wrapped together in regret and sadness. But finally, with a sigh, Francesca sat up, wiping at her cheeks to remove the tears that had escaped.

"Are you certain?" he asked.

She nodded. "I—I lost a child that I was carrying, and the doctor told me I would probably never have another one. He was right. I never conceived after that." She gave him a small, glancing smile, and stood up, moving away. "Now you understand."

"I understand that you have carried a burden of sorrow for years," he replied carefully, standing up. "But is this why you refuse to marry me?"

"Yes, of course!" Francesca swung to face him. "Do not play dense with me. The Duke of Rochford cannot marry a barren woman. You have to produce heirs. You have a duty, a responsibility to your name, your family."

"Pray, do not tell me about my duty," he retorted, his face tight. "I have lived with it all my life. Since I was eighteen, I have done my utmost to live up to the name, to avoid tarnishing or betraying it in any way. Indeed, I have sought to improve it. But I am not going to sacrifice my life on the altar of Rochford. I am more than just the Duke of Rochford. I am Sinclair Lilles. And I will marry as I wish—not for my family, not for the name, not for the estate, but for *me!* You are the woman I want for my wife. You are the one I love."

Francesca stared at him. "You—you love me?"

He looked back at her, puzzled. "Yes, of course.

Isn't that what we have been talking about? I love you. I want to marry you."

Francesca's knees felt suddenly weak, and she went to the chair and sat down. "I...but—you never said it."

He gaped at her. "Never said it? I asked you to be my wife. Indeed, I asked you three times! Why else would I ask you?"

"Because my family is old and well-connected. I would be acceptable. You explained all those things to me when you asked me to marry you the first time. You told me how right and agreeable it would be for the two of us to marry. How we knew each other well and our families were—"

"I was trying to convince *you,*" he retorted. "Not myself. I knew I wanted to marry you, and it had nothing to do with your family."

"You desired me. I understand that. I am aware that my face and form are pleasing to men."

"You are more than pleasing to me. You always have been. When I saw you dancing at my house that Christmas, your hair up and your skirts down for the first time, I was dazzled. I lost my heart utterly and completely. Francesca...I burn for you. I am like a schoolboy again. Whenever you enter the room, my knees threaten to turn to water."

"Truly?" Francesca tilted her head, a pleased smile curving her lips. "But when we were engaged, you never—well, you hardly even kissed me."

He let out a groan. "My God, Francesca! You were

eighteen, barely out of the schoolroom. Did you think I was going to grab you and ravish you?"

"No, of course not, but—I did not think you *loved* me."

"You are so exasperating, I could shake you. I was trying to play the gentleman, however little I felt like it around you." He took her hand and raised it to his lips. "I lay awake at night, thinking of you, too filled with lust to sleep. I still do."

"But—that is not love."

"Desire alone does not last for fifteen years. That is how long I have loved you. No matter how I tried not to, I could not stop. There was no other woman who woke my interest."

"Do not try to tell me that you have been celibate for fifteen years."

"No. I will not lie to you. There have been other women, but none that I loved. None I would have married. When you broke it off, I did my best to hate you, and then I tried to forget you. It was like a knife in me every time I walked into a party and saw you there with Haughston. So I stayed away. I spent more time at my estates and less in London. Then Haughston died and I— It is wicked of me, but I admit it, I was filled with happiness the day I heard of his death."

"Why did you never say anything?"

"What was I to say? You still held a low opinion of me. How was I to convince you that Daphne had lied? After all those years, it seemed an impossible task. And

I—well, sometimes my pride is my own worst enemy. I told myself I would not grovel to you. Your love for me had died years ago. I saw no signs that I could bring it back. We had a sort of friendship. And perhaps… perhaps I was not brave enough to risk breaking my heart again. But this last year, it seemed…easier, I suppose, between us. When you told me Daphne had confessed what she had done, I hoped that you might come to feel differently about me."

"Then why did you start looking for a wife? Why did you ask me for my help?"

"Sweet Lord, Francesca, what was I supposed to do?" His face contorted with frustration, and he swung away from her, beginning to pace. "You told me that you wanted to make it up to me by finding me a wife! It was clear that you had no feeling for me. But I realized—well, at first I was furious, and I wanted to lash out at you, but then I saw that this was a way to allow me to spend time with you. I thought that I could subtly woo you under the guise of letting you find me a bride."

"So instead of courting those girls…"

He nodded. "I was trying to court you."

Francesca could not hold back a little giggle. "What fools we both are."

"Yes," he agreed. "I think perhaps we are." He pulled her into his arms. "I love you, Francesca, more than anything or anyone in the world. I want to marry you."

"But your heir…" She resisted, not leaning into him.

"Blast the heir. My cousin Bertram can inherit, or his sons. And if he manages to produce none, then it will pass to some other distant relative. I will be dead then, anyway, and I do not think I will care. What matters to me are all the years remaining to me…and spending them with you."

He reached down and tilted up her chin. "Francesca…beloved…you are the only woman I want for my duchess. Will you marry me?"

Francesca looked up at him, and it was a moment before she could speak past the lump in her throat. "Yes, Sinclair. I will marry you."

THEY WERE MARRIED two days later in Lilles House in London. The ceremony was simple, with no family or friends except Irene and Gideon to witness as the duke slipped the Lilles wedding ring upon her finger.

Rochford had obtained a special license before he had asked her to marry him that day in her garden, and he called in his favor to Lady Mary's fiancé, Christopher Browning, asking him to marry them posthaste. He had no intention, Rochford told Francesca firmly, of allowing her to slip away again. And Francesca, smiling, had agreed. In truth, she wanted to waste no more time being anything other than his wife.

Afterwards, when their friends had left, Rochford took her hand in his and said, "Come. I have a present for you."

She laughed as she followed him upstairs. "Another

gift? But you have positively showered me with gifts. All the jewels…the dresses I ordered yesterday from Mlle. du Plessis."

"Those are but a drop in the bucket," he assured her with a grin. "It is my intention to buy you so many clothes that even you will not be able to wear them all. And slippers. And jewels. We will buy every gown and bauble in Paris on our honeymoon. I have years to make up for, years when I could do nothing, had no right to do anything for you, and I had to stand by and watch as you struggled."

He led her into his bedroom and across to the small dressing room beyond. Unlocking a door in the wall, he revealed a closet of shelves behind it, many of them filled with jewelry cases. He removed a mahogany jewelry box and carried it out to the bedroom, setting it on a table.

"More jewels?" Francesca laughed. "How many jewels can the Lilleses have?"

"A positively vulgar amount, I assure you," her husband replied. "However, these are different. They do not belong to the Lilles family. They are yours."

Intrigued by his words and expression, Francesca pulled open the bottom drawer of the small chest. In it lay a sparkling tiara. Her eyes widened. It was a tiara that had belonged to her grandmother. She had given it to Francesca when she married Lord Haughston. Francesca looked over at Sinclair, her eyes wide.

"I don't understand."

He nodded toward the box, and she continued opening the drawers, taking out necklaces and bracelets,
earrings and rings...all sorts of jewelry that had once
belonged to her. The Haughston parure of emeralds
Andrew had presented her with on their wedding
day...a brooch of pearls and sapphires that Dom had
given her...the pearl necklace from her parents.

"These are the things I sold!" Francesca stared at
him. "You—you bought them?"

He nodded. "I saw a necklace once at the jeweler's
and recognized it as one you had worn. I was certain,
and I managed to worm the information out of the man.
He admitted that your maid had been selling things for
you. So I bought it, and I told him to bring everything
else you sold him to me."

"So that is why I was able to get such good prices
for them! I thought it was Maisie's amazing bargain-
ing skills." Francesca laughed, tears filling her eyes. "I
never dreamed that it was you...."

"The gold and silver pieces are downstairs in the
butler's pantry."

"No! You bought all those, too? You did not need to
take those, as well."

"I doubted that most of them meant much to you, but
I wanted to make sure—" He broke off and shrugged.

"That I got the best price for them," Francesca finished.

"I am sorry. I could not buy your wedding ring back.
He told me he had already sold it."

"It doesn't matter. *None* of them matter." She smiled

at him, her face glowing, struggling to hold back the tears in her eyes.

She understood now the depth of his caring. What he had done for her all these years, silently, expecting nothing in return, thinking that she loved him not, knowing that she had believed lies about him—yet despite all that, he had secretly purchased the things she had sold only because he wanted to help her. Because he could not bear to see her struggling with her poverty. She saw now, too, how often he had manipulated things so that she could make money—the bet he had made with her last year about finding a husband for Constance, the way he had led his great-aunt to her to arrange a wife for Gideon, the allowance for food he had arranged with her butler when Callie stayed with her, which she was sure had been far in excess of what was needed.

She swallowed hard and took his hands in hers. "All that matters is that you wanted to buy them. I love you more than I can ever tell you."

"That is good. Because I love you even more."

He raised her hand to his lips and kissed it. His hand curled around the sapphire bracelet he had given her after their bet. She had worn it and the sapphire earrings today; her dress had not mattered, but those gifts from him had.

He rubbed the sapphires thoughtfully with his thumb. "I thought that I would have to pay a great price for these. I feared you might have sold it somewhere else. The other day, when I saw you wearing it and my earrings…why did you not sell them?"

"I could not sell those," she told him, her unshed tears shining like jewels in her eyes. "They were all I had of you."

"Oh, my love." He pulled her to him, hugging her fiercely. "Now you have all of me. You always shall."

He bent his head and kissed her.

EPILOGUE

Christmas, Eighteen Months Later

MARCASTLE WAS DECORATED for the season, with mistletoe and holly and boughs of fir all over the enormous house. Christmas was still several days hence, but the guests were already gathered. Callie and Brom had arrived two days earlier, as had Irene and Gideon. Constance and Dominic had driven in the night before, carrying with them a fresh snow. The dowager duchess was installed in her usual room in the south tower, well away from the nursery wing. Francesca's parents, the Earl and Countess of Selbrooke, were not far from her, as was Great-Aunt Odelia. Eighty-one years old though she might be, she was not about to miss as momentous an event as this. It had been thirty-nine long years since the last christening of the future Duke of Rochford.

For it was this that had brought all the visitors, not Christmas Day, though of course everyone planned to remain for that celebration, also. At three months of age, Matthew Sinclair Dominic Lilles, the fifth Marquess of Ashlocke, on whose shoulders the mantle of Duke of Rochford would one day fall, was being christened. The vicar of St. Swithin's, the same man who had married the baby's parents a year and a half earlier, would preside over the ritual, along with the local vicar, who regarded the younger man with some jealousy and was careful to guard his rights as the priest attached to St. Edward the Confessor Church, the Lilles family's home church for generations past.

It was an event unlike any that had been seen in recent memory at Marcastle. The duke and duchess's wedding celebration had been denied to the locals, and as a consequence, everyone was determined to make these two weeks a very special time. There were balls and teas and all sorts of indoor amusements planned, as well as outdoor activities to suit the weather, including skating on the small pond, which had fortunately frozen hard just before the snow and was likely to remain so.

The servants had spent weeks preparing the house, repairing, cleaning and decorating with a vengeance. The duchess, after only a year and a half, was well-loved by all, and they were determined to do her proud. Goods had been ordered from as far away as London, as well as from Norwich and Cambridge. Cook had been busy night and day, whipping her charges along remorselessly, and extra servants had been hired on to help cook, clean and serve.

The subject of all this festivity, a cherubic infant with soft black curls and pink cheeks, was sound asleep in his bed, unaware of the fate that awaited him in less than an hour. Just down the hall from him, the nursery rang with shrieks and giggles as sixteen-month-old Ivy FitzAlan darted around the nursery table, stopping to peer around the corner at her pursuing father. Dominic, Lord Leighton, showed little signs of catching her, preferring to stop his crawling on hands and knees and pop out around the leg of the table to cry "Boo!" This, of course, set off another shriek and more giggles as Ivy toddled off once again.

Her mother, Constance, barely showing in her second pregnancy, sat placidly watching the chase as she talked to Irene, who sat beside her on the sofa. A year-old boy, his hair a riot of golden curls, stood at Irene's knee, his hand fisted in her skirt to maintain his wobbling stance, and watched Ivy and Dominic, letting out occasional shrieks of glee.

The two women had not met until last Christmas at Redfields, when all the families had gathered there and at Dancy Park for the festive season. They had quickly become friends, however, and had continued their friendship through a voluminous correspondence. Still, even letters could not contain everything, and there was still a good deal of news to catch up on.

Much of it would have to be repeated, of course, to Callie when she returned. She was in her bedroom, nursing her own five-month-old son, Grayson, while Brom and Gideon were ensconced in the library downstairs, doubtless conducting one of their many discussions of business, a subject that would keep them occupied for hours if one of their wives did not pull them out of the place to attend the christening.

"Almost time, love," Constance pointed out to Dominic. "Best let Nurse put Ivy to bed for her nap." She refrained from adding that the game Dom had been playing with their daughter would make that task rather more difficult than usual.

"I know. I know. I have to change for the ceremony." Francesca's brother stood up, grabbing his daughter and swinging her high in the air, then kissing her stomach noisily before turning her over to the patiently waiting nurse. "It's not every day a man becomes a godfather."

Irene, too, handed her own Philip over to his nurse after a final loving nuzzle of his sweet-smelling, chubby neck. She linked arms with Constance as they strolled out of the room, followed by Dominic.

"You know, I never thought I wanted to be a mother," Irene said. "Now I can barely stand to leave him. He's almost walking now. It's as if his life is just rushing by me."

Constance nodded her agreement. "I know. It seems only yesterday that Ivy was the size of Grayson." She sighed. "Poor child. I don't know what she is to do— growing up with all these boys. She'll doubtless be wild as a March hare—or maybe just a terrible flirt."

Irene laughed. "I am sure she will be as calm and lovely as her mother."

The three of them paused to glance in the door of the

room where Matthew lay sleeping. At the foot of his bed stood his parents, both gazing down lovingly at the child.

Outside the room, the other three glanced at each other and smiled the knowing smile of fellow parents, then walked off down the hall.

Francesca linked her hand through Sinclair's and leaned her head against his arm, releasing a happy sigh. "I still cannot believe it. Every time I look at him, he seems like such a miracle."

The duke bent to kiss his wife's sun-bright hair. "He *is* a miracle."

Francesca smiled. "Yes, and perhaps there will be others."

Rochford suppressed a groan. "Hopefully not too soon."

Francesca's pregnancy had been nine months of worry for him, and much as he loved his son, he was not looking forward to a repeat of the experience. He curled his arm around her, pulling her close to his side.

"Happy?" he murmured, bending his dark head to her golden one.

"Utterly so," she agreed. "I never thought I would have a child, and now to have one so healthy and beautiful and perfect…" She went up on tiptoes to kiss Sinclair's lips. "And to love my husband so, as well."

"After eighteen whole months of marriage, too," he jibed. "Now *that* is a miracle."

"No. No miracle at all," she replied, all seriousness

now. "For I will love my husband the rest of my life. I think that is why I was able to conceive, you know—it took love."

"If that is what it takes, then, God help us, we shall have an enormous brood."

The duke kissed his wife again, more lingeringly this time. At last he straightened with a regretful sigh. "We have to go now. We cannot be late, or we may have the two vicars dueling over the baptismal font."

Francesca chuckled. "We may have that before it's all over, anyway." She turned to look once more at her baby. "It seems a pity to wake him up."

"We'll manage." Rochford scooped him up, wrapping the blanket tightly around him, and the baby merely squirmed for moment, then nestled against him, sound asleep.

With the sleeping baby securely in the crook of the duke's arm and Francesca's hand looped through his other, the three of them swept out of the room to join their families in a celebration of the future.

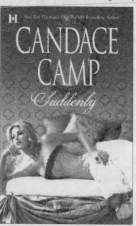

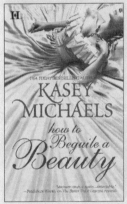

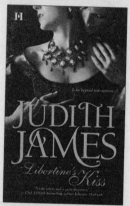